RELUCTANT SPY

Presented to the
Clayton Community Library
by

CLAYTON BUSINESS

&

COMMUNITY ASSOCIATION

RELUCTANT SPY

Iris Collier

Thorndike Press
Waterville, Maine USA

This Large Print edition is published by Thorndike Press, USA.

Published in 2003 in the U.S. by arrangement with Piatkus Books Ltd.

U.S. Softcover   ISBN 0–7862–5431–9   (General Series)

The text of this Large Print edition is unabridged.
Other aspects of the book may vary from the original edition.

Set in 16 pt. New Times Roman.

Printed in Great Britain on acid-free paper.

ISBN 0–7862–5431–9 (lg. print : sc : alk. paper)

To Christopher

CHAPTER ONE

He left the Master Mariner's tavern at half past ten. He hadn't intended to stay so long, but the place had been a welcome haven from the storm, the ale was excellent, the company convivial. The wind lashed his face as he turned towards the Point and into Broad Street, heading to the house where his sister Agnes lived with her shipwright husband Tom and a lively brood of small children. The rain was easing off but he could hear the waves dashing against the harbour wall, and, looking up, he saw the ragged clouds scudding across the sky, hiding the moon, and he thanked his lucky stars that he'd crossed over from France the night before.

He carried no light, relying on his familiarity with the streets of Portsmouth to get him home. He'd drunk too much, and he thought longingly of his bed, although it was a bit of a crush sharing a room with Agnes's brood. Tomorrow, an early start. He'd booked his passage to London for the next day with a fellow wool merchant. Not many hours to go before he'd have to get up as the carrier wanted to be on his way by first light. He should have left the tavern earlier, before it got dark. He shouldn't have drunk so much. Agnes would be worried. Tom would curse

1

him for keeping him from his bed. He didn't want to cause trouble. He didn't see his sister all that often. Usually he crossed over from Calais to Dover, but this time he had work to do in Le Havre. Work. Always work. Through the heavy fumes of alcohol he thought back to that last night in Le Havre, his conversation on the boat; that is, what conversation he was able to have on a boat that reeled and lurched its way across the Channel like a drunkard.

The narrow streets were deserted. All law-abiding folk were in bed at this time. A few figures were huddled in doorways. He heard someone laugh. Someone swore. Then there was the sound of breaking wood, the crash of an object hurled against a wall. Portsmouth Point was a sinister and violent place at night. Now he turned left into Fish Street, a dark, cobbled alley-way, where the overhanging houses almost touched one another. Agnes and Tom lived at the end of the street where the houses were more substantial. As he turned the corner, thanking God that he would soon be in his bed, two dark figures, lurking in a doorway of one of the houses, stepped out into the street. He didn't have time to turn round. Certainly he didn't have time to draw his dagger. One of the shadows darted forward. The knife slid into his back just below the shoulder blades. He felt a numbing pain. He turned to face his attackers, stumbled and fell. He didn't feel the second stab that pierced

2

his heart. The two men pulled out their daggers, wiped them on their cloaks and hauled him into the gutter.

'Get his purse. Be quick,' one of them said.

The other cut the purse, well-filled with money, and stuffed it down the front of his jerkin. Then, wrapping their cloaks round them, they disappeared into the night.

In the house in Fish Street, Agnes grew seriously worried. Where was Bartholomew? He wasn't usually as late as this and the tavern was only a few minutes' walk away. Tom had fallen asleep. There was nothing for it, she would have to go and find her brother by herself.

'Damn him,' she thought, as she put on her cloak. 'Drunkard that he is. Never knows when to stop, that's his trouble.'

*   *   *

The monks had gone. Four of the bells had gone. The silver plate had been carted away. And his friend, the kindly, expansive Prior Thomas, was now rector of a church in Shoreham. His house, where he had enjoyed so many good dinners and listened to beautiful music, was deserted. Already the villagers were creeping up in the night and helping themselves to the stones and the lead from the roof. Jackdaws had made their nests in the window embrasures. The cloisters were silent.

3

Last autumn's leaves had drifted into the corners and lay around in heaps. Nicholas felt immensely sad. Another age. Another time. Only two years ago he'd been standing here with the Prior and discussing improvements to the buildings. And now, centuries of prayer, almsgiving, teaching and healing had been swept away by parliamentary legislation orchestrated by the King and his minion, Thomas Cromwell. Soon, bit by bit, the stonework, the timbers, would all vanish. Buttercups and cow parsley would grow on the once well-tended grass of the cloister garth. Soon, all would vanish. Just a few foundations and marks on the earth for future generations to wonder over and try to imagine what the Priory had looked like in its heyday.

He walked into the church where, not long ago, the monks had chanted the daily office. The choir stalls were still there; the chantry chapel was still there, not finished because the workmen had not had time to complete their work before the King impounded it. He walked up to it and admired, as he always did, the fine carvings on the pillars; carvings of children climbing trees, cherubs playing lutes, angels blowing trumpets, and the strange collection of mythical beasts, objects of the sculptor's imagination. A fitting resting place for his wife Mary, now at rest in the graveyard for seven years, but soon to be brought in here, to this tomb where she would remain for ever.

Then, when his time came, he would lie beside her, just as, in life, they had shared a bed together.

He glanced up at the painted ceiling. It was his ceiling. He'd paid for it. It was his family history that was recorded there in the heraldic imagery. His family's motto, Toujours Loyal, was written on one of the shields. Loyal, he thought resentfully, that was a joke. Of course he supported King Henry. Only a fool would oppose him, or someone thirsting for martyrdom. But Henry expected much from his servants, and was miserly with his rewards.

He heard the church door open and he turned round. Alfred Hobbes, the Vicar of the parish church of Dean Peverell, had come in to disturb his peace. He was a small man, with the face and features of one of the smaller rodents. He walked up to Nicholas, his face registering a sly obsequiousness which set Nicholas's teeth on edge.

'Good morning, Lord Nicholas. We don't often have the pleasure of seeing you here. Not now that your friends have gone,' he said, waving a hand round the deserted choir.

Nicholas looked at him sharply. 'Yes, my friends have gone. More's the pity. And now I suppose the place will go to rack and ruin.'

'Not necessarily,' said Hobbes with a cunning look at Nicholas. 'We could move the parishioners in here. After all, they still have to worship God, and now that the monks have

5

left, they would be pleased to come in here on Sundays.'

'So you want to be Prior, eh?' roared Nicholas, scarcely able to control the urge to seize Hobbes and shake him until his teeth rattled. 'Curb your ambition, Vicar, or you'll be out on your neck. Remember, I'm still the patron of your living. Nothing's going to change that. Let the parish worship where they've always worshipped. The other side of that wall. When change is needed it will be up to me to decide what to do. Meanwhile, get back to your flock. They'll need you more than ever now that the monks have gone.'

Pushing Hobbes in front of him, Nicholas walked back to the main door. They stepped out into the June sunshine. It looked so beautiful, so peaceful. It was hard to believe that only two years ago the monks were evicted. He remembered seeing the sad procession of the brothers filing out of their choir, carrying their rolled-up mattresses. Some had set off down the road without a word to anyone, without one look behind them. Others had been met by their relatives who took them off in carts or on horseback, watched by the crowd of subdued villagers who had turned up to mock and jeer, but had fallen silent as the monks made their dignified exit. All gone. Now new men were in power. New faces at Court, a new Queen, already five months pregnant. Queen Jane. The King had married her a mere eleven days after his previous wife, the bewitching Anne Boleyn, had been executed in the Tower.

'Have you any news of Mistress Warrener?' said Hobbes, looking slyly up into Nicholas's face. 'They say she's well set up at Court. Queen Jane is much taken with her, I hear.'

'Vicar, get back to your own church, and attend to the souls of your flock. Mistress Warrener is well.'

Hobbes sighed. 'Her father misses her greatly. It's time she paid us a visit.'

'That's for the Queen to decide. Now, be off with you. But damn me, who's this?'

A horseman stood by the lychgate. Both horse and rider were caked in dust and splattered with foam from the horse's mouth, and sweat from his body. Nicholas's heart missed a beat. Not again. Not another summons to Court. He thought he'd finished with all that. Was he never to live in peace and finish off his chantry chapel?

Ordering the Vicar to get back to his church, Nicholas went towards the rider who dismounted and removed his hat.

'The King, Lord Nicholas, wants to see you. It's urgent, he says.'

'Can I not sleep in my own bed, and leave tomorrow?'

The man shook his head. 'The King says you are to start at once.'

Nicholas looked despairingly at the

messenger. Was it always to be like this? Either the King was coming to see him, or he was to go to the King. There was never any warning. No time to put his own affairs in order. Fortunately, his horse, Harry, was in superb condition. He had to be. He would have to travel along the treacherous roads of Sussex in record time. Henry was not a patient man. Fortunately it was high summer. The nights were short, the roads deeply rutted, but passable. And there was a full moon.

He walked over to where he'd tethered Harry to a hawthorn bush by the roadside, the messenger following him. He had a good idea what the King had in store for him. Find someone; someone the King wanted rid of. Arrest him. Bring him to trial and make sure there was enough evidence to convict him. Henry wasn't too bothered with the niceties of the criminal law when it came to getting rid of people he didn't trust, but he liked to go through the motions of a just trial. There weren't many people Henry trusted, Nicholas thought, as he mounted Harry, who whinnied and pawed the ground impatiently. Except, for some unknown reason, he trusted him, Nicholas Peverell, lord of the manor of Dean Peverell, a small estate in the County of Sussex, close to the cathedral city of Marchester.

Followed by the messenger, Nicholas rode up the village street to the crossroads, and then up the long drive to his manor house which had been his family seat ever since the first Peverell settled there after the Conquest of England by the Duke of Normandy, five hundred years ago.

At the heavy, oak, Norman door, he stopped and waited for the messenger. 'You're welcome to stay here for the night,' he said. 'Refresh yourself. I'll set off as soon as I've given instructions to my servants.'

Then he tugged on the bell rope, the gate-keeper opened the door and they clattered into the courtyard.

CHAPTER TWO

'The King, Lord Nicholas,' said Thomas Cromwell evenly, 'is enjoying a day's hunting; a necessary recreation in his busy life. However, he sends his regards and says he hopes you'll join us for dinner this evening. There's to be some music, I gather, and an exceedingly good menu has been ordered.'

Nicholas cursed inwardly. It was always like this. The ride from Sussex had been long and hard and it had taken its toll on Harry who'd been left behind at Merrow. And all for nothing. Henry's hunting expeditions usually lasted all day, or until he'd worn out eight or more horses. Henry liked to play the waiting game. The summons to Court. Then the agony of being kept in suspense not knowing why the King had sent for him. But Nicholas was used to it. It didn't do to read too much into this assertion of royal authority.

Cromwell, too, enjoyed playing his master's power games. Looking at him, Nicholas saw the gleam of satisfaction in his crafty eyes, hastily concealed by an ingratiating smile. After all, Nicholas could be the next favourite. Cromwell knew it was best to keep in with favourites; especially when one's own position might one day depend on that person's goodwill.

Nicholas found it hard to conceal his dislike of Cromwell. Even his appearance irritated him. A plain, stout man. A man of the people, a Londoner, Cromwell was dressed, as usual, in a long, dark-coloured robe trimmed with expensive fur, his only vanity. His pale, podgy face, always inscrutable, today showed signs of fatigue, and his hand which held a letter was tightly clenched with tension. Here was a man, thought Nicholas, who had served one master, Thomas Wolsey, well, and had been passed on to serve a royal master, one who had the power of life and death over his subjects. He knew Cromwell had risen to high office through his ability to manipulate Parliament. He'd been responsible for procuring the King's divorce from Queen Catherine and for making the King Supreme Head of the Church in

England. This man, thought Nicholas, was the architect of the King's power. The King owed everything to him. But for how long? Once Cromwell had outlived his usefulness, was he to suffer the same fate as Sir Thomas More and Queen Anne? Henry, Nicholas knew only too well, had no hesitation in ridding himself of anyone he tired of. Looking at Cromwell, Nicholas shuddered. There, he thought, could be me, if the King had a mind to it.

At that moment, however, Cromwell was the picture of affability. He told Nicholas that a room had been made ready for him above the gatehouse. A small room, but then he was only to be there for one night. He would be comfortable. He would enjoy tonight's feast.

Nicholas was growing impatient. He was tired and needed to rest. 'What does the King want me for?' he asked, cutting short Cromwell's platitudes.

Cromwell looked at him in astonishment which Nicholas knew was feigned. Cromwell knew very well what was in the King's mind. He'd probably put it there in the first place. 'Lord Nicholas, how should I know why his Highness has sent for you? He needs your services; that's all I know. As a Justice of the Peace you know all about legal procedures. You are a friend of sheriffs. You know how to deal with cases of sudden death.'

'Sudden death? In Marchester?'

'Not in Marchester. Oh, nothing to worry

11

about; just a small matter. It's probably of no consequence at all. A wool merchant, by name Bartholomew Tyler, was stabbed to death in the back streets of Portsmouth. Let me see now . . .' He referred to the piece of paper in his hand. 'Yes, here we are. Five days ago. The evening of the fifteenth of June.'

'Five days ago! Too late to start an investigation. Besides, Portsmouth is way out of my jurisdiction. They have their own Sheriff. They've probably caught the murderer already. I am not the only man responsible for the upkeep of law and order in the south of England.'

Cromwell shrugged his shoulders dismissively. 'The Coroner will put you right on the facts. The Sheriff will get on with his side of the business. But you know how it is with these lowly officials. They can't see the wood for the trees. Now you, Lord Nicholas, with your great experience . . .'

'I, too, am but a lowly official, Baron Cromwell,' said Nicholas emphasising the new honour recently conferred on Cromwell by the King. 'I also know it's none of my business what goes on in a neighbouring county. The Sheriff of Portsmouth will deeply resent my interference.'

'Not if the King sends you, my Lord. Just think about it. Would we really bother to summon you here only to put you in charge of a run-of-the-mill robbery which ended in

12

death? Yes,' he said, seeing Nicholas's enquiring look. 'Tyler's purse was taken. But that could have been a deliberate attempt to put the authorities off the scent.'

'But what other motive could there possibly be? A merchant. Portsmouth's full of them. Incidentally, what was he doing when he was attacked?'

'He'd been out drinking. It was late. He was on his way home, or rather to his sister's house in Fish Street where he was staying.'

'Then he should have stayed there and not gone wandering off to alehouses. Portsmouth's a dangerous place after dark. Robberies arc two a penny, especially in the area down on the Point.'

'I agree with you. Tyler should have stayed in if he wanted to be safe. But he wanted a drink. Now, Lord Nicholas, this little matter of the death of a wool merchant is the reason why you're here. The King wants you to go to Portsmouth and clear the matter up. We want the thieves caught and punished—severely and publicly as a warning to others. The King cares deeply about the safety of his subjects, and he doesn't like to think that it's not safe to walk the streets after dark.'

'But what, in God's name, is so special about Bartholomew Tyler? I can't tell you how many people are murdered after dark all over the kingdom, and robbed of their purses. There must be at least three people a week in

13

Marchester alone who are attacked and I'm not called in to investigate. I preside over Quarter Sessions, and I sentence them, not catch them.'

'As I said, the King wants you to go. Portsmouth is very special to him. He wants his subjects to be safe there. Now, I suggest you take a rest, refreshments will be brought to you, and we will see you again at dinner. I believe one of your friends, Mistress Warrener, will be singing for us. Queen Jane is very taken with her. As one of her ladies-in-waiting she enjoys a privileged position.'

Despite his self-control, Nicholas's heart missed a beat at the mention of Jane. He hadn't seen her for a year; not since she'd been invited to Court to sing to the King. Had she changed? Would she recognise him? Worst of all, had someone at Court engaged her affections? Cromwell, he could see, knew how much he admired Jane. If he knew she was being courted by someone, he wasn't going to reveal it. Like his master, Cromwell enjoyed the game of cat and mouse. And in this case, he, Nicholas, was the mouse.

The interview was over. Nicholas left Cromwell to his machinations, and walked across the courtyard of Hampton Court, Wolsey's palace which the King had coveted and taken from him. His room was where he'd stayed before, at the top of the turret by the gatehouse. It was small, but adequate, one used to put up short-stay visitors. A room for the King's servants, not courtiers. Cold beef, bread, and a tankard of ale were laid out on a wooden table by the small window. There was a jug of water and a bowl, and after washing the dust and sweat off his face and hands, Nicholas ate the food. Then he threw himself down on the hard, wooden bed and in seconds was asleep.

* * *

A knock on the door jolted him awake. A servant entered carrying a pitcher of water and a garment draped over one arm which he dumped on the chair.

'His Highness sends his regards,' the man said, 'and hopes you will accept this gift of a coat. He hopes it meets with your approval. He'll be ready to meet you in fifteen minutes in the banqueting hall.'

He bowed and left the room. Nicholas, dazed with sleep, got up, realised it was later than he thought, dashed some cold water over his face and shoulders, and picked up the coat. It was a splendid jacket made of fine royal-blue wool. Tudor roses were embroidered in gold thread on each point of the collar and the buttons down the front looked as if they were made of real silver. A good gift, thought Nicholas. But why such an expensive one? The King never gave away gifts without there being

15

an ulterior motive. Most likely it was a bribe. And his heart sank at the thought of what was in store for him.

*   *   *

The King and his servant were standing together, deep in conversation, when Nicholas was shown into one of the ante-rooms off the Great Hall. They stopped talking when they saw him, and the King walked across to greet him.

'Well, Peverell, here you are safe and sound, thank God. I'm glad to see you. That's a magnificent jacket you're wearing! I hope you like it. Cost me something, I can tell you. I spent a fortune on those buttons. But only the best for my friends, eh Thomas?' he said turning to look at Cromwell for confirmation.

'Your Highness honours me with your favour,' said Nicholas, bowing low. The King turned back to him and put an arm companionably round his shoulders. Nicholas felt a sense of relief. The King was in a jovial mood. Long may it last, he prayed.

King Henry, Nicholas had to admit, was in fine physical shape. Despite a day's hunting, he still seemed full of vigour. Admittedly, his girth had increased remarkably since he'd last seen him, but that was only to be expected as time went by. He still had the upright stance of a man in his prime, though, feet apart, radiating strength and power. His large, ruddy face showed no signs of excess fleshiness and his red-gold beard still thrust forward aggressively. The eyes were the same, small, calculating, revealing nothing of his thoughts. Here was someone, thought Nicholas, who was absolutely in control of himself and anyone else who happened to cross his path. He was surrounded by minions who obeyed his every whim. He was Henry Tudor, power personified.

Yet Nicholas wasn't frightened of him. Of course he was wary. He wasn't taken in by his affability. Too often he'd seen Henry's mood change. The good humour could evaporate in an instant, the face would become suffused with blood, and the eyes narrow to two tiny slits. King Henry in a rage was an unforgettable sight. But somewhere underneath this powerful exterior Nicholas sensed a lonely man, one who was desperately insecure. He could never have close friends. Too many people jostled for his favours. Too many people watched his every move, made plans for their own advancement should he fall sick or be killed in a tournament. How many people had gasped in horror when he'd fallen from his horse last year whilst jousting. How many had rushed forward to calculate the extent of his injuries. Even his friends watched his every move. It was only last February, at the King's palace at Greenwich, that Nicholas had been talking to one of the King's closest friends, Lord Montague, who had been drinking unwisely at dinner. He'd turned to Nicholas and said, 'He will die one day, suddenly; his leg will kill him and then we shall have some jolly stirring!' Nicholas had pretended not to hear but he had made a mental note that Montague's days were numbered if he couldn't control his tongue.

The ante-room had now filled up with courtiers. The smell of roast meat was overpowering, and the King was becoming restive.

'Time to eat. Let the Queen be seated first though. Come Peverell, you shall sit next to me tonight. I want everyone to see how well that coat suits you. It does you proud. The colour's just right. I envy you that thick mane of brown hair, not a grey hair in sight. Mind you, I think I look well myself, don't you think? Not bad for a man turned forty.'

He swivelled round on his small feet and the full skirt of his gold-embroidered doublet swirled round him revealing his enormous codpiece, the symbol of his manly power.

'Your Highness, as always, looks in the best of health,' said Nicholas.

'Hm—my leg plagues me; especially after a day's hunting. But it's only a trifle. I can still ride a horse and pleasure a woman, eh Thomas?' he said, stopping in his pirouetting to poke Cromwell in the ribs.

18

'Your Highness is full of vigour,' said Cromwell obsequiously, 'as your Queen bears witness.'

'How right you are, Thomas. Yes, my beloved Jane. The best of my wives. Soon to be the mother of my son, God willing.'

Amen to that, thought Nicholas. Let him get his son, then he'll stop changing his wives like someone in a Christmas game.

'Now, Peverell,' said the King, suddenly serious, and ignoring the press of the courtiers around him. 'I understand Thomas here has briefed you about this little matter of Bartholomew Tyler. I want it cleared up once and for all, you understand. I can't have my subjects robbed and murdered in the streets of my towns. Get it cleared up, Peverell.'

Nicholas bowed. 'I'll do my best, your Highness. But one small question I must ask— what was so special about Tyler that the Sheriff and Coroner of Portsmouth can't sort out the matter of his death between them? Why call in an outsider?'

'I've told you. I want to make my streets safe at night. Law and order, Peverell. The prime function of government. Surely you know that. Now, let's away to eat. Venison tonight, and quails, my Queen's favourite dishes. Oh yes, one more thing. When you catch the person or persons who murdered Tyler, bring them here to London. They will have to be interrogated.'

'Interrogated, your Highness? But surely . . .'

'No buts, Peverell. Just do as I say. We'll talk further on this later on. I've got another job for you. Whilst you're in Portsmouth, you might as well kill two birds with one stone. Now, is the Queen seated yet?' he asked the Master of Ceremonies who stood ready by the door.

'She is, your Majesty.' he said.

'Then tell them to make ready. Come Peverell, sit next to me, and let's talk of music and love and pleasant things instead of murder and robbery.'

To the shrill sound of a fanfare of trumpets and pipes, Henry, with his arm round Nicholas's shoulders, led them into the Great Hall which was his most recent addition to Wolsey's palace.

Peverell strolled into the Great Hall, very conscious of the King's arrn weighing heavily on his shoulders. He tried to relax, to smile, but on all sides he was aware of the envious glances of hundreds of pairs of eyes. He was, for one night, the new favourite. But not for a moment was he lulled into a false sense of security. He could sense something was wrong. Henry was worried. He, Nicholas Peverell, was to be sent on a dangerous mission; he wished to God he could read the future and know what was in store for him.

But first he must bow to Queen Jane. She sat there, at the high table, a diminutive figure,

20

her pregnancy concealed by the table. Her face, with its delicate, pale complexion, was composed as she acknowledged his greeting. She looked happy and confident in the knowledge that she was carrying King Henry's child. Next to her sat Jane Warrener.

For a moment, time stood still. Jane, his beloved Jane, who had helped him two years ago when they had unearthed a conspiracy against the King in Sussex. Jane, who had laughingly declared herself his spy, whom the King had snatched away to adorn his Court. Nicholas had heard that Queen Jane had taken to her and that she was one of her ladies-in-waiting, but not for a moment had he expected her to be in such an exalted position as to be seated at the Queen's right hand at a royal banquet. And never had he expected her to have changed so much. She had always been beautiful; now her beauty was dazzling. The beautiful oval face with the brilliant blue eyes was still the same. But now there was rouge on her cheeks, her lips looked full and red, and her eyes seemed brighter than ever. The copper-coloured hair was drawn back and tucked into a green-velvet head-dress studded with pearls. There were pearls in her ears and she wore a necklace of pearls round her slim neck. Her green silk dress was cut low in the front and edged with tiny seed pearls. The bodice was tight fitting and set off her full breasts to perfection. Nicholas was speechless.

Queen Jane was only of middling height and her pregnancy had filled out her face and figure so that she looked stocky beside Jane who was as slim as a willow wand. Jane, he realised, had grown up. The Court had changed her. How beautiful she'd become. She must have hundreds of admirers, he thought. And of course, she must have forgotten him?

'You know Mistress Warrener, I hear,' said the Queen, turning to look at her companion. 'She's from your part of Sussex, I understand, Lord Nicholas.'

Nicholas collected himself and bowed. 'Yes, I know Mistress Warrener very well. I am glad to see she has blossomed in your service, your Highness.'

'She is a sweet girl with the voice of an angel as we shall hear presently.'

Nicholas looked at Jane who inclined her heard politely. But there was a sparkle in her eyes and he knew she was the same Jane that he had known since she was a child. She had learnt the ways of the Court. She'd become a person in control of herself, whose face gave nothing away.

The King was getting impatient and calling for quails and wine. Nicholas bowed to Jane and the Queen and took his seat next to him. The feast had begun. Course after course was brought in by servants staggering under the weight of the serving dishes. Every type of fowl and fish was offered to him and the King, who ate heartily, and invited Nicholas to help himself off his loaded plate. Despite the long ride, Nicholas had no appetite. The scene seemed unreal as if he were living in a dream. The huge room with its elaborate wooden ceiling, the glowing Flemish tapestries covering the walls depicting scenes from the chase and Greek mythology, the smell of the rich food, the strong wine, the heat and the press of people round him made him feel light headed and he drank more than he should to give himself strength. And above all, he was aware of Jane Warrener sitting just a few feet away from him on the other side of the Queen.

'Peverell, you look tired,' said the King suddenly. 'Come, let us take a turn outside and get some fresh air. I can't have you falling asleep on us. We haven't heard Mistress Warrener sing yet, and we have yet to sample a great dessert of a fairy palace made with hippocras and quince jelly, my favourite.'

Nicholas was grateful to leave the Great Hall and walk with Henry in the cooler air of one of the galleries. The windows were open and he could see out into the royal gardens where shadows were creating mysterious shapes, and roses filled the air with their scent.

'It's good to be here, out of that noise and heat, Peverell. I only hope it's not too much for the Queen. We are very conscious that she is carrying a priceless burden which, by the grace of God, will be my son. We do so much long for a son, Nicholas,' said the King sadly. 'How can I sleep peacefully in my bed and know that I am without an heir? When I die, anything could happen to this country of ours. We could be torn apart again by civil war.'

'Your Highness has two fine daughters,' said Nicholas, touched by the King's display of vulnerability. 'Both are in good health and likely to live for a long time.'

'But they are daughters, Nicholas. Only daughters. They'll marry, like daughters always do. And who will they marry? Foreign princes. Then England will be governed by a foreign power. They could marry one of my nobles, of course. And where will that lead us? To conflict and warring factions, just like my father had to face when he came to the throne. No, daughters will only give us trouble. We need a son.'

'They might not marry, your Highness. One of them might choose to rule alone as your daughter and in her own right.'

'Not marry? Don't be a fool, Peverell. It's unheard of for a royal princess to remain unwed. No, I must have a son to succeed me. I had thought of making Fitzroy my heir. He was a brave boy and dear to my heart, but, alas, God took him for His own last year, and we have no one to replace him. His mother was a strong lass. I loved her well enough. But away with these sad musings, my beloved Jane is five months with child and the doctors are confident it will be a boy.

'But whilst we have a moment to ourselves, there is another matter. When you finish the business in Portsmouth, I want you to proceed to Porchester. The governor of the castle is Sir Charles Neville, recently appointed. He was in the service of Westmorland but, after the rebellion in the north, I sent for him to come south and look after our coastal defences. It was too dangerous to leave an ambitious young man up north where I can't keep an eye on him. Now, I want you to report on his progress—see what he's doing, keep him up to the mark. You know what I mean?'

'Surely Lord Southampton has overall responsibility for coastal defences?'

'He's busy building me a castle at the eastern end of Portsmouth. He can't be everywhere at once. No, I want you to pay Neville a visit.'

'You mean you want me to be your Highness's spy?'

'Oh, come, come, Peverell, don't be so melodramatic. You know as well as I do that sound government depends on knowing what's going on. How would I have put down the northern rebellion if I didn't have inside information? Now, see Cromwell tomorrow before you leave, and get him to produce letters of introduction. Neville won't give you any trouble. He's a nice enough fellow, about your age, I should think. Incidentally, how old are you, Peverell?'

'Thirty-four, your Highness.'

'Hm . . . you're getting on. But you're still a handsome fellow. Neville must be a few years younger than you. He's a bit green to be given such a position of responsibility, but I like to give young men a chance to show their mettle. Now see that you get plenty of exercise,' he said playfully poking Nicholas in the ribs, 'if you want to look like me in ten years' time. Come, it's time we rejoined the company. It's getting late and I have much business to attend to tomorrow. That fool Cromwell told the French ambassador to come and see me at half past eight. I doubt whether I shall be in a fit state to receive him.'

Back in the Great Hall, the tables were being cleared of the previous courses. To more fanfares the dessert was brought in and a great pink jelly castle was put in front of the King. He spooned the sweet, aromatic pudding on to Nicholas's plate and urged Queen Jane to eat heartily. Then, after demolishing the edifice, he sat back with a sigh of satisfaction and clapped his hands.

'Now, silence for Mistress Warrender. You must concentrate, Peverell. Just listen to how much she has improved under our tuition.'

The company fell silent, as Jane stood up and walked to the centre of the room. A young man with dark, Italianate looks stepped forward carrying a lute. One of the servants brought him a stool which he perched on facing her. Nicholas was overwhelmed by the sight of her, tall and slim, her dress glowing in the light of hundreds of candles. Suddenly, he knew that he would never forget this scene. And he realised that he loved her. He always had. But he also knew that he'd lost her. They'd grown away from each other. Her place was here with the Queen. She'd keep the Queen company and grace the Court with her beauty and her voice, whilst he was only lord of the manor in a small village in Sussex.

The company had fallen silent. The servants had come in from the kitchens and stood in silent groups round the edge of the room. Then the young man glanced at Jane, and began to play. Jane turned to the King and began to sing a song of extraordinary sweetness. Her bell-like voice had matured since she had sung for the Prior in Sussex. It was fuller, more accomplished as she took in her stride the intricate runs and changes of key which the music demanded. The song was about unrequited love, a young man inconsolable in the knowledge that his mistress no longer loved him. When she'd finished, the King turned to Nicholas, his face flushed with pride.

'That was one of my songs, Nicholas. Now wasn't it damn fine?'

'Your Majesty amazes us all with your many talents,' said Nicholas automatically, his eyes

27

never leaving Jane who stood there so confidently with all eyes upon her.

Other songs followed, some composed by the King, some by the former court composer, William Cornish, and some by Italian composers whom Nicholas had never heard of. Jane's Italian was flawless and Nicholas felt a surge of pride in her achievements and glad that she had continued her education at Court.

When she went back to her place, Henry turned to look at Nicholas and there was just the trace of a twinkle in his eyes.

'I think, Nicholas my friend, that you still harbour strong feelings for Mistress Warrener. Now put that all out of your mind. I want her here at Court. My Queen wants her to be present at the confinement and sing lullabies to our son. She's only a lass, Nicholas. One day we'll find her a husband, but she's not to be wasted in that dung heap of a village of yours. No offence, of course,' he said, noting Nicholas's start of annoyance, 'but let's face it, what can you offer a girl like this down there in Sussex, compared to what we can offer her here? You'll only tie her down with a baby every year. Soon that voice will become shrill and she'll turn plump and pious, weighed down with household cares. No, she must stay here. The Queen loves her, she's receiving a first-class education that will be wasted on you, she'll be a friend to my two daughters— Elizabeth already loves to listen to her singing.

Now let's drink another flagon of this excellent claret and then we should retire early. But first, a toast to you, Peverell, just between ourselves. Success to your mission, and safe return. And to the downfall of our enemies!'

'To the downfall of your Highness's enemies,' said Nicholas automatically, his eyes still fixed on Jane who was talking animatedly to the Queen.

CHAPTER THREE

That night the Queen retired early. Usually, Jane would sing to her or entertain her with light conversation before she went to bed. Sometimes the Queen would summon a group of her ladies to eat sweetmeats and drink mulled wine whilst they recounted the Court gossip. It was the time of day which Jane enjoyed very much. She had become attached to the Queen ever since she had been summoned to the Court and the Queen had taken her under her wing. The Queen had come to value Jane's lively wit and entertaining conversation and in return Jane appreciated the motherly concern of the older woman. Now, with the pregnancy advancing, Jane's support was increasingly valued. The Queen knew how tenuous her position was. She'd seen what had happened to Anne

Boleyn when she'd not given the King the son he'd longed for and he'd grown tired of her. And now, even though the King showered her with tokens of his affection she was sufficiently experienced in the ways of the world to know that if she lost the baby, or the child turned out to be a girl, the King's eyes would start roving elsewhere and he would soon find ways to cast her off. Jane understood the Queen's fears and felt sorry for her. So much was expected of this one event and it didn't do to disappoint King Henry.

After they had prepared her for bed, the Queen dismissed her ladies-in-waiting. Jane was ordered to stay. She blew out all the candles leaving just one burning on the bedside table. Then the Queen lay back on her pillows and patted the side of the bed.

'Come and sit beside me, Jane, for just a little while. You sang so beautifully tonight and I saw that his Majesty was impressed. You must never leave us.'

'Your Highness knows that I would never consider such a thing. My place is here beside you as long as I can be of use to you.'

'That will be for ever. You are a great comfort to me, Jane. You give me strength at a time when I most need it, but I know that one day you will want to leave us. A woman without a husband is a poor, sad thing.'

'I am grateful for your concern, your Highness,' said Jane perching herself on the

30

edge of the bed at the Queen's bidding, 'but I have no thought of matrimony. My only concern is to serve your Highness and be with you when we celebrate the birth of your child.'

'Thank you, Jane, I shall need you when my time comes. I am full of misgivings. Sometimes I feel that I haven't long for this life . . .'

'You mustn't say that, not even think it. Your Highness is young, in perfect health. The doctors say there is no cause for concern.'

'I know all that, but the fact remains I am not as young as you, Jane, and childbirth is a hazardous business as you know. Our graveyards are full of young wives and their infants. Nature is cruel to women. But, tonight, I want to talk about you, Jane. Someone as young and beautiful as you should not go unwed and you are not made to be a nun. Now tell me, who was that young man whom the King favoured tonight? He seemed a little disconcerted when he saw you, and I sensed that you, too, were not indifferent to him. Is he an old admirer? He seems a very presentable young man, good looking, strong, a nice open face, sensitive, not one of your country bumpkins. What was his name now? I've forgotten.'

'Lord Nicholas Peverell, your Highness. He's lord of the manor of Dean Peverell in Sussex. My father is one of his tenants.'

'Now that is interesting. Would you like to be lady of the manor, Jane?'

31

'Your Highness knows that I live only to serve you. You have done so much for me, educated me as if I were your daughter, given me these lovely dresses and honoured me with your confidences.'

'You have deserved it, Jane. You have given us all so much. I hope we shall always be friends. Now, let's dispense with these tiresome formalities. I think "madam" would be sufficient when you address me. Friends should be close to each other. It is significant that we both have the same Christian names; we were meant to be close. Come, let me hear you address me as you would any other noble woman.'

Jane slid off the edge of the bed and dropped her a deep curtsey. 'Your Highness, madam, honours me with your friendship. I hope I shall be worthy of it.'

'Then come and kiss me and reassure me that this Lord Nicholas won't spirit you off to rural Sussex before the birth of this child. I couldn't do without you, Jane.'

'Madam, I promise. I shall serve you as long as I am needed. Matrimony doesn't appeal to me. I want only to serve you.'

Jane leant forward and kissed the Queen gently on her forehead. She looked so pale and vulnerable lying there with her golden hair spread out over the pillow. Jane waited until the Queen's face lost its anxious expression and relaxed ready for sleep.

'Thank you, Jane. Now leave me to rest. Sleep well yourself, you have much restored me. As long as you are here I know nothing will happen to me or to my child.'

Jane stayed until the Queen's eyes closed and her breathing became deep and regular. Then she went into her own room next to the Queen's chamber. The King wouldn't trouble the Queen tonight, Jane knew. Nothing must upset the precious burden the Queen was carrying.

Jane didn't bother to light a candle as the moonlight, which was streaming into her room, was light enough. She took off her head-dress with a sigh of relief and shook out her hair. Then she carefully untied the lacing on her dress as far as she could reach and slipped it off over her head. She took it over to the window and gave it a shake. How beautiful it was, she thought, with the moonlight glinting on the gold embroidery, and for a moment she thought back to the simple linen dresses she used to wear at home. Her parents, although indulgent, could never have afforded to buy her a dress such as this. Even the nightdress which she now put on was made of fine lawn and trimmed with lace as delicate as cobwebs. She hung her dress up in the cupboard along with all the other dresses the Queen had given her, and then she lay down on her bed. Whether it was the effect of the moonlight, or the scent of the flowers drifting in from the garden outside, or her conversation with the Queen, sleep eluded her.

She knew Nicholas wasn't far away. She'd found out where his room was and how long he was staying. She was told that he was due to leave early in the morning so she wouldn't be able to see him as the Queen would want her services as soon as she woke up. It had been a shock to see him tonight and she was surprised at the feelings he'd aroused in her. He'd seemed different away from his home territory, less arrogant, and oblivious to the envious glances of the other courtiers when he came into the Hall, so obviously the King's favourite for the evening. He ought to be on guard when he spoke to anyone as she knew that one remark to a servant meant that the whole Court would know about it before the day was out. There wasn't a servant in the place who wasn't in some courtier's pay. Eavesdropping was a recognised and lucrative pastime. Nicholas ought to be warned.

She said her prayers and shut her eyes but sleep still eluded her. Her mind was full of images of Nicholas and she couldn't block them out. She got up, draped a cloak over her shoulders, and put on a pair of embroidered slippers. Then, quietly, she opened the door and looked out into the passageway. Everything was quiet. Silently as a shadow she went down the stairs to the courtyard which was flooded with moonlight. There was no one about. Keeping to the edge of the courtyard where the shadows were darkest, she made her way over to the gatehouse. The main gate was locked, of course, but the door leading to the rooms at the top of the tower was open. She climbed the stairs and paused outside Nicholas's room suddenly appalled at what she was doing. What would people think if anyone caught her? What gossip there would be when they heard that Mistress Warrener had succumbed to temptation and was caught playing the whore? They'd laugh and say that was what happened when a country girl was raised up above her station. She knew she had enemies. Some people were jealous of her musical talent and resented her position in the Queen's household. She ought to be sensible, turn round and go back to her room.

But something made her stay. Something drew her forward and she gently knocked on Nicholas's door. Then the awful thought came to her that the Household Chamberlain might have changed the rooms and lodged Nicholas elsewhere. If he had done this, then who would confront her when the door was opened? She turned to run back down the stairs, but it was too late. Before she'd got to the top stair, the door opened and Nicholas stood there in his nightshirt looking at her in astonishment. Without a word he ushered her into his room and closed the door.

They stood there looking at each other. She

felt embarrassed, at a loss for words. What was he thinking? Why didn't he speak? Then she thought of all those meetings they'd had in the past. She hadn't been embarrassed then; why should she be now? They'd been good friends. Surely that couldn't change.

'My Lord, forgive me for coming but . . .' To her surprise she found herself stammering. Was he so shocked that he'd become tongue-tied?

'Jane, what is it? What's happened?' Nicholas finally managed to say.

'Oh nothing, nothing important. It's just that I was so surprised to see you tonight and wanted so much to speak to you, but the opportunity didn't arise. I couldn't let you go without saying a word so I took the risk of coming to see you now. We were such good friends, Nicholas. Surely you haven't forgotten that?'

'I wanted to speak to you, too, Jane. But you looked so grand, so inaccessible, sitting next to the Queen that I thought you'd not remember me.'

'Inaccessible? How can you say that. You were sitting next to the King, remember? How could I speak to you? But please, Nicholas—forgive me, but that's what I called you not so long ago—tell me about my father. Is he well? Does Aunt Hannah look after him? He always had a delicate chest. Does she know how to treat it?'

'Your father is in excellent health,' said Nicholas formally, fighting down the urge to take her in his arms and cover her face with kisses. 'He delights in tormenting his sister and spends his days grumbling that no one can look after him as well as you can. He also plots with his friends how he can transport the stones away from my Priory without anyone seeing him. He's building himself a fine manor house with the money the King paid him as compensation for your removal to Court. He's doing well.'

'Compensation? You mean the King actually bought me?'

'I suppose you could put it like that. The King buys everyone, as you know. But let's put it another way. He offered your father a large sum of money for any inconvenience he would suffer as a result of your leaving him. He was pleased to accept it. It cushioned the blow of your departure, so to speak.'

'But this is quite dreadful. The King bought me! It makes me feel like a slave.'

'No, don't take it like that. Oh God, why didn't I keep my mouth shut? Your father would expect compensation, don't you see?'

'No, I don't see. And how much was I worth, may I ask?' said Jane backing towards the door. She'd never felt so angry in all her life. She'd made a terrible mistake coming here. She'd risked her reputation for what? Only to learn that her father had sold her like one of his household chattels. And Nicholas didn't seem to think it anything out of the ordinary. He was just like all the others— insensitive, tainted with the same brush as all the other courtiers who believed that everyone and everything had its price.

'Jane, stop. Please don't go. Please don't be offended. The King hasn't bought you. You could leave tomorrow.'

'Indeed I could not. I've just promised the Queen I'll not leave her, not, at least, until after she's given birth.'

'That's not the same as being bought. You're not under any legal obligation to stay. You haven't signed any contract. You've made a promise, that's all. That was your choice.'

'But I have a moral obligation if promises mean anything.'

'That's different from being a slave where moral obligations don't come into the picture. You are a free agent and your father's a very happy man, rest assured.'

'Yes, he would be,' said Jane bitterly. 'He values money above anything else. Well, I hope he got a good price for me. Enough to build himself a manor, you say?'

'With the help of the walls of my Priory, yes; and with the large sum the King paid him he can hire labourers. Mark my words, he's on his way to join the ranks of the landed gentry. But let's put all this out of our minds, Jane. Have you forgotten how we were such good friends, how we rode together and talked together and saved the King's life?'

'That was your doing, Nicholas.'

'But without your help it wouldn't have been possible. But what really brings you here tonight? Not just to ask after your father. You knew I would look after him.'

'I know. I'm sorry I got angry. It's just when I saw you tonight I was sorry I couldn't talk to you. I wanted to ask so many things. What happened to the Prior after he was turned out? And the Priory? What's left of it, I mean, after my father's finished with it? And what brings you to Court, Nicholas? What does the King want with you?'

He laughed, and suddenly she knew it was all right. Nothing had changed between them. They were still partners. She would still be his confidante. She hoped they could still be friends.

'The King wants me to sort out a piece of unfinished business, that's all. He doesn't trust anyone to do a job properly. He wants someone to keep an eye on the others. A case of *quis custodiet ipsos custodes?* I think. I shouldn't be away long. Then I'll have to report back here.'

'And don't forget there'll be someone keeping an eye on you, Nicholas. That's one of the reasons I had to come and see you tonight; to warn you. The King favoured you tonight. Everyone would have noticed that; everyone will start murmuring. Lots of people will be jealous; they are probably already plotting your downfall. Don't ever relax your guard, Nicholas. However much the King honours you, heaps favours on you, he can change as quickly as a summer cloud can turn to rain. Don't rely on Cromwell. He will use you, have you watched, and if things go wrong he'll be the first to denounce you and you will go to the Tower like so many others. I've seen it happen only too often. And I couldn't bear it, Nicholas, if anything happened to you.'

She wanted him to understand, not to take life so lightly. She knew he couldn't tell her what his mission was, but she could guess it was important and therefore potentially dangerous, otherwise the King would not have bothered to send for him. And this time she couldn't help him. She had to tend the Queen. He was on his own.

Nicholas was touched by her concern. He moved towards her and put his arms round her shoulders. 'Jane, don't worry about me. I am going on an insignificant mission to investigate a person of no consequence. Come, don't get alarmed. I shall come to no harm.'

'How can you say that? You don't know what's in the King's mind; nor does Cromwell. You could be about to walk into a hornets' nest.'

'And you won't be there to pour salve on my wounds,' he said smiling down into her eyes.

'You weren't meant to be serious, Jane. You were meant to bring happiness to people. Now go back to the Queen and don't give me another thought.'

'I shall always think about you,' she said, turning to go.

'And I, Jane, have never stopped thinking about you,' he said, pulling her closer to him. 'When I saw you tonight, I knew that I've always loved you and will never stop loving you. And when this business is finished, I shall come back and ask for your hand in marriage. The King cannot expect to keep you here for ever like a vestal virgin, unless of course . . .'

He paused and Jane looked up at him steadily. 'There is no one else, Nicholas, and there never will be. I shall wait for you, but I know that the Queen will not want to release me until after her child is born. But I shall be here and I will be your ears and eyes at Court just as I was once your ears and eyes in our village. At least I can tell you who are your enemies.'

'Still my beautiful spy, Jane? But you, too, must take care. Spying is a dangerous game.'

'Especially at the Court of King Henry. But don't worry about me. I have been here long enough to know the dangers and keep out of trouble. The Queen will want me with her more and more now as her time approaches, but I can listen and observe. I am used to saying nothing. Nothing is expected of me except to sing and keep the Queen happy.'

'Then I shall return as quickly as I can. A pity you can't come riding up to me as you once did on Melissa. You must miss the freedom, Jane.'

'You don't know how much I have yearned to gallop over the soft green turf of the South Downs and breathe in the smell of the sea. Here the air is stale and oppressive. I am only allowed out when the Queen wishes to take the air and that will be less often as her time comes. The King has a dread of the pestilence which rages in London at the moment and keeps the Queen under lock and key here at Hampton Court. The Court will not move to London this summer.'

'One day, Jane, we shall, once again, ride together. Think of the woods and meadows around Dean Peverell. Think of those days when we spoke together in my garden and remember that you will always be in my mind, you will always be my beloved spy.'

'And God keep you safe, Nicholas.'

Then he turned her face to his and kissed her, and for a moment there was just the two of them together and the outside world seemed far away.

CHAPTER FOUR

'Of course he's buried, Lord Nicholas. What else do you expect? It's eight days since we picked him up from the corner of Fish Lane. We can't leave a corpse hanging around in this weather; he'd be stinking to high heaven by now.'

Nicholas struggled to control his irritation. Jack Nott, Sheriff of Portsmouth, was not going to be cooperative. A huge man, over six feet tall, with broad shoulders and a barrel chest, he stood with his back to the empty fireplace, glowering at Nicholas. He was a man who had seen action at firsthand, Nicholas thought, judging by the scar on the right side of his face which had only just missed his eye. With a dark, shaggy beard and a mane of coarse brown hair tumbling around his shoulders, he looked like a wild mountain bear. Dressed in a soiled linen shirt and leather trousers, his sword propped up in one corner of the fireplace, he looked ready for action at a moment's notice.

The Under-Sheriff, Daniel Wheeler, by contrast, sat patiently at the far end of the large oak table which took up most of the space in the Sheriff's office. He had a roll of parchment in front of him which Nicholas had just handed him; it was the letter of introduction written by Thomas Cromwell at Hampton Court on the day of Nicholas's departure. Wheeler was a diminutive man with a small, weaselly face surrounded by sparse, nondescript hair, and he'd said very little so far. However, Nicholas had been warned by his friend, Richard Landstock, Sheriff of Marchester, that the two of them made a formidable team, used to dealing with the world's villainy and deeply resentful of any interference, the King's or anyone else's.

'I'm sorry to trouble you, Sheriff, but we are particularly interested in this man, Bartholomew Tyler. The more information you can give us about him, the better.'

'Well, you are troubling us, my Lord. We're busy men, Master Wheeler and myself. Tavern brawls, smuggling, fighting over the doxies, murders and muggings are all two a penny here in Portsmouth. Sometimes we catch the perpetrators; most times we don't. Our jail is full of ugly-looking characters, but we can't keep them there for ever. There are laws, you know.'

'I'm well aware of that. Let me remind you that in my county I am Justice of the Peace. Our Quarter Sessions never lack customers.'

'Well, then, what in Hell's name are you doing here? We've got enough on our hands at the moment, what with Southampton building a castle just down the road and demanding this and that and stealing all the town's labour

44

force. There's not a ship's carpenter or stone mason to be had for miles around. And now we've got to put up with you.'

Nicholas, trying to control his temper, walked over to the window and looked down into the harbour where ships were making ready to leave on the flood tide. It was a busy, noisy scene: ships' crews arguing and shouting orders to each other, shipwrights hammering away at the timbers, seagulls screeching as they fought over scraps of food thrown overboard. What did it matter if a man had been murdered eight days ago? Life was rushing on down there in the port. No one had any time to rake over dead ashes. The Sheriff, he could see only too well, had all his work cut out to keep some semblance of law and order in this rowdy town, seething with life and indifferent to death. But the fact remained that he, Nicholas was under orders, and the King wanted an arrest.

'Sheriff, you'll have to hear me out,' said Nicholas, suddenly realising he was not going to get anywhere by being conciliatory. He turned to face Jack Nott. 'I'm here because the King's sent me. It's not my wish to be here, I've enough work to do on my own patch. No, let me finish,' he said, putting out both arms to check Jack Nott's rush towards him. 'For some reason which I don't understand, this Bartholomew Tyler is important to the powers that be. The King wants the killer, or

45

killers, caught and brought to London for interrogation. This is no ordinary murder.'

'So it appears. To London, eh? To the Tower?' said Jack Nott, stopping in his tracks.

'Most likely. We need to know who's behind Tyler's death.'

'There's politics here, Jack,' said Daniel Wheeler quietly. 'Best hear him out.'

His voice seemed to have a calming effect on the Sheriff who sat down at the head of the table and shouted for ale to be served.

'Well, sit yourself down, man,' he said to Nicholas, indicating a chair near him, 'and let's get on with the business. The sooner we finish, the sooner you'll leave us in peace.'

'That suits me, Sheriff,' said Nicholas, joining him at the table. 'Now first of all, have you got a principal suspect yet?'

'God damn you, no,' shouted Nott. 'It happened at night, down on the Point, everyone with any sense was in bed, as Tyler should have been. But what does he do? He wanders off to the Master Mariner's with a purse full of money and gets himself killed. What else can you expect? And, so far, no witnesses have come forward.'

'Coroner says there were probably two attackers,' said Wheeler. 'Tyler was stabbed in the back. He must have turned round to face his attackers who stabbed him twice in the chest, one blow entering his heart. Now it would take two men to carry that out. It's easy

46

to put a knife into a man, but it takes time to get it out. You'd need two men to inflict those sort of wounds.'

'Thank you, Master Wheeler,' said Nicholas looking gratefully at the Under-Sheriff. 'Now we are making progress. Where was he staying?' he said, accepting a tankard of ale from the servant who had just come into the room with three tankards of ale and a jug on a tray. They waited whilst the servant served them all, left the jug on the centre of the table, and then went out.

'He was staying with his sister, Agnes Chandler. Her husband's one of the shipwrights who still works on His Majesty's ships down in the shipyards, despite the Earl of Southampton's efforts to persuade him to come and work for him. It seems that Tyler came in that afternoon of the fifteenth of June on a Flemish ship, and went off to book himself a place with a carrier who was leaving for London on the following day.'

'And where did he go to find this carrier?'

'At the Mariner's, of course. That's where they all meet, the carriers, the sea captains. Most business is conducted there.'

'So he had some friends, apart from his sister, that is?'

'I don't know if you could call them friends. Contacts more likely.'

'It would pay you to speak to the Chandlers,' put in Daniel Wheeler. 'They'll be able to tell you more about Tyler than we can. They might be able to let you see his room, for documents and so on. They would also know his address in London.'

'We know that. We've contacted his wife, who knows nothing about his business, except he's a wool merchant, and like hundreds of others in that trade does business in Flanders and some of the French towns.'

'A prosperous man, by the sound of it,' said the Sheriff, draining his tankard and pouring himself out some more before passing the jug on to Nicholas who waved it away. 'I think we can safely assume that the motive for his murder was simple robbery. Now, you tell the King that we shall be doing our utmost to catch the thieves. We've got our men planted in every tavern in Portsmouth, and that's no easy task, let me tell you. My men all rely on informants, and between them all there's not much goes on that we don't get to know about. We'll catch the rogues, rest assured.'

'Thank you, Sheriff,' said Nicholas standing up, 'you've been most useful. Now, if you could tell me where I can find the Chandlers, I'll go and see them straight away.'

'Tom Chandler'll not be at home right now,' said Wheeler. 'But his missus'll be there. There's a whole brood of children to be taken care of. They live in the last house in Fish Lane, off Broad Street. Biggish house; the only stone house in the street. You can't miss it.

Shipwrights are doing well at the moment what with the King wanting all these new ships.'

'Well, I wish you luck with the Chandlers,' said the Sheriff, draining his tankard and getting to his feet. 'I don't think you'll get much out of them, mind, but you might be lucky. I'll certainly pass on anything that comes in which might be useful to you. Let me know where you're staying. You're welcome to leave your horse in my stables if you want. But tell me why, in God's name, is the King so interested in Bartholomew Tyler?'

'And that,' said Nicholas walking over to the door, 'is what I'm going to find out. Good afternoon, gentlemen.'

*   *   *

Nicholas found the Chandlers' house in Fish Lane without any difficulty. Most of the houses were made of timber and plaster, with thatched roofs and overhanging top storeys, but the Chandlers' cottage, right at the bottom end of the lane was a small stone house with a tiled roof which seemed to have been there since the beginning of time; a house worthy of a master craftsman. The front door was opened by a young girl with an untidy mop of hair who ushered him into the living room where the mistress of the house, Agnes Chandler, was seated at one end of the large table which filled most of the room. She was

49

spooning porridge into the open mouth of a healthy-looking baby and the rest of the family, two boys and two girls, were seated round the table busily dipping pieces of bread into bowls of broth and stuffing the bread into their mouths. They hardly bothered to look up when Nicholas came in. One of the girls had spilt some of her broth on the oak table and started to draw pictures with it, using the crust of the bread as a paint brush. The girl who had opened the door rushed forward with a shriek of protest and took the bowl away from her. A row would have broken out if Agnes hadn't looked up from feeding her baby and shouted at them to be quiet otherwise she'd tell their father how impolite they'd been to a visitor.

Nicholas felt like an intruder. Agnes, still young, with a pretty face, untidy blonde hair and a plump, firm figure had her hands full. However, she made him welcome and asked the girl to fetch some ale. Then, when the girl had brought in the jug of ale, she handed the baby, who had gone to sleep, to the girl who carried him over to the cradle in the corner of the room. She lowered him in gently and drew up a chair beside him and began to rock the cradle with her foot whilst she took up a piece of coarse, blue material and began to sew on a patch.

The children finished their soup and ran out into the street to play. Agnes indicated the chair next to her and Nicholas sat down.

'You've come to ask about Bartholomew, I expect,' she said sadly. 'That's why most people come to see me these days. The Sheriff's men come most days and there's not much more I can say. Are you one of his men, sir?'

'I suppose you could say that. My name's Nicholas Peverell, and I hope you don't mind telling me what you know about your brother's movements on the fifteenth of June. I'm sorry you have to go through it all again. This must be a most distressing time for you.'

'Yes, sir. Tom's taken it very badly, and as for me, although Bartholomew was my eldest brother and I hadn't seen him for some time, he was still family. It's terrible to think that this should have happened to him whilst he was staying here. He seemed so cheerful and not at all put out by the children. He brought us all presents, sweetmeats for me and two bottles of wine for Tom, and some balls and tops for the children.'

She turned her head away and began to cry silently to herself. Nicholas waited until she'd recovered before he continued with his questioning.

'You say Bartholomew wasn't a regular visitor, Mistress Chandler?'

'That's right. You see he'd made his way in the world, London, Antwerp, all those places where he had to go on business, and we'd lost touch with him. But it was nice to see him,

51

although we had such short notice, and he seemed content with what we could offer. We wanted him to stay longer but he was keen to get on his way, although I had a feeling he would've liked to stay on if he could.'

'Do you know why he decided to come here this time?' said Nicholas.

'It was in the way of his business, so he said. Usually he crossed over to Dover from Calais. It's a straight run to London and plenty of carriers to take him. But this time he had business in Le Havre—someone wanting to buy a whole lot of broadcloth, I think. He deals in broadcloth as well as wool, you know. Anyway, there was a boat leaving for Portsmouth and the captain could take him so he decided to come here. It was a bit of a rough crossing I gather, so it took them a long time, but he had company on board, so he said, and the time passed quickly enough.'

She paused, lost in her own thoughts. 'What happened when he got here, Mistress Chandler? Take your time,' said Nicholas gently.

She made an effort to collect her thoughts. 'Oh he enjoyed his meal with us, we had some good fish and fresh pork. He gave us the presents and we talked until it was time for us to go to bed. We're not ones to stay up late, these days, sir. Tom and me can't wait sometimes to close our eyes. Well, Bartholomew then said he'd go down to the

Mariner's then and fix up his journey to London for the following day. Tom wanted to go with him, but I was firm because Tom needs his sleep as much as I do and Bartholomew could lie in bed the next day if he wanted to. Bartholomew said he wouldn't be long, and off he went, and that's the last we saw of him.'

Her eyes filled with tears, and Nicholas felt guilty at putting her through the ordeal again. The servant girl had stopped rocking the cradle as the baby was asleep. She now put down her sewing and came over to Agnes.

'Mistress, can I fetch you something? Some water? Milk? Or I could make a hot, herbal infusion?'

'Some water, Anna if you please. Then go and see what the children are doing outside. We shan't be long.'

Anna fetched the water and Agnes drank thirstily. Then she handed the beaker to the girl who went outside into the street where the sounds of children's laughter came wafting in through the open front door.

'I'm sorry to ask this, but I understand it was you who found Bartholomew later that evening?'

'Yes, sir. It was getting really late and Tom went to bed. He always falls asleep the moment he puts his head down, but I couldn't sleep as I was worried about Bartholomew. So I went downstairs and into Fish Lane, and there on the corner I found him lying face down.'

'Did you do anything to him? Turn him over? Try to revive him, that sort of thing?'

'Oh no, sir. He was beyond all that. There was blood everywhere. It was horrible, horrible; I shall never forget it.'

'And you didn't see a knife?'

'No, they'd made off with that. They just left him to bleed to death. They'd taken his purse, of course. Have they caught the thieves yet, sir? Do they have anyone in mind?'

Nicholas shook his head. 'I'm afraid not. The Sheriff and his men are doing all they can. But tell me, Mistress Chandler, after you'd found Bartholomew, what did you do next?'

'I ran back here and woke Tom up. He went to get the Sheriff.'

'Did Bartholomew have a bag with him? Maybe with his night things in it, or his papers. After all, he was just returning from a business trip.'

'There is a box upstairs,' said Agnes. 'The Sheriff's been through it but you could take another look if you want. Come, let's go up to where he was going to sleep. We've got a moment before the children come in.'

Nicholas followed Agnes up the steep wooden staircase that went straight up into the one big room which was almost filled by two large beds, one a four poster with curtains drawn back for the day time. There were two small truckle beds beside them. At the far end of the room was a doorway and Agnes took him into a small room where there was a bed and a table with a chair beside it, and a cupboard in one corner of the room. On the table stood a wooden box with a metal clasp.

'This is where we put guests,' said Agnes. 'Bartholomew would have slept in this bed.'

Nicholas pointed to the box. 'Was that Bartholomew's?'

She nodded. 'Go ahead and open it if you want. It's not locked.'

Nicholas went over to the box and lifted the lid. Inside there were rolls of parchment, each roll neatly tied together with linen ribbon. He took one out and untied it, and the individual documents fell apart. They were all lists of different amounts of cloth bought and sold over a period of one month. There were names, places, dates. Bartholomew had done business in many places: Brussels, Bruges, Ghent, Ypres, Calais, Le Havre; all towns known to be connected with the wool trade. The pattern appeared to be that Bartholomew mainly sold raw wool to clothiers who turned it into the fine woollen cloth for which Flanders was famous. Sometimes he sold the coarse broadcloth which the working population wore, the sea captains, the farmers, townsfolk. The fine cloth was for the gentry. It made fascinating reading, but hardly relevant to a murder enquiry. He put the documents back in the box and fastened the catch.

'I could, if you agree, Mistress Chandler, take this back with me to London and give it to Bartholomew's wife. She'd know where to find his fellow wool merchants. Someone ought to deal with these orders.'

She looked at him with a smile of relief. 'Thank you, sir. Tom was worried about them; he knew someone would want to see to all those orders. You see, Bartholomew was highly respected by his Guild. He was very high up, I understand. He seemed to know all the important people in London. He told us over his supper that he'd met Cardinal Wolsey himself, and this man Thomas Cromwell. He'd eaten dinner with the Earl of Southampton when he came to London. So many grand names, he had us all in a state, I can tell you. To think a member of my family should've rubbed shoulders with all these great men. It seems his Guild gives banquets and all these men are invited. Bartholomew told us his dearest wish was to meet the King, but that'll not happen now.'

'Instead he had to make do with Cromwell.'

'Oh, he'd met the good Thomas More before he died, and Queen Anne—she was on her way to be crowned when he saw her. Poor lass. I know she led the King a right dance, but she didn't deserve to die.'

They went downstairs, Nicholas carrying the box under one arm. As he made to leave the house, Agnes asked him if he had lodgings for the night.

'Of course, I expect the Sheriff will be putting you up, but if not, you are welcome to stay here.'

'Thank you, Mistress Chandler, but I shan't be ready to sleep yet. I'll have to go to the Mariner's and I expect they'll have a room for me and a meal.'

'Then I'll send James to warn them you'll be coming and they will get a room ready for you. It's no trouble, I assure you,' she said as Nicholas began to object, not wanting to put her to any trouble. As James, the eldest boy, ran off, Nicholas asked if she knew the name of the boat which had brought Bartholomew to England.

'Oh yes, sir. It's still in port. Tom's been working on it as the captain wanted some repairs done. I think it's ready to leave. If you want to speak to the captain, you ought to go now. He'll be putting to sea at the next high water which is later on this evening. It's going to be a good, clear night, with a bright moon, so he'll want to be on his way.'

'And the name of the ship?'

'Some Flemish name. Tom says it means Flemish lion, or lion of Flanders. The captain's called Hans something or other. That's all I know. Good luck, sir,' she said, as Nicholas set off down the street. 'I hope you'll soon bring us news of Bartholomew's murderers.'

*   *   *

Down in the outer harbour, the *Vlaamse Leeuw* was getting ready to go to sea. The big, square, rust-coloured sail was half furled, the timbered sides had been newly painted and its name picked out in gold letters. As Nicholas looked down into the ship's waist, a man's face appeared out of the main hatchway. It was a brown, weather-beaten face topped with a shock of straw-coloured hair.

'Who wants me?' he said with a thick, guttural accent.

'My name's Nicholas Peverell and I'm investigating a murder. May I ask who you are, sir?'

'Hans Artevelde. You're one of the Sheriff's men, I suppose. Come aboard if you must.'

Nicholas stepped over the gunwale on to the deck of the ship, and was told to go below. The head disappeared and Nicholas followed it down the companionway into a warm, comfortable room. There were four bunk beds, a table covered in charts, two chairs and some cupboards above the bunks. A small charcoal brazier glowed in one corner and the smell of frying meat and onions filled the room.

'Well, now, what can I do for you? Best be quick about it. My mate will soon be joining me and he'll want his supper before we leave.'

'When you made your last passage from Le Havre do you remember bringing with you a man by the name of Bartholomew Tyler?'

'Ay, that I do. A very friendly man, a good sailor. We had a bit of rough weather on that crossing—that's why I've had a few repairs done—but Mr Tyler wasn't bothered. He was up on deck with the crew and the other passenger and they kept each other company whilst drinking my beer. Would you like some?' he said indicating a leather jug on the table. 'It's beer, mind. None of that cat's piss you call ale. That won't last a voyage. We drink beer in Ostend where I come from. It's made from hops and lasts for months. Here, help yourself.'

Nicholas poured the strong, frothy beer into one of the tankards and drank deeply.

'It's excellent,' he said wiping his mouth on his sleeve. 'Keeps the cold out, I should think.'

'It's our life blood. We'd not get far without it.'

Hans went over to the little stove and began to prod the meat with a long-handled knife. 'What more do you want to know about Mr Tyler,' he said. 'I'm sorry to hear he was murdered the night he left my ship.'

'Can you remember the name of his companion?'

'Oh yes. We all know Jacques Gallimard. A Frenchman, of course, but he couldn't help that. He spends a lot of time crossing the Channel. A merchant, like Tyler. Does business in the French ports and over here.

We all know him.'

'What's his business?'

'That's not my business, is it?' Hans said, grinning across at Nicholas, pleased with his joke. 'He's probably a wool merchant, like Tyler. Both prosperous. Mr Tyler was the stupid one to go walking round Portsmouth late at night with a purse full of money on his person.'

'This Monsieur Gallimard, do you know where he was going after he left your ship?'

'Good God, man, that's not for me to ask. I don't talk to the passengers, especially when the wind's blowing a gale and there's a steep sea running. I only give the orders and tell the others to keep their heads down. I was only pleased that those two gave me no trouble.'

'And when they left the ship, did they leave together?'

'Not that I could see. They shook hands and went their own ways. Mr Tyler, I know was to stay with his sister here, down by the port. And now, if you don't mind, here comes my crew. I hope you catch Mr Tyler's murderer. He was a nice man, generous too. He paid me well.'

A pair of leather sea-boots, followed by two sturdy legs covered in strong, baggy trousers came down the companionway, followed by the rest of the man, sturdily built with the same shock of yellow hair as the captain's. He was followed by another man, no more than a boy. They stood silently at the foot of the stairs staring at Nicholas and glancing hungrily at the stove. It was time to go.

Thanking the captain for his hospitality, Nicholas climbed up on deck and walked the short distance to the Mariner's tavern, where a room had been made ready for him and a trayful of food, cold pie and bread and cheese, was brought up to him.

The landlord had nothing more to add to what Nicholas already knew. Only the name of the carrier, John Trimble; and that he'd left on the sixteenth of June without Tyler, of course. The landlord had liked Tyler. A sociable fellow, he said. Didn't seem to be the sort of man who'd have enemies. Splashed his money about, though, and that was a stupid thing to do in that town. Word soon gets round, he said, especially where money was involved. Tyler was asking for trouble and trouble came his way.

That night, Nicholas slept uneasily, his mind full of images of Hans and his crew setting sail from Le Havre with Tyler on board and a Frenchman named Gallimard. He thought of the convivial Tyler who brought presents for his sister's family. A man proud of his achievements who couldn't resist boasting about them. A man who knew his way around northern Europe, who had contacts in France and the Flemish towns. A man who knew Cromwell. Who was he? thought Nicholas as he saw the cold light of dawn disperse the

61

darkness in his room. Unfortunately he'd taken the answer to that question with him to the grave.

CHAPTER FIVE

In the early hours of the morning Nicholas drifted off into a heavy sleep only to be woken up by a knock on the door. Telling the man to come in, he forced himself to wake up. A servant entered carrying a tray with a platter of bread and cold meat and a jug of ale on it which he put on the table.

'Someone to see you, sir. He's downstairs. Says he'll wait.'

'Tell him I'll be down as soon as I can.'

Cursing silently that he'd overslept, Nicholas got up, pulled on his clothes and went downstairs.

A man was talking to the landlord in the tap room and he turned when he saw Nicholas. The landlord made himself scarce.

'A message from the Earl of Southampton, Lord Nicholas. He would like to see you as soon as possible. He'll be at the castle most of the morning.'

Nicholas called for the landlord and asked him to send someone to fetch Harry from the Sheriff's stables. Then he returned to his room, splashed cold water over his head and ate the bread and beef. Bartholomew Tyler's box was on the floor by his bed and he put it away in one of the wall cupboards. He decided to leave it there with the landlord as there wasn't much point in carrying it with him to Porchester. He felt sure his visit there would be brief as Neville was bound to resent his interference. He could pick the box up on his way back to London.

Harry was well rested and impatient to be off. Telling the landlord he'd be requiring a second night's lodging, he set off along the coastal road towards the castle which was being rebuilt to defend the eastern approaches to the city of Portsmouth. The weather was hot and sultry and the sea stretched away to the horizon like a length of blue silk, the tiny waves lapping at the water's edge like an edging of lace.

He should have been in high spirits on a day like this: Harry was in fine form, he'd done all he could to investigate Tyler's death and he was still on speaking terms with the Sheriff. But he felt uneasy. As if someone was watching him. So strong was the feeling that he reined Harry in and twisted round in his saddle to see if he was being followed. No one appeared to be taking any interest in him. Some horse-drawn carts, piled high with goods, were lumbering along at the side of the road. The fishermen were mending their nets next to their boats which were pulled up on the beach. Some country people were returning from the city's markets. Some people were standing around staring out to sea where the Isle of Wight rose out of the water like a sleeping leviathan. No one was following him.

Deciding that his feeling of foreboding came from a bad night's sleep, he urged Harry forward and covered the short distance to the castle in a very short time.

Great changes had taken place since he'd last been there, two years ago. King Henry wanted a chain of forts along the south coast and he'd elevated Sir Ralph Paget to the peerage as the Earl of Southampton and made him Lord Admiral of the King's Fleet and put him in charge of the building operations. Since Nicholas's last visit the keep of the old castle had been demolished and a new building was rising out of the thick, defensive walls. He rode through the postern gate into the main courtyard where stone masons were chiselling away at huge blocks of Portland stone and the noise from the carpenters' hammers was deafening.

As he handed Harry to a groom, Southampton saw him and picked his way over to him through the debris.

He hadn't changed a bit, thought Nicholas. A big, vigorous man, a soldier to his fingertips, with a strong weather-beaten face, cropped hair and well-trimmed brown beard, he was dressed for action in leather hose and jerkin and a linen shirt unlaced down the front for comfort in the hot weather. He clapped Nicholas boisterously on the back and shook his hand forcibly.

'It's good to see you again, Peverell,' he said. 'I'd heard that you were giving us a visit. Not more bad news, I hope? Don't say the King's coming down to see me again? He expects me to build him a castle in a matter of weeks and curses me when I tell him we can't do the impossible.'

'As far as I know, the King's still at Hampton Court. He'll stay there most likely until Queen Jane gives birth.'

'And when will that be?'

'The child's expected in October.'

'Then let us pray that the King gets his heart's desire and Queen Jane is safely delivered of a boy.'

'I'll say amen to that. But you sent for me. Is there anything I can do for you?'

'Not unless you can haul blocks of stone into place and saw wood. I wanted to see you, Peverell. That's all. Catch up with the Court news and find out why you've come here. You're neither a naval man, nor a soldier, are you, Peverell? And I'm sure you're not here to enjoy the sea breezes. But come, let's have a drink and you can tell me your news. Here, clear this lot away,' he called to one of the carpenters, 'and bring us some ale.'

He brushed some wood cuttings to one side,

clearing a space for the jug of ale when it came. He dragged up a bench for Nicholas and one for himself and sat facing Nicholas straddling his bench as if he were riding a horse.

'Well, out with it, what brings you here?' he said pouring out a tankard of ale and handing it to Nicholas.

'I'm on a murder investigation, Sir Ralph,' said Nicholas evenly.

'Sheriff's business. Nothing to do with you.'

'Seems it's the King's business. He wants to know who murdered Bartholomew Tyler, and why.'

Southampton whistled. 'Tyler? I thought that was over and done with days ago. The man's in his grave by now and surely the case is closed. Verdict, death by wounds inflicted by person or persons unknown.'

'The King's not satisfied that the Sheriff has done all he can to track down the killers, but I'm satisfied that the Sheriff is doing all he can. As time passes, it becomes more and more difficult to catch the murderers unless witnesses come forward, and in this case there don't seem to be any. Tyler might have been an important man, prosperous, top man in his Guild, knew influential people at Court, but he wasn't a careful man. He carried his purse tied to the belt round his waist and walked home through the streets of Portsmouth late at night on his own. He was an easy prey. Have you any ideas as to who might have wanted him out of the way, Sir Ralph?'

'I'm not a Sheriff's man, Peverell. I've got to build the King his castle and look after his ships, not conduct a murder investigation. But what do you know about this man Tyler? Why was he so special that the King sends you here to interfere with the Sheriff's business?'

'He was a much-travelled man. I've got a box of his containing all the orders he collected from customers in the Flemish towns and the French coastal towns. He was a likeable sort of chap and was on dining terms with Thomas Cromwell.'

Southampton took a long draught of ale. 'That fellow? I don't trust him an inch. He's got a finger in every pie and mark my words, Peverell, he's got it coming to him. The man makes enemies and as soon as the King tires of him he'll end up in the Tower, if not Tyburn.'

'That may be so, but at this moment, it's Cromwell who's in the saddle.'

'You say this Tyler was a friend of Cromwell so there's probably more to his death than meets the eye. I'm sure you know that Cromwell likes to keep up-to-date with what's going on. He'll be watching you, that's for sure, and me, too, most likely. Do you know, Peverell, for one moment I thought he'd sent you down here to keep an eye on me! His agents are everywhere. Has it ever occurred to you that Tyler could be one of Cromwell's spies?'

'But he was a wool merchant. Spent his time travelling round Europe.'

'Precisely. The King has enemies everywhere, not only in this country. Remember the Pope excommunicated him only four years ago. That makes him an outcast on the continent. You've also got to remember that the Emperor Charles is nephew to the late Queen Catherine. He'll want her daughter, Mary, his niece, to be next in line for the succession. Now we have the late Queen's daughter, Elizabeth, who is illegitimate in the eyes of the Emperor. If Queen Jane produces a boy, then there's no hope for Princess Mary. The Emperor'll not like that. It's complicated, Peverell. The King faces Yorkist plots at home and continental disapproval at the same time. He's isolated, and he's uneasy. It only needs the Emperor Charles to join forces with his brother-in-law, the King of France, and we could face a powerful alliance prepared to invade us and depose King Henry.'

'I'm grateful to you, Sir Ralph for your lucid analysis of the international situation. But I understood that there's no love lost between King Francis and the Emperor. In fact I thought they were fighting each other.'

'Oh, they'd call a truce if they thought there was any possibility of a successful invasion of England.'

'And you think Tyler could be involved in all this?'

'He could have been. There are lots of Tylers beavering away in Flanders and France, collecting information and sending reports back home. Good God, Peverell, they're all at it. Take the French ambassador now, nice as pie, full of Gallic charm, he'll have his spies. He's allowed to send dispatches back to the French King. Who knows what's in them? Some, I daresay, Cromwell will have intercepted and will've read, but many will get through. The more I think about it, the more I think that this Tyler was in Cromwell's pay and he found out something important and someone wanted him silenced.'

'The captain of the ship who brought him over said he spent much of the voyage talking to a Frenchman.'

'Well, there you are. The Frenchie fellow would have left the boat and straight away reported Tyler to someone who ordered his death. Now I wonder what Tyler could've found out? It must have been important. No wonder the King wants these forts built. It used to be sufficient to have Porchester well fortified. I used to be the Lieutenant there, you know. But it's not enough now. Portsmouth is where our fleet is. We're very vulnerable, Peverell, if the King of France and the Emperor combine forces.'

Nicholas stood up, his head suddenly

clearing. The pieces of the puzzle were suddenly coming together. 'You mentioned Porchester, Sir Ralph. That's my next port of call. I'm to inspect the defences and report back.'

'Good God, Peverell, the King does trust you. Mind you, Neville will not take kindly to you poking your nose into his business. There's no talk at Court is there of war against France?'

'No more than usual. The King has always wanted to reclaim those lands in France which we used to own. However, for the last year he's been preoccupied with clearing up the north of the country after last year's rising. He's become more distrustful of late, though. Thinks we're all against him.'

'He's made many enemies. But what about you, Peverell? You're loyal, I suppose. The Peverells always have been and you've nothing against the King, have you?'

Nicholas suddenly became aware of a growing crowd of people clustering round them. The conversation had taken a dangerous turn. Southampton ought to guard his tongue.

'Me? Oh I keep my head down. I only want to lead a quiet life, but it appears it's not to be. But it looks as if you're wanted, Sir Ralph. Look at all these people.'

Southampton took the hint. 'Get away with you,' he roared. 'Can't you see I'm busy? Get back to your work, damn you.'

He jumped up and physically thrust the crowd of people away. He looked at Nicholas ruefully. 'Damn the lot of them. I hope to God they didn't hear too much of our conversation.'

'It doesn't pay to talk too openly. But tell me about Sir Charles Neville. What do you know about him?'

'Neville? I can't abide the man. Porchester used to be my responsibility,' he said as they walked back towards the postern gate. 'Then the King ordered me here and put Neville in my place. He's young, appears to be harmless enough, but he's cheated on me, and one day I'll get my own back.'

'What's he done, Sir Ralph?' said Nicholas, beckoning the groom to bring Harry forward.

'Done? Why the bastard's gone and made the King a higher offer for the Priory at Porchester. As soon as the canons left, I made the King an offer for it which he accepted. Then along comes Neville and offers him more. Now that's dirty business, Peverell. And if a man cheats on me, well, by God I'll pay him back. You can tell him that. I make no secret of it. Well, I've work to do, and by the sound of it, so have you. But one piece of advice I'll give you. Watch your back. It's an unenviable job being the King's spy. Mark my words, he'll throw you to the lions if things go wrong. You might think you're his friend, but friendship is a luxury the King can't indulge in.

Everyone is a potential traitor in his eyes. Remember that.'

They said their farewells and Nicholas rode slowly back to the town. Bartholomew Tyler had been a pawn in a deadly game of international chess. But who were the other players? And what was he, Nicholas Peverell, supposed to be? Another pawn? He was surrounded by shadows, faceless people, watching him, watching everyone. No one could be trusted—not even the landlord of the Mariner's, not even the Sheriff; not even the Earl of Southampton.

* * *

Arriving at the Mariner's, Nicholas gave Harry over to one of the stable boys with instructions to feed him well. Then, shouting to the landlord for pie and ale to be sent up to him, he went up to his room and straight over to the cupboard where he'd put Tyler's box. He took it out and carried it over to the table by the window. He lifted the lid. The rolls of parchment were still there, neatly arranged in rows. One by one, he lifted them out and began to read them carefully. A knock at the door interrupted him and he opened it and took the tray of food from the boy and put it down on his bed. Then he went back to scrutinising the lists of orders.

They were all orders for wool or woollen

cloth. The names of the customers were carefully written at the top of each order: Jan Vydt from Ostend, Cornelius Woestijne from Ghent, Karel Ruysbroek, Bruges, Leon Smet, Ypres and Pierre Tancarville from Le Havre. Five merchants, all wanting to buy English wool and woollen cloth. But suppose there was more to them than meets the eye? Suppose they were some of Tyler's contacts in Flanders and France? Suppose, thought Nicholas with growing excitement, these orders were coded information which Tyler was to carry back to Cromwell. The more he stared down at these rolls of orders the more certain he became that this box contained the information which Cromwell wanted. Coded information; a pity he, Nicholas, hadn't the key.

The key! How extraordinary that a box containing information as important as he supposed wasn't safely locked up. But it had been unlocked when Agnes Chandler showed it to him. So what had Tyler done with the key? There was only one thing for it, he'd have to go and find that key if he wanted to ensure the safety of the box's contents.

Putting the box back in the cupboard and leaving his food untouched, he walked the short distance to the Chandlers' house and was once more admitted to their living room. He asked Agnes about the box, if she knew whether it had been locked when her brother arrived at her house. She didn't know, because she only looked at it after he died and it wasn't locked then. Puzzled, he returned to the Mariner's and ate his midday meal.

Maybe, he thought, he was making a mountain out of a molehill. Perhaps he should take the contents of the box at their face value. Perhaps they were just what they appeared to be: lists of orders to be carried out in London for delivery to continental customers. But even so, a merchant of Tyler's status would surely have locked away his business affairs. Unless he forgot to lock it—and he didn't seem to be the sort of man who was that careless. Unless . . .

And here Nicholas paused, wiped his mouth with his napkin, and left his room, calling for his horse. This time he rode to the Sheriff's house and was told that he was busy at the town jail. When he got there he found Jack Nott sorting out a dispute between two seamen charged with disorderly conduct after a long night's drinking. He handed the two over to his underlings when he saw Nicholas and walked over to join him.

'I'm sorry to come at an awkward moment, Sheriff,' said Nicholas.

'All moments are awkward, Peverell. One thing after another. Those two almost killed a man last night and can't remember a thing about it. Now, how can I help you?'

'When you found Tyler's body, did you find anything on his person? A key, for instance?'

'What sort of key?' said Nott, scarcely able to control his irritation.

'A small one. Tyler had a box which contained his business transactions and it's unlocked. Seems odd that a man of his professionalism leaves his business affairs unlocked.'

For a second Nott paused, as if his mind was elsewhere; then he turned his attention back to what Nicholas was saying.

'You'll need to speak to the Coroner about that. My men removed the body and the Coroner examined it. As far as I know he didn't find anything. Mind you, his purse had been stolen and that might have had a key in it. You could go and ask him. His court's not sitting this afternoon so you'll find him at home. Leave your horse here and young Dick will show you where he lives.'

Shouting for someone to take Harry away, and summoning Dick, a young boy of no more than ten years old, the Sheriff went back to his work. Nicholas left the jail with Dick who took him to the Coroner's house just a couple of hundred yards away from the jail.

The Coroner was sleeping off a heavy midday meal and wasn't at all pleased at being disturbed. But he remembered Tyler, had searched the body thoroughly and was certain there had been no key.

Another dead end. It seemed as if Tyler had been content to carry his business transactions around in an unlocked box. And that ruled out the likelihood that the documents contained information about his secret dealings on the continent as anything confidential he would surely have locked away.

Collecting Harry from the Sheriff's stables, he rode back to the Mariner's tavern. The landlord was waiting for him and was curious to know where he'd been. Nicholas brushed him aside and started to go up the stairs to his room, but paused on the bottom step.

'Have I had any visitors? Any messages?'

'Oh no, my Lord. Rest assured that if anyone had come to see you I would tell you immediately. Will you be wanting dinner?'

Nicholas ordered dinner to be sent up to his room later. Then he went to his room, checked that the box was still in the cupboard and sat down on the edge of the bed. His investigations seemed to be leading nowhere. He still had no idea as to who murdered Tyler. But he did know a bit more about Tyler himself. However, the question of the key still worried him. It was so unlikely that Tyler didn't lock away his business transactions. After all, he wouldn't want anyone else to steal the names of his clients. And why did he have this feeling that the landlord was lying when he'd asked him if he'd had any visitors? He'd been too slick with his answer, too obsequious in his manner. He'd sounded false. And why did he have the same feeling that the Sheriff had been hiding something when he'd asked about the key? The Sheriff had been preoccupied with his own business, of course, but all the same he'd seemed evasive and he'd been over-anxious to get rid of him. It was all very confusing.

*　　　*　　　*

He went to bed soon after dinner so as to make an early start for Porchester the next day. This time he slept heavily. He didn't hear the creak of the stairs as someone came up to his room. He didn't hear his door open. But he did hear the cupboard door open. He opened his eyes, and through the heavy veils of sleep he saw the back of a man standing in front of the cupboard. He sprang out of bed, and instinctively tried to grab the man round the neck. But the man stepped aside and reached for the heavy pewter candlestick on a table by the side of the bed. Nicholas was thrown off balance and, before he could recover, the man raised the candlestick and struck Nicholas down with the strength of someone felling an ox.

CHAPTER SIX

The box had gone, of course. Raising himself off the floor, his head throbbing with pain, his brain confused and disorientated, it was the first thing he thought of. He looked up at the cupboard, the door open, and saw, in the ghostly light of dawn, the empty shelf.

He groaned and collapsed back on the floor. How stupid he'd been, how naive, not to have taken the box and its contents more seriously. But now the bits were beginning to fall into place. Someone knew what that box really contained under the camouflage of routine business transactions. And it was most likely that the person who'd stolen the box had also removed the key from the person of Tyler, who, probably, he had murdered, or at least had been a party to the murder. Now, the box was in the hands of the King's enemies—yes, he would have to think of them as enemies from now on—and he, Nicholas Peverell, had let it go. It would have been so easy to have got another key cut by a locksmith, and he could have put the box in a safer place until he was ready to take it to London. In fact, with the light of hindsight, he should have left immediately for London and taken the box to Cromwell. But he'd been slow. Slow and stupid. But no longer.

He sat up and clutched his head between his hands. Fortunately, there was no blood, only an egg-sized bump. But the dizziness was a problem, and he hauled himself to his feet and perched on the edge of the bed waiting for the faintness to go. His body was weak, but his mind was clearing. It now looked very likely that Tyler had been one of Cromwell's agents. Probably, he had acquired some information relating to a continental alliance against England; the proof Cromwell needed to put the country on war alert. The threat, almost certainly, was to come from the Netherlands, where the Emperor's sister, Mary, ruled as regent, and also from Francis, King of France. The details of that plot could have been in the box, in some sort of coded form. And how relieved the enemy would be now that they knew their plans were safe and Cromwell was still in the dark. But what were their plans? Nicholas thought. Was the alliance planning an invasion of England? If so, when? And where would an invasion force land? One thing was certain; Southampton would have to be warned, and Sir Charles Neville, who was responsible for the fortifications at Porchester Castle.

He staggered over to the table by the window where there was a jug of cold water and a bowl. Lowering his head, an action which caused darts of pain to shoot across his head, he dowsed his head and shoulders with the water and rubbed himself dry with the linen towel which the landlord had provided. He felt his strength returning. Pulling on his clothes, he went downstairs. The house was silent, the landlord and the servants still asleep. He wanted to find out how the thief had managed to get in last night as most alehouse keepers were fanatically security conscious.

The front door was bolted from the inside. He went into the tap room and examined the windows facing onto the street. All were firmly bolted on the inside. He went into the kitchen at the back of the house where the embers of the fire still glowed red. The only window here was in the larder at one end of the kitchen. The door was open and stepping inside he examined the tiny window which opened out onto the narrow alley at the back of the alehouse. It opened when he pushed it and there were scuff marks on the windowsill. So that's how he'd come in. Not easy, the thief had been a big man, Nicholas remembered, and he'd be carrying a box when he left. Maybe he'd sent someone in through the window to let him in by the front door. When they left, they would have gone through the same procedure in reverse.

There were now sounds of life overhead, and a servant girl came into the kitchen rubbing the sleep from her eyes. She took one look at Nicholas and shrieked with fright. She would have bolted back upstairs had Nicholas not grabbed hold of her and told her who he was. She was young and painfully thin and was shaking with terror when Nicholas spun her round so that she had to look him in the face. Then he asked her if anyone had come to the alehouse yesterday afternoon asking about him.

'Sir, please don't hurt me,' she stammered, 'we had lots of visitors. How could I know what they wanted? Master doesn't tell me.'

'Did anyone ask for me?'

'You sir? I don't know your name, do I? Now please let me go. I have to get the fires going before Master comes down.'

She was a poor, pitiable child. Her arms were as thin as sticks and her body undeveloped; but he had to ask her one more question.

'My name is Nicholas Peverell. Did you hear anyone say that name?'

'Maybe. Only once. Someone came just before you returned. I was getting the supper ready and heard that name mentioned. That's all. Oh God help me, here comes Master. Please let me go.'

Nicholas released her and she scuttled off towards the fire just as the landlord came in. He stopped in his tracks when he saw Nicholas.

'What the devil! I'm sorry, my Lord, but I didn't expect to see you here at this hour.

What's happened? Your head . . .'

'I've been robbed, that's what's happened. I tried to stop him and got this for my pains,' Nicholas said, pointing to the bump on his head. 'Now, landlord, this is serious. The thief stole the box I was looking after. Inside were important documents. Why didn't you tell me someone was asking for me yesterday afternoon? Why did you lie to me?'

'I didn't think anything of it. A man called late in the afternoon and I was busy. We run a good business here, as you know. He asked me, just casually like, if you were staying here. I said you were. I pointed out your room, and he said he'd come back later.'

'Which he did; at a somewhat later hour, and not by the front door.'

'How the devil did he get in?'

'He found a way. Now landlord, I want you to tell me what that fellow looked like.'

'I didn't see him very well. I'm sorry about the theft of your box, my Lord. I'll report the matter to the Sheriff, of course, as soon as I can. Now sir, if you'll excuse me, I have breakfast to get . . .'

'That can wait. Now come here, and let me jog your memory.'

Nicholas took hold of the landlord, who was still only half awake, and shook him like a terrier shakes a rat. Then he gradually tightened his hands round his neck until his face turned a dark red and his eyes bulged with terror.

'Tell me who he was, or, by God, I'll strangle you with my own hands.'

The man was writhing around in Nicholas's grasp and strange noises were coming from his open mouth. Nicholas relaxed his grip but still kept hold of him.

'I've never seen him before. You've got to believe me. He was a foreigner, that I do know, because he spoke our tongue badly.'

'Was he a Frenchman?'

'I don't know. Foreigners all sound the same. He spoke funny, that's all I know.'

'Did he say where he came from? Where he was staying?'

'No, no, of course not. It was none of my business.'

Nicholas stared at the man, now trembling with fear. He was probably lying. He'd surely want to know the name of someone asking after one of his guests. Probably he'd been warned not to tell anyone of the visit. Probably the landlord had been too terrified to ask. Perhaps money had changed hands. Whatever had gone on, he, Nicholas, was unlikely to find out. But he'd been taught a lesson. People were watching him, ruthless people with a lot at stake. From now on he would have to be on his guard. For all they knew, he could have memorised the contents of the box, and so could be the next target.

Pushing the landlord away, he shouted for

breakfast and went up to his room, where the sunlight was now streaming in through the window. Another day; another move in the deadly chess game. But from now on, he thought, he was not going to be a pawn; he would be a major player.

* * *

'My God, Peverell, you've taken quite a beating. Let me get our doctor to take a look at that bump on your head,' said Southampton, looking at Nicholas in concern. 'Seems you've got yourself involved in something serious here. Mind you, you're only speculating about the contents of Tyler's box. There was no mention of a specific plan for an invasion, was there? You say there were documents inside, documents recording Tyler's business affairs. What leap of the imagination had made you come up with the conclusion that the country is about to be invaded by foreign powers? Sit down, man,' he said as Peverell began to sway on his feet, 'and let me get the doctor.'

He pushed a bench towards Nicholas who collapsed on it with relief. They were standing in the newly-built keep of the castle where building work was going on all around them. 'Forget the doctor. There's nothing he can do. I haven't broken anything. The dizziness will soon pass. But you must take the theft of

84

Tyler's box seriously, my Lord. A thief wouldn't take the risk of breaking into a house and knocking out one of the occupants and stealing a box which contained nothing more than the names of business associates. You know as well as I do that if he'd been caught, he'd be facing a charge of breaking and entry, theft, and causing grievous bodily harm. He'd swing for that. I admit that I didn't find any evidence of invasion plans, but I think, in the circumstances, we ought to look at the worst possible situation. Just take a look at what's happened so far: someone gets murdered; the King and Cromwell take the matter seriously. Seriously enough to summon me to Court and send me down here to find out who the murderers are. Then I find out that Tyler has continental contacts. He carries a box containing their names. You agreed with me that he could be one of Cromwell's agents. Then the box gets stolen. Why? Surely it must be because the contents of the box are not what they seem.'

'You don't know that, Peverell. You could be leading us all up a blind alley. But I have to admit that we mustn't dismiss the possibility that Tyler was on to something and was making his report to Cromwell. Of course, I shall expect the worse. I would not be doing my job properly if I didn't. I shall alert the fleet out at Spithead, and get this fort completed as fast as I can. In any case the outer walls are finished and we can mount cannons on them on the seaward side. That way we can stop any hostile ships from reaching Portsmouth Harbour. At least we have plenty of time to get ready. An invasion force with naval backing cannot be assembled overnight! But you ought to go and alert Neville. Porchester Castle is in a bit of a backwater but will be useful if any ships get past our guns at the Point.'

'We'll be relying on Neville to crush any invasion force.'

'Leave the military tactics to me, Peverell. When I want your advice I'll ask for it. No invasion force will get up as far as Porchester; we'll see that it doesn't. What do you think we've got a fleet for? However, I'm very grateful to you for coming to see me, especially with that sore head. I hope you're wrong about Tyler and his box. But, rest assured, I'll take the matter seriously and get the defences ready. Whatever the outcome, it's not a bad idea to keep the ships on the alert. Now rest a bit. Have some refreshment, and let my doctor put a poultice on that bump on your head. It quite ruins your beauty, and my Lady Ursula won't like that.'

'Lady Ursula?'

'Neville's wife. She's a bit susceptible to good-looking men.'

*　　　*　　　*

After a brief rest, Nicholas set off for Porchester. As he crossed the bridge from Portsea Island to the mainland he looked out across Portsmouth Harbour where, in the soft, late afternoon light, the still water shone like a mirror. It was a scene of such peace that all the talk of invasion seemed irrelevant. Nothing, he thought, could ruffle the calm of that place where fishing boats, with sails furled, floated on the water like swans asleep.

Turning west along the main coastal road, he saw Porchester Castle ahead. It stood on a promontory, facing the harbour, its massive walls, which had stood there since Roman times, presenting a formidable defence against any invaders from the sea. He rode up to the gatehouse and presented himself to the gate-keeper who let him into the outer bailey. He rode into this large courtyard, surrounded on all sides by thick, defensive walls which were punctuated by twenty bastions built at regular intervals along the walls. From these bastions cannons could be fired at the enemy. There were none in place now, Nicholas noted. In fact the place looked completely deserted. Ahead of him, at the far side of the courtyard was the watergate where visitors crossing the harbour by boat could land. To the right of the watergate stood a partially ruined building which appeared to be a church. He wondered if it was ever used now, or whether Sir Charles

Neville had his own chapel.

To his left, stood the mighty tower of the main keep of the castle. It was surrounded by more encircling walls and was approached across a moat and a drawbridge which could be raised in the event of an attack. Nicholas clattered across the bridge and through the gateway into the inner bailey, the courtyard of the main castle where the Constable had his house and guests could be accommodated and entertained in other buildings, built during the previous centuries and frequently used in times past by royalty. King Henry, himself, Nicholas remembered, had been here two years ago with Queen Anne Boleyn and they had spent the time hunting in the surrounding forests.

Not long ago, he thought, this courtyard would have been full of people: soldiers, servants, prisoners of war. Now, all was quiet and appeared deserted. It was clear that its days as a defensive fortress were numbered. During the long wars against France, this castle had been used by the kings of England for assembling armies and storing bullion to pay for the wars. Edward III had stayed here and sailed from here to his victory at Crécy. Henry V had sailed from here to defeat the French at Agincourt. Now times had changed. Southampton was the man of the moment. Portsmouth, with its dockyards, its forts defending the mouth of the harbour, the

King's fleet waiting outside the harbour in the Solent, had replaced Porchester Castle. In the soft, early evening light, the huge fortress seemed to Nicholas to be like a magical place, where knights in armour guarded an enchanted princess. A place where princes set out to play dragons and find the holy grail.

He dismounted and looked around him, the feeling of having wandered into an enchanted castle growing stronger by the minute. Ahead of him was a strongly built house, to the right of which stood the massive keep where soldiers would have lived in times past. Behind him was a fine building which he thought was probably the royal palace built by King Richard II. Here, King Henry would have stayed. On the other two sides of the courtyard were more buildings; all appeared deserted. Suddenly, a groom stood beside him, and led Harry away to be fed and stabled. Nicholas shook himself awake. This might be a place of enchantment, but he couldn't see that it would serve any useful purpose in repelling an invasion fleet. He needn't stay here long, he thought. He'd soon be back with the Earl of Southampton, in Portsmouth, where the action was.

He crossed the courtyard to the huge Norman doorway of the Constable's house. The door swung open on well-greased hinges, and Sir Charles Neville came out to greet him.

CHAPTER SEVEN

He wasn't a bit like Nicholas had imagined him to be. He had assumed that, as Neville was the Constable of a castle, he would look like a soldier; someone like Southampton. A man with a military bearing. But this man was as unlike a soldier as it's possible to be. He could have been taken for an artist, a painter, a musician, an actor, still wearing his costume; maybe a courtier who had never seen action on the battlefield. He was of medium height, slightly built, with dark hair curling on to his shoulders. A lean face tapered neatly into his high shirt collar. His doublet was made of black velvet embroidered with silver thread, and his slim legs were encased in fine white silk. Nicholas felt his heart sink. So this was the man who might have to repel an invasion of seasoned French and Flemish mercenaries!

Neville greeted Nicholas pleasantly enough; it was obvious someone had given him warning of his visit because he showed no surprise. He ushered Nicholas into the main room of his house. It was a long, low room with an inglenook fireplace in which logs were smouldering. A long, central table, laid up for a meal, took up most of the room. Ten chairs were placed at intervals round it. The stone walls were covered with brilliant tapestries depicting hunting scenes and on the south wall there was a very striking tapestry showing ships unfurling their sails and about to leave harbour. The rushes on the floor were plentiful and smelt clean and sweet.

'Welcome to our modest home, Lord Nicholas,' said Neville, his voice pleasant and well modulated. 'We are indeed honoured by your visit. It's not often that we have such an exalted visitor.'

'The pleasure is mine,' said Nicholas formally, and handed over Cromwell's letter of introduction which Neville read and gave back to him.

'We heard you were in the vicinity. News travels fast in these parts,' said Neville in response to Nicholas's enquiring look. 'We have a room ready for you, and perhaps, after you have refreshed yourself, you would like to join my wife and me for some wine before dinner. There's no hurry. We eat about eight. A little late, I know, but my wife prefers it that way. Come, James will take you to your room.'

James, a young boy, appeared as if on cue and led Nicholas upstairs to a room at the front of the house which overlooked the inner courtyard. Nothing could have been more peaceful. Nicholas felt himself relaxing. There was a jug of hot water standing on an elegant oak table by the window, with a bowl beside it. As he set about washing the dust of the journey from his face and hands, he felt as if he was in the comfortable home of a well-to-do country gentleman. He glanced round the room, noting that the furniture was all exquisitely made, much of it by Italian craftsmen. No expense had been spared. The curtains round his four-poster bed were made of costly damask, heavily encrusted with intricate embroidery. The sheets, which had been turned down for him, were made of the finest quality linen and had been scented with lavender. The water in a pewter jug standing by the bed tasted fresh and very cold. Nicholas drank thirstily.

He stood at the window looking down at the silent courtyard. He felt like a spectator at a play that hadn't yet started. The cast was assembling; when would the play begin?

This feeling of enchantment continued for the rest of the evening. He was the only guest and the three of them were waited on by six servants who anticipated his every need. His glass was filled with a fine Burgundy wine and replenished before he had emptied it, and only the choicest morsels of flesh and fowl were presented to him. They sat at one end of the table, Neville at the head, Nicholas sitting opposite Lady Ursula.

If Neville was the courtier, Lady Ursula was the enchanted princess. She looked older than her husband, her body full and voluptuous, her face flawless with dark blue eyes which seemed almost black, a full mouth, and glossy dark hair smoothed back under a French hood, a style made popular by Anne Boleyn. The edging of the hood was heavily encrusted with precious jewels and rubies glowed in her ears and hung round her neck in a lavish necklace which must have cost a king's ransom. Her cream-silk dress was low-cut revealing beautifully-shaped breasts. The edge of the bodice was decorated with pearls, and the front of her dress was studded with tiny seed pearls which shimmered in the candlelight. She ate very little and drank only water and spoke hardly at all. But she watched Nicholas intently and he, very conscious of her scrutiny, kept his eyes fixed on her husband who ate heartily, and drank a great deal.

The conversation was of a general nature, ranging from the pleasure of hunting in the forests around Porchester to the boredom of living in such a backwater. Lady Ursula came to life at this point and bcmoaned the fact that they were so far away from Court and decent company was non-existent.

'You, Lord Nicholas, are the first guest we've had this month. My Lord of Southampton comes to give Charles his orders, but he never stays long—he only comes to argue with Charles over the Priory which we've bought. I feel I shall die of boredom here and will be buried in that crumbling church or simply tipped into the surrounding mud flats.'

'No fear of that, my dear,' said Neville with more than a hint of sarcasm. 'Your relatives would be on to me like a pack of hounds. I suffer, you know, my Lord, from being married to a member of the Woodstock family, with royal blood in its veins—descendants of the third Edward, as she'll no doubt delight in telling you. All the family are very rich, so that's a compensation.'

'And, may I ask, for what do you need compensating, my dear husband?' said Lady Ursula, her eyes lighting up with glee at the prospect of an argument.

'For being married to the dullest and most bad-tempered wife in the county, that's why.'

'And what about me? Am I to have no compensation for being married to the most inadequate fop in the King's realm? Still, I suppose you do sing well, I'll give you that. Why don't you sing us something before we retire? Do you like music, Lord Nicholas?' she said looking him full in the face.

'It gives me great pleasure, madam.'

'Well that's something. The only music Southampton recognises is the sound of cannon fire. You'll sing to us, Charles, won't you?' she said, turning towards her husband. 'Let James bring your lute.'

Without any hesitation, Neville got up and draped himself elegantly over a tall stool which one of the servants had put in place in front of the hunting tapestry. He looked as if he had simply stepped out of the scene to entertain them whilst they rested from the chase. He sang the songs of the old troubadours—songs of courtly love and unrequited passion. His voice was a melodious tenor and he handled the lute skilfully. Nicholas, in his exhausted state, with his head still throbbing painfully, felt his senses reeling. Gradually he felt himself drawn into a fairy tale, a tale of chivalry and brave knights. He was also aware of Lady Ursula's scrutiny. Glancing across at her, he met her eyes, and she held his gaze. Her eyes were like two magical pools, full of mysterious lights, and he felt himself drawn under her spell. The pains in his head eased and his body relaxed and he gave himself up to her enchantment.

When the music stopped, Nicholas begged for more. He wanted the spell to go on for ever. He didn't want to think of Cromwell and Bartholomew Tyler and coastal fortifications. An enchantress had beckoned him into her world and he wanted to stay there.

At last Neville put down the lute and grinned across at Nicholas. 'You'll sleep well now, my Lord?' he said.

Nicholas rose unsteadily to his feet. The prospect of bed suddenly seemed very attractive. He thanked them both for their hospitality and found his own way to his room. Tomorrow, he thought grimly, he'd examine the fortifications of the castle which, as far as he'd seen so far, seemed sadly lacking. He opened the window to breathe in the cool night air pleasantly laden with the salty tang of the sea. The waning moon glided out sedately from behind a cloud and cast a soft light over the courtyard. The sky was dark and mysterious, studded with stars—like precious jewels on a lady's dress.

He pulled off his boots, undressed and lay down on his bed. He left the curtains open so that he could feel the cool air on his body. His pillows were soft and sweet-smelling. He felt his body relax into sleep, with the image of a woman's face in his mind—a woman with glowing eyes and a smooth white face. But as he drifted into sleep the face changed. The eyes came to life, sparkled and challenged him. The face became framed with glorious coppercoloured hair; Lady Ursula had become Jane Warrener.

*   *   *

Much later, he couldn't tell what time it was, he was woken from sleep by the unmistakable noise of a horse's hooves clattering over wood. The wooden drawbridge! he thought, as he sat up. So, it appeared they had a visitor. He got out of bed and went to the window. The breeze had stiffened, the smell of the sea was very strong, and he realised that the tide had come in and was probably lapping over the steps leading up to the watergate. However, the man he was looking at was on horseback and would have come in by the land gate. He was tall, wrapped in a dark cloak, his cropped head uncovered. Nicholas couldn't see his face as it was turned away from him. He was talking to Neville who was dressed in a long robe of some dark-coloured material. They walked over to the keep, deep in conversation. Neville pushed the door open and they disappeared inside.

For some reason or other, he found the scene disturbing. There shouldn't be mysterious night visitors in an enchanted palace. Then he pulled himself together. Of course it was perfectly reasonable for Neville, as Constable of the castle, to expect visitors at all times of the day. And just because he had a beautiful wife who possessed powers of enchantment, it didn't mean that he ignored the responsibilities of his position. Tomorrow, he thought, he must shake himself out of his lethargy and get down to business. In the meantime, there were still a few hours to go before daylight. Sleep called.

*   *   *

Next morning he breakfasted on cold beef and wild duck and went out early with Neville to inspect the castle. They first took a look at the building on the south side of the courtyard.

Once a royal palace, it was now in a state of neglect. It was hardly ever used, Neville said. The last time anyone came to stay in it was when King Henry brought Queen Anne Boleyn there two years ago. It just wasn't worth spending money on it for repairs. The keep, though, was a different matter altogether. Neville pushed open the massive, wooden door and they found themselves on the ground floor which was full of servants preparing food and washing out clothes in huge vats of hot water. The atmosphere was close and steamy and only dimly lit by torches fastened to the walls as there were no windows. If Neville's house had been the magic castle, this was its powerhouse. Nicholas asked how the servants communicated with the main house as he'd seen no signs of servants since he'd arrived, except for the six who waited at table.

'We have an underground passage that connects this building to my house. I don't like food cooked on my premises; nor do I like the place cluttered with servants. It's easy for them to cook and wash here and bring the food straight on to the table. In that way, we are not disturbed.'

'A sensible arrangement,' said Nicholas evenly, thinking of his own house where the servants not only ran the place but seemed to regard him as an intruder. 'Did you build the passage?'

'Oh no. It's always been here. I simply enlarged it and removed any obstructions. By the way, there's always hot water here—you only have to ask for it and you can have as much as you like. I like to take a bath twice a week; you are welcome to do the same, if you have a mind to it. Just have a word with James and he'll arrange it all.'

Nicholas thought that, after the bruising he'd suffered and all the dust and sweat he'd accumulated after days of hard riding, a bath would be welcome. Neville stepped over to an old man, who, with his bent back and straggly hair and beard looked like one of the gnomes in a fairy story, someone who spent his life mining for gold in a secret mountain.

'Hugh will see to it,' said Neville as he came back to Nicholas. 'He's in charge of the hot water. Now let's go up to the next floor.'

They made their way up a winding stone staircase set in the side of the keep and stepped out into a room full of soldiers. At least, it seemed to Nicholas, there was a large number of people present, and judging by the pikes propped up against the wall, and the pile of helmets in one corner, they must have been soldiers. Most of them were sitting round a large table eating from wooden bowls. In the centre of the table chunks of bread were stacked on a pewter plate. There were several pewter jugs containing either ale or water, dotted along the table. The room had narrow slits in the walls that let in the fresh air and light. Nicholas counted ten men. They looked at him and Neville resentfully as they entered the room, but when one of their number shouted an order they scrambled to their feet.

'Don't disturb the men at their breakfast,' said Neville calmly to the soldier in command. 'I only want to show our guest how well defended we are.'

'With this handful of men?' said Nicholas incredulously. 'But there's only ten of them.'

'My Lord of Southampton seems to think that's enough to defend this place stoutly.'

'We'll do our best,' muttered the commanding officer.

'However,' said Neville, 'he has promised to send reinforcements, and they should be arriving any time now.'

'What do they do all day?' said Nicholas, feeling reality receding once again. 'They can't stay here all the time. They're not prisoners.'

'Certainly not. They patrol the walls, search the premises, and soon will be moving cannon into place.'

'Soon?'

'I've just heard we are to be supplied with new cannons. Very up-to-date and they're to be mounted on the bastions facing the harbour. We are to stop enemy ships from landing here—it seems.'

Nicholas looked at him sharply. There was more than a hint of sarcasm in Neville's voice and it didn't do to mock the military arrangements which he, as Constable, would have to put into effect.

'So that must have been the person I saw last night, Sir Charles. Was he the person who brought you news of the cannons?' said Nicholas.

'He was one of Southampton's messengers,' said Neville looking sharply at Nicholas. 'I'm sorry we disturbed your sleep, my Lord.'

'Oh it is of no consequence. I slept the sleep of the dead. It was only the sound of the horse's hooves crossing the drawbridge that woke me up. I soon went back to sleep. But I'm sorry you were disturbed in the night, Sir Charles.'

'Oh, my job has no off-duty hours. When my Lord of Southampton wants to speak to me, anytime will do to suit his convenience. He seems to have some fanciful idea that we are soon to be attacked. I can't think that it's a matter of great urgency for us here, stuck up at the wrong end of the harbour, and we're not expecting a land attack, it seems. Southampton's the one who should be getting a move on with that fort he's building. Still, no doubt he thinks these fine men will protect our shores when all else fails. And whilst we're waiting, they eat their heads off at my expense. On with your breakfast, men,' he said, as they turned to go.

'They exercise in the yard later, and patrol

the outer walls. In their off-duty time they play dice and drink. I draw the line at women though. They only cause trouble,' he said as they climbed the stairs to the next floor.

There were four more floors, all of which revealed nothing of interest. They seemed to be used for stores as there were piles of blankets and rough clothing, and one room seemed to be the armoury, judging by the pile of harquebuses lying on the floor. From the top of the keep, Nicholas stared out across the harbour, still peaceful in the calm, summer weather. In the distance he could make out the outline of St Thomas's church and the sturdy shape of the fort defending the entrance to the harbour.

'We're the end of a bottle-neck,' said Neville as they stood together with the wind buffeting their faces. 'Portsmouth provides a very effective stopper. We're quite dispensable, you know, Lord Nicholas. Tell the King that, when you make your report to him. Southampton is the man of the moment. I am here simply because the place should have a Constable and I was available. Southampton can't stand the sight of me, as you must have gathered. He'll see to it that I remain a custodian of a castle that has long outgrown its use. Meanwhile, I moulder away. Admittedly, with my wife's money, we have a very comfortable life, but at my age I should be in a much better position. This job is for an old man; someone at the end of his career, not at the beginning. The King has no business to keep me here, a man of my accomplishments. I have been badly treated, Lord Nicholas. Tell that to the King when you next see him.'

'Why not tell it to him yourself? He can be quite reasonable sometimes, when you catch him in the right mood. He doesn't like to be surrounded by discontented people.'

'Lord Nicholas, not once have I been summoned to Court. All communication with the King is brought to me by Southampton, or one of his minions. But, by God, Peverell, there's one thing I have got—the Priory. The canons have been turned out and the King's accepted my offer. I outbid the Earl of Southampton. What a triumph! Ursula fixed it, of course. She asked one of the members of her family who's at Court to negotiate with the King. Ursula arranged for the money to be sent and we are now in possession of the Priory. It's a fine building on a prime site, surrounded by forests; and it's all mine!'

He was becoming very excited and Nicholas could see that he was as happy at stealing a march on Southampton as a child who has been given a toy better than the ones his friends have received. Neville might never make a soldier, but he would become a substantial landowner. Probably he'd become a member of parliament, if he played his cards right; maybe a member of the King's Privy

103

Council. Ursula would like that.

'Have patience, Sir Charles. You are still young. Honours will come your way when you've become lord of the manor of Porchester. You'll get summoned to Court, right enough.'

'Let's hope so. Meanwhile I have to keep up this pretence of being a soldier and a commander of men. I've been given ten soldiers to play with and I shall keep them busy. But let me show you the rest of my fortress. It's a pleasant day for a stroll and I want to get out of this wind. Tomorrow, you can enjoy the pleasures of the chase, if you like. You may take your pick of my horses if you'd like a change from that black beast of yours. My wife will accompany you as I've many things to see to. She's quite taken a fancy to you, you know. I'm afraid she finds me a dull sort of fellow. But it was the King's wish that I should marry her and at least he found me a rich heiress. Unfortunately, she's not suited to being the wife of the Constable of a fortress which has outgrown its usefulness.'

As he followed Neville down the stairs to the ground floor of the keep, Nicholas wondered why the King should go to the trouble of finding Neville a wife when he was perfectly capable of finding one on his own.

The rest of the day passed pleasantly enough. They strolled along the top of the outer defensive walls, examined the places where the cannons were to be mounted, and went down to the watergate to talk to the captain of Neville's boat which was for his personal use only. There was no doubt in Nicholas's mind as to what he would say in his report on the defences of Porchester Castle. It would truthfully record a dismal state of neglect and apathy. Should an enemy get through Portsmouth's defences, Porchester would be a walkover, leaving the southern shores of the country wide open to an invasion.

CHAPTER EIGHT

The next morning, Nicholas ate his breakfast on his own in the main hall. Suddenly Neville walked in and seemed in high spirits.

'A fine day for the chase, Lord Nicholas,' he said breezily. 'Ursula will meet you by the gatehouse when you're ready. She's checking out the hounds at the moment because there's talk of a plentiful supply of game of all sorts in the forest. You should have good sport.'

'You'll not be riding with us, Sir Charles?' said Nicholas looking up enquiringly.

'Not today. I've got to get over to my Priory. The masons are waiting for me to give them instructions and the sooner they complete their business of turning the church into a private house, the easier it will be to keep

Southampton at bay.' He saw the joke and gave an abrupt laugh. 'You see how both of us hunt today. You to shoot deer, and I to ward off Southampton's attack on my property. So we'll meet again at dinner. Take care Ursula doesn't press you too hard. She's unstoppable once the hounds raise the scent. Just listen to them now! A fine orchestra tuning up. I hear she's got Gaston out today. Keep well clear of him; he's got jaws of iron and can rip off a man's arm if it gets in his way. Good hunting, Lord Nicholas!'

Neville left the room and Nicholas jumped to his feet, pushing away the remains of his breakfast. He went out into the outer enclosure and there, by the gatehouse, a group of horsemen had assembled. In the midst was Ursula, beautifully mounted on a powerful bay gelding with a slender neck and a delicate head which showed its Arab blood. She looked perfectly at ease sitting side-saddle, her body swaying gracefully to the horse's movements. She was dressed in a dark-blue hunting dress which emphasised her voluptuous body, a neat hat, decorated with swan's feathers perched on her head, concealing her hair. She raised her whip in greeting when she saw Nicholas and urged her horse towards him.

'Good morning, my Lord,' she called down to him. 'Come and take your pick of our horses. You'll see we keep a good stable. Some we breed for strength, some for speed.

Gervase, here,' she patted her horse's neck, 'is a combination of both. No one can beat him when he chases the hare.'

'He is indeed a fine beast, but I intend to use my own horse. Harry can do with the exercise and he's a past master of the chase.'

'As you will. We'll have to put him to the test and have a race; Gervase against Harry. I daresay the stable lads will be placing their bets.'

Nicholas gave the order for Harry to be brought from the stables, and he came prancing out into the sunshine, full of energy and the joy of living. He welcomed Nicholas with a delighted whinny and thrust his elegant head into his outstretched hands. Nicholas stroked his glossy nose to quieten him and spoke gently.

'Come on, old fellow. You've had enough of good living, let's show this lady what we can do. You're on show today.'

He mounted Harry and went over to join the rest of the party, most of whom were servants carrying the equipment needed for the hunt: the crossbows, the quivers full of arrows, the long knives, and the baskets of food.

Harry sensed the excitement and pranced around alarmingly. The baying of the hounds, still incarcerated in their kennels, whipped him up to fever pitch. He knew the sound only too well and was eager to be off.

'Release the hounds,' shouted Ursula.

One of the huntsmen raised the short, curved horn to his lips and the eerie note sent shivers down Nicholas's back. Its effect on the hounds was immediate. The baying grew to a frenzy, and, once released from the kennels, they hurled themselves round the riders in a delirium of enthusiasm. Those horsemen who had whips used them energetically to keep the hounds away from the horses' hooves. Nicholas, used to his own pack of bassets and greyhounds, bred for their keen scent of smell and speed when chasing the fallow deer, looked in amazement at the motley assortment of dogs milling round the riders. By far the biggest and most ferocious looking was a huge mastiff with a great ugly face, its jagged teeth showing as it opened its jaws to emit a deep-throated roar. Nicholas caught Ursula's eye and pointed to it enquiringly.

'Gaston,' she mouthed back at him. 'We hunt boar today.'

Deciding to keep well clear of the hellish Gaston, Nicholas looked at the other dogs. There were bloodhounds, of course, essential for tracking, several dogs of unknown breed, some of them looking as if they'd seen better days and were in poor condition. There were a few bassets, but on the whole they were a mixed bunch. They were all ravenous, not having been fed that day, and eager to get started.

Ursula raised her whip as the signal to be off, and with the sound of the horn ringing in their ears and the deafening roar from the dogs, they clattered over the drawbridge and headed towards the forest which then covered that part of Hampshire.

The hours passed in a blur of sensations—the clamour of the hounds desperate to pick up the scent of some forest creature, the dappled light falling on to the forest paths, the excitement of riding Harry who had entered into the spirit of the chase with great enthusiasm. He had no difficulty in keeping up with Ursula's Gervase. Nicholas urged him on, always keeping the white swan's feathers in sight.

The woods were full of game of all kinds, but the hounds were kept strictly under control, the huntsmen checking them if they set off on a false trail. They frequently scented fallow deer, which occasionally Nicholas saw flitting like ghosts through the undergrowth; but the huntsmen were after bigger game. Gaston was their leader. Gaston was the king of the boar hunt.

At midday, they stopped briefly for refreshment. The servants led the horses away for a brief rest, and a great basket of food was produced and laid out on a cloth placed on the mossy forest floor by a stream of clear, running water. Ursula looked flushed and very beautiful. Her hair, as dark and glossy as

Harry's shining coat, had escaped from under her hat and cascaded down her back. They ate quickly, game pie, legs of chicken and wild duck, ale for Nicholas, and the water from the stream for Ursula. They said little, Ursula tearing the flesh off the chicken legs with sharp, white teeth. Both were aware that the hounds were eager to be off again, and the Master of the hounds was having difficulty in restraining them.

Suddenly, Gaston gave one, deep-throated call. It was an unearthly note and had a devastating effect on the other hounds.

'He's scented boar,' said Ursula, running to her horse. Quickly they mounted and now, with Gaston leading them, they followed him deeper into the wood under the thick canopy of trees where the sunshine hardly penetrated. Gaston was silent now, his body stiff with tension, the hairs along his neck raised, his nose close to the forest floor. They paused at a pile of fresh droppings and Ursula nodded to the Master of the hounds.

'He's on to it, and the boar's not far away. He'll lead us to it. Keep the others back, and keep them silent.'

They reined in their horses and followed Gaston, who, with head lowered to the scent, weaved his great body in and out of the thickets. Riding became more and more difficult as the boughs of the trees barely cleared their heads. Then Gaston gave a great, urgent bark. He'd seen the boar. It came crashing out of the undergrowth and stood there, staring at them balefully, its huge tusks ready to strike. One of the greyhounds could not be restrained. He leapt forward and hurled himself at the great beast only to be skewered on the sharp tusks and tossed aside contemptuously to the edge of the track.

'Stop them, you fool,' Ursula shouted, 'leave it to Gaston.'

Gaston now dropped down on his belly and slithered along the track towards the animal who stared at him with its small, piggy eyes. Suddenly, the boar decided not to risk an encounter, and he wheeled round and crashed off into the undergrowth where the horsemen couldn't follow him. Then Gaston rose to his feet and dashed after him, the huntsman blew his horn, this time the shrill call of the tally-ho, and the rest of the pack plunged after Gaston into the thicket.

The horsemen couldn't penetrate the dense undergrowth so they followed the path round to the other side of the thicket, where there was a glade in front of a giant oak tree whose massive branches blocked out the sunlight. Ursula signalled them to stop. In silence, they waited. Nicholas could hear the hounds and the boar crashing round in the bushes, he could feel his heart beating rapidly; he could sense the dark, mysterious atmosphere of the forest glade as he waited for the beast to emerge. Minutes passed, then, with a great crashing sound, the huge boar came out of the thicket and turned to confront the hounds with its back to the tree.

He was concerned. Nicholas expected the huntsmen to advance with knives and despatch the beast quickly. But that wasn't Ursula's intention. She watched, with mounting excitement, as hound after hound leapt at the boar only to meet its death on its lethal tusks, as sharp as swords.

'For God's sake, call off your hounds. Don't you want to save them?' shouted Nicholas sickened by the sight of so much blood. Soon the glade would be slippery with the blood and entrails of gallant hounds not bred to attack an enraged boar.

She glanced at him with a look of contempt. 'Does the sight of blood sicken you?' she said.

'Indeed it does, madam, especially when it is spilt unnecessarily.'

'We want to tire the beast,' she said, her face flushed with excitement. 'Then we'll release Gaston.'

'Then release him now and put an end to this slaughter,' he said.

'Oh, don't worry about the hounds. We only bring the old and useless ones on a boar hunt. Their purpose is to do what they're doing at this moment, to tire out the boar at bay.'

'It's a cruel way to end the life of a hound that has served you well all its life. Call them off, madam. This is not good sport.'

Ursula shrugged her shoulders, and nodded to the Master who was holding Gaston with the utmost difficulty. The mastiff was in a frenzy of rage at being held back. His fur was drenched in sweat and his great jaws dripped saliva. But, when released, he became a different animal. He knew it was no use hurling himself against those sharp tusks like the others; his method was to attack the rear of the animal. He crept forward, the boar watching him suspiciously with bloodshot eyes. Then he lunged forward and clamped his teeth on the boar's hind quarters, a bite which severed the tendons and caused the blood to stream down on to the ground. The boar let out a shriek of pain and whirled round, trying to knock Gaston off against the tree. But Gaston held on. Shaking his head, he worried away at the boar until the animal was in a frenzy of agony. Then, just for a second, Gaston released his grip, only to fasten his teeth into the boar's soft underbelly. This time he dragged his jaw along the creature's body, tearing open his belly and causing the entrails to tumble out into the glade. The boar gave a terrible shriek of pain and collapsed.

'Enough,' roared Nicholas, beside himself with anger. 'Despatch him now. He has suffered enough.'

'Not yet,' said Ursula, her eyes fixed on the gory spectacle, 'he can still fight back.'

113

'Aye, that's his nature; he's a brave beast. He deserves a brave end. Despatch him now, or, by God, I'll do it myself.'

He jumped down from Harry, drew out his dagger, and approached the dying animal, whose eyes seemed to look at him beseechingly. With a swift movement he slit the beast's throat, and he died instantly, with Gaston still clamped to his belly.

'Lord Nicholas, how dare you interfere?' Ursula screamed, as he returned to Harry and mounted him. 'I am in charge of the hunt. Remember you are my guest. I give the orders.'

'That's as maybe, madam, but I can't stand cruelty to man nor beast and you go too far. Now call off that mastiff, give the pack their due, and let's away. I've had enough of this cruelty. We do things differently in my part of the country.'

'Then you are a weakling and a coward, like my husband. There's nothing wrong with the sight of blood.'

'No, madam, only when it's shed unnecessarily for the pleasure of the spectators.'

He turned Harry and urged him away from the scene, not wanting to see the hounds gorging themselves on the boar's entrails. He knew this was a necessary part of the kill, but it always sickened him.

Ursula, still furious, rode after him. 'Let's

114

put you to the test, my Lord. There's an open field not far from here. Let us race our horses and see whether you are as feeble a horseman as you are a huntsman.'

'I'll not put my horse's life at stake, madam, but I'll gladly race Harry against your gelding.'

They rode on in silence until ahead of them was an open stretch of countryside intersected at the far end by a ditch and a high fence.

'To the ditch,' she said, 'over it and back here to the start. Let's go.'

She was off before he had time to collect Harry. But the horse seemed to sense what was going on. With a snort of rage he leapt forward and flew after Ursula's horse with a tremendous surge of energy. Harry knew he was being tested; he'd show them what he was made of!

Nicholas gave him his head, and with a speed that took Nicholas's breath away, Harry steadily drew near the flying figure ahead of him. Nicholas checked him to let Ursula clear the ditch and fence, then urged him over. He took the obstacle with effortless ease, turned, braced himself, and repeated the performance. Then, like an arrow released from the bow, he raced after the other horse. Soon the two horses were level. Gervase was beginning to tire, and Ursula had to resort to the whip. With a contemptuous flick of his tail, Harry passed Gervase and arrived back at the start with no obvious signs of tiredness.

Ursula rode up, her face taut with anger, her horse flecked with foam. 'It seems that your horse has been well rested at our expense, Lord Nicholas,' she said when she'd recovered her breath.

'He's been bred for speed and endurance, madam; not many horses have outstripped him.'

'Then you must allow us to use him. He's a stallion, I see, and he could sire excellent foals from my mares.'

'He could indeed. But he's not for hire.'

'Then you must let me buy him. You can name your price.'

'He's not for sale, not at any price. But I thank you for your excellent stabling. However, you'll be relieved to know that you won't have to feed either of us for much longer as I have to be away tomorrow.'

'Surely not so soon, my Lord. We can hunt hares tomorrow—the best of all sports.'

'I think I'll decline, madam. I've no stomach to see hares ripped to pieces by uncontrolled hounds. If you want to see bloody spectacle, madam, then I suggest you go to the bear pit in Portsmouth and watch the Saturday afternoon performance.'

They rode home in silence, Ursula white with anger. Once back in the castle, Nicholas saw to Harry and went to his room after calling James to prepare him a bath of hot water.

Not long after, there was a knock on his

116

door and James told him his bath was ready in the bathroom which was down in the cellar of the house. Nicholas was desperately in need of a soaking in soothing hot water, and he followed James down into a good-sized room where a tub of hot water filled the place with steam. Herbs had been sprinkled on the water, and helped by James, who tugged off his boots, Nicholas undressed and stepped into the bath, sinking gratefully down under the sweet-smelling water. Telling James to leave the towel on a chair, he ordered him to leave. Then he gave himself up to the enjoyment of a relaxing bath. But it was difficult to forget the scenes of the day's hunt. A keen huntsman, he liked to hunt wild animals which provided food for himself and his household throughout the year. But he always gave consideration to the animals which were hunted and to the hounds which hunted them. He could not stand cruelty and he made it a rule that a cornered animal should be despatched quickly and mercifully. His hounds were trained to raise the scent, follow it, lead the huntsmen to the quarry and then they would despatch it as quickly as possible. But today he had witnessed carnage and it had been instigated by a woman. And he had been sickened by the sight of it.

Suddenly, he became aware that he was not alone. Someone had come into the room. Through the haze of steam he made out the figure of Ursula. She was dressed in a loose

117

robe and her hair was unbound. She was emerging from the steam like a ghostly wraith, and as she came to the side of the bath she let the front of her robe fall open.

'Come, Lord Nicholas, let me massage those tired muscles of yours. I am expert at rejuvenating a spent body.'

She leant forward and picked up a cloth which hung over the edge of the bath and dipped it into the water. She was completely naked under the robe and he saw her silky smooth breasts glistening with oil. She smelt of some pungent herb and he felt his pulse quicken. She squeezed out the cloth over his chest and laughed with glee.

'Let us see, Lord Nicholas, if you are as feeble in the sensual arts as you are in the chase. But, somehow, I think you are not going to disappoint me.'

For one moment, Nicholas was tempted. She was undoubtedly one of the most beautiful women he'd ever seen, but then he remembered that look of excitement on her face when she'd watched the mastiff torture the boar. Yes, he would enjoy her, he thought. There was no doubt about that. Any man would. But afterwards he would regret it because there was no compassion in her and love was an unknown word. He rose to his feet and stood there dripping with water. She stepped back, admiring him, letting her robe slip off her shoulders.

'My Lord, you are a fine man, as well made as that magnificent horse of yours. Come, let me mount you and we shall ride together and have good sport.'

She picked up the towel off the chair and he stepped out of the bath, took it from her and wrapped it round his waist. Then he kissed each of her breasts and pulled her robe around her.

'Madam, you are the personification of beauty. But you are my host's wife, and it would be churlish of me to take advantage of you.'

'Then you are a weakling, a poor, feeble specimen of a man. You don't deserve a wife or a mistress. Go and find yourself some pretty boy.'

He pushed her aside and picked up his clothes where James had put them. Suddenly, he looked up and saw Neville standing by the open door. He looked furious.

'Lord Nicholas, I expected you to enjoy the pleasures of the chase with my wife, not the pleasures of the bath house. I require an explanation.'

'I shall be only too pleased to oblige, Sir Charles. But first, allow me to put some clothes on.'

119

CHAPTER NINE

It was too late to leave that evening as Harry needed to rest before embarking upon another journey. Nicholas ordered food to be sent to his room and after James had cleared away the dishes he began to think about the report he was going to have to write on the defences of Porchester Castle.

But he found it difficult to concentrate; his mind was too full of the images of that day's events—cruel images of dogs tearing at the cornered boar, and the seductive image of Ursula offering herself to him in such a blatant manner. There had been a row, of course. Neville had gone through the performance of the aggrieved husband, an act which Nicholas had found intolerable and he'd stormed out of the bath house and retired to his room. One thing was certain, however; he must leave tomorrow morning at first light and speak with Southampton. Porchester, as a defence against an invading force, was useless. Neville, as its commanding officer, ineffectual. If Tyler had been bringing back information about an invasion force assembling on the continent, then Neville should be removed as soon as possible, and the defence of the south coast put into the hands of the Earl of Southampton.

The trouble was, he thought, there were no

certainties in all of this. It was all speculation. And the one man who might have enlightened them was dead, and his report, if it was a report, stolen. Maybe it was all a fuss about nothing. Maybe Tyler had been murdered and robbed for the obvious financial reason. But someone had wanted his box badly enough to risk a break-in and an attack upon the occupant of a room. One day they would know the answers, but meanwhile he would be serving no useful purpose in remaining in Porchester, especially in the company of an irate husband and his wife whom he had just spurned.

His reverie was interrupted by a knock on the door. Thinking it was the servant, James, coming back to see if he needed anything for the night, he told the person to enter. To his surprise, the door opened and Neville stood there. He looked anxious and tense, not at all like an avenging husband.

'Lord Nicholas,' he stammered, 'I'm sorry to disturb you, but I have to speak to you.'

'If it's about this evening's episode I have nothing more to say. I told you what happened. Do I have to spell it out to you?'

'Think no more about it; it's of no importance. I know my wife only too well. She's a devil with a beautiful face. No man, not even my captain of the guard, can satisfy her. She put Southampton through his paces but he had to cry "enough". No, I've come about another matter.'

'Then come in and sit down.' Nicholas pushed forward another chair. For a moment they sat in silence, Neville hunched in his chair, a picture of dejection.

'My wife is my own problem, I realise that,' he said quietly. 'King Henry did me a disservice when he arranged my marriage. She has money, it's true, but I have to pay a high price for it. This place doesn't suit her; she needs constant amusement. And children. They might have settled her down, though I can't see that she has any maternal feelings in her at all. However, there it is. I can't help her in that area. So we are locked together in a state of perpetual animosity. But you are not going to leave us tomorrow, are you, Lord Nicholas?'

'That is my plan. I've seen all I need to here. Enough to write my report, that is.'

'I hope you might reconsider your departure. One of Southampton's messengers told me today that tomorrow ten cannons are arriving here to be installed along the seaward bastions. The men have already started to build the pulleys and tomorrow they should be in place. You'll need to see them installed and check that they're in good working order so that you can put that in your report.'

Nicholas hesitated. The last thing he wanted to do was to stay in this castle longer than was absolutely necessary. However, he could see

Neville's point. He couldn't leave the moment the castle's defences were about to be strengthened.

'When are they due to arrive?' he said.

'By midday. They are on their way now, but oxen travel slowly, especially with heavy loads. I should be grateful if you would stay. This is a step in the right direction and I would be relieved to know that your report contained some cheering news. Also, the men will work better if they know that the King's messenger is watching them.'

'Then I'll stay, provided I have my meals brought up here. I like to eat alone.'

'Certainly. But you won't be embarrassed by my wife any more. She will be hunting tomorrow, it is her one pleasure, and I shall leave instructions that she is to stay in her room at mealtimes. In that way, we can eat our food in peace. Rest well, Lord Nicholas, and we'll meet again in the morning.'

Neville left the room, and Nicholas got up and crossed over to the window and looked down into the courtyard. Dusk was falling and the keep and the other buildings were bathed in a soft, warm light. Yes, it was an enchanted place, he thought, but the enchantress had turned out to be a seductive devil with a taste for blood.

*   *   *

He slept fitfully, waking up suddenly in the early hours to the sound of horse's hooves clattering over the wooden drawbridge. He got up and looked down into the courtyard where the same sight met his eyes which he'd seen before—Neville, dressed in a long night robe was leading a horseman over to the keep. Clouds had built up from the west during the night and had covered the moon, so Nicholas couldn't see the rider's face. It was odd, he thought, how Neville received his visitors at night. The Earl of Southampton was only ten miles away. Surely, he needn't send messengers at night, unless it was a matter of extreme urgency.

It was all very disturbing, he thought, as he went back to bed. Mystery surrounded this place. Not only did it have a beautiful witch, but also a custodian who acted strangely. He wasn't what he seemed. There was more going on than Neville was prepared to tell him. And why had Neville been so anxious for him to stay on? Any other husband who had found his guest staring at his wife's naked body would have ordered him out of his house immediately. He wouldn't have given a moment's thought to the arrival of ten cannons, or whether his guest was going to mention them in his report; unless he was extremely ambitious and cared nothing about his reputation as a husband. It was all very odd, and Nicholas was glad to see the dawn and the arrival of James with jugs of fresh water.

Daylight did nothing to disperse his troubled thoughts. The low clouds hung over the castle like dark curtains and the air felt heavy and oppressive. There would be a storm by nightfall, he reckoned. Meanwhile, the soldiers were clattering around in the yard, dragging ropes and planks of wood over the drawbridge into the outer yard. Throughout the morning, pulleys were erected by each bastion for hauling the cannons up to the top. At noon, the first of the oxen arrived, lumbering through the gate, pulling its cart laden with a heavy cannon and a pile of shot. The other carts followed, some carrying extra soldiers as well as cannons and soon the outer bailey was full of lowing oxen, men heaving cannons into place, and the captain of the guard bellowing orders to all and sundry.

The cannons were of a formidable size, Nicholas noted, and newly cast. Each shot looked a good forty pounds in weight. It could have a devastating effect on enemy shipping. They were mounted on two-wheeled carriages and the job of hauling them on to the top of the bastions was no easy task, even with the strong blocks and tackle which the men had been preparing. Once on top of the bastion they had to be positioned with the barrel of the gun protruding through the turrets. As the walls of the bastions were not all of the same height, sometimes they had to make platforms to raise the guns. It was heavy, tiring work, especially in the sultry heat, and by the evening the men were exhausted, and there were still four more cannon to position. And tomorrow they would have to be fired.

That night, the storm broke. Great sheets of lightning flashed across the sky over Portsmouth Harbour. The crash of the thunder seemed to mock the sound which the cannons would make next day. It all seemed pointless labour to Nicholas, lying awake and thinking over the day's activities. The likelihood of an invasion fleet actually reaching Porchester and getting in range of the cannons and being hit by such a notoriously inaccurate weapon seemed very remote. But the storm passed and by morning the air had cleared and the sunlight streamed into his window.

That morning was spent in getting the rest of the cannons into position and then the moment came when they had to be tested. Only two men knew how to fire them, and they had to teach the others how to load the shot, pour in the gunpowder and apply the lighted taper. Above all, they had to realise the importance of keeping their fires going.

By the afternoon, progress was being made. Such large guns had a formidable recoil which two of the men learnt to their cost—one had a leg broken, and another was hit in the chest—

so ropes had to be fastened to the walls of the bastions to stop them inflicting any more harm. Then the gunnery practice continued until most of the men could aim reasonably straight at the target which had been floated out on the water of the harbour.

In the midst of this chaos, Nicholas was aware that a group of horsemen had arrived at the land gate. Leaving the men to their work, Nicholas went down to join Neville who had gone to greet the new arrivals. As he walked across the courtyard, he noticed that one of the horsemen was none other than the Earl of Southampton. What had happened to bring the Admiral of the Fleet here when he knew perfectly well that they would be involved in erecting the cannon which he himself had ordered? Had he come to check that there were no problems, he wondered? Southampton was deep in conversation with Neville but both stopped talking when Nicholas, very conscious of the fact that he was dishevelled and his face was blackened with gunpowder, the result of a cannon misfiring, came up.

Southampton dismounted and Nicholas was suddenly aware that everyone had gone strangely quiet and the Earl couldn't meet his eye.

'Lord Nicholas,' Southampton said, turning to look at Nicholas with a strange expression on his face, a mixture of contempt and sorrow.

'I've come here on an errand which fills me with sadness. I have been ordered to arrest you, and I have no other course but to obey that command. You must make ready to leave immediately and I have been instructed to convey you to London.'

'By whose orders, my Lord?'

'The King's orders. Here is the warrant.'

He handed the piece of paper to Nicholas who read it in such amazement that for one moment he thought it must have been a hoax. But one look at Southampton showed him that this wasn't a joke, it was deadly serious.

'On what charge?'

'Treason, my Lord. I am to convey you to London and lodge you in the Tower at the King's pleasure. Now, as we have been on friendly terms in the past, and in view of your noble standing, you can give me your word that you will not attempt to escape. In that way you will not be bound and you can ride on your own horse. Do you give me your word?'

Nicholas looked helplessly around him at the stony faces. He could not believe what was happening. How was it possible that he, the King's loyal servant, should be arrested on a charge of treason? It had to be a horrible mistake. Once he'd spoken to the King, all would be well, he thought. So, he gave his word that he would not try to escape and Harry was brought out of the stables. They were to leave immediately. He mounted and prepared to ride off with Southampton on one side and a guard on the other but he allowed himself one look back at the crowd which had gathered to witness his shame. Then he saw Neville standing on his own with a smile of triumph on his lean face. Then Nicholas saw it all. He'd been tricked! Neville had outwitted him. Neville had wanted this to happen all along. He wanted Nicholas out of the way and in such a fashion that no one would believe a word he said. Why, he thought, as they left the castle, had he not obeyed his instincts and challenged Neville? Why had he not left immediately and reported the night visitors to Southampton? Why had he been so reluctant to mistrust Neville? Probably Neville coming to see him in his room the night before last and asking him to stay on and watch the erection of the cannons had been part of a strategy to keep him in the castle whilst he built up his case against him. Probably Ursula had been part of the plot. Now he would be accused not only of treason but also of adultery with his host's wife. And he, Nicholas, had walked straight into the trap. But what was in it for Neville? What was he up to?

They rode at speed, stopping outside Guildford to spend the night at an inn, Nicholas with a guard on each side of him. At Putney, he left Harry at a posting house, and was taken to London by boat. At dusk they reached the watergate of the Tower. The tide was in and the gate opened to receive them. As Nicholas stepped out on the weed-covered steps where so many people had landed before him, he realised that he was lost. No one came out of the Tower alive; not when the charge was treason.

As the gate shut behind him, and he was taken up the steps to his lodging place in the grim fortress he realised that he had failed utterly. It was only fifteen days since the murder of Bartholomew Tyler and he was now a prisoner in the Tower of London.

CHAPTER TEN

Orpheus sat on a rock centre stage, playing his lute and singing a haunting song about the sadness of a life without love. All around him crouched the beasts of the forest, a motley collection of lions, deer, boars and some creatures that looked as if they had jumped straight out of a bestiary—grotesques with humped backs and long, prehensile tails and gaping mouths full of jagged teeth.

The performance was going well and Jane, waiting for her cue, could see that the Court was entranced. Orpheus finished his song and the consort of viols reinforced with shawms and a tabor struck up a peasant dance. The wild beasts then jumped up and cavorted

130

round the Great Hall of Hampton Court like a band of demons escaping from Hell. Even the Queen laughed when one of the monsters lumbered up to her and prostrated himself at her feet.

The band stopped, Orpheus began to play a gentle tune on his lute, and Jane came on to the improvised stage dressed as Eurydice in a simple tunic with her hair bound back with ribbons. As happens in masques, Orpheus fell in love immediately and began to woo her with his music. Eurydice, shy at first, soon succumbed to his music and began to sing with him. Their voices were well matched. Orpheus, one of King Henry's Welsh guards, whose father had fought with the King's father at Bosworth Field, had a fine baritone voice, and his dark, Celtic face had the right air of melancholy about it. Eurydice sang with a clear soprano which had matured under the training she had received at Court, and the two fell deeply in love. One by one the beasts crept back on stage and sat at their feet rolling over on their backs as a sign of submission to the god of love.

Then, with an ominous chord from the viols, one of the page boys, dressed as a snake, slithered across the floor, impervious to the warning cries of the courtiers who had forgotten their wine and sweetmeats and had become involved with the performers. The snake's costume was made of some shiny, bright green material decorated with sinister black markings covered with silver glitter. His hideous face was picked out with chevron markings and he'd been given a huge, forked tongue which he could operate from inside his costume by pulling a string. As he approached the stage, he hissed ominously.

Soon, all the beasts saw him and crept away ashamed of themselves for deserting the couple, but terrified of the snake. The viols began to utter agitated discords, and the shawm wailed a warning. Then Eurydice looked up. Too late, the snake rose up and leapt at her, fastening his imaginary teeth into her arm. Eurydice gave one shriek, and fainted. The snake slithered off, the beasts came lumbering back, and Orpheus broke into a powerful lament. As the beasts carried away her body, and the scene shifters removed the rock and brought in the gateway to Hades, Orpheus accompanied her body, singing his lament as only a Welshman can, and reduced the audience to tears.

The Master of the Revels had taken liberties with the plot, and the beasts accompanied Orpheus to King Pluto where he begged for his sweetheart to be returned to him. As the King listened to Orpheus's impassioned plea, the page boys and the court dwarves, dressed as demons, danced round Orpheus, mocking him with rude gestures, but unable to harm him.

King Pluto was moved by Orpheus's singing and relented. Then the moment came which the audience had been waiting for. At Orpheus's passionate cry, Eurydice—Jane—sat up on her bier which the beasts had placed on the floor in front of King Pluto, and sang the song of joy which was the climax of the masque. Then she got off the bier and the lovers fell into one another's arms, King Pluto looking on benevolently. At the end, Orpheus took her by the hand and led her away, the Master of the Revels having been asked to change the plot in view of the Queen's condition.

The masque ended with a riotous wedding feast, where beasts, grotesques, and the devils from Hades cavorted round the hall. The courtiers leapt to their feet and joined in, dancing vigorous reels to the loud, peasant music, whilst Eurydice lay in Orpheus's arms.

'Eurydice, Jane, my darling girl,' he whispered, 'when shall we be married? The King has given his consent. We can be married in the Chapel Royal whenever you say the word.'

But Jane was in no mood for Daffyd Owen's wooing. She disentangled herself from Daffyd's clasp and dragged him on to the floor to join the others in a wild reel. Her hair had broken loose from the ribbons and tumbled down her back. With her feet encased in jewelled slippers, she looked entrancing and

Daffyd could only look on completely enthralled.

Finally, with a crash on the tabors, the dance ended and everyone collapsed with exhaustion. Then King Henry, who had not danced out of respect for his wife, clapped his hands and called for Jane. She went over to where he sat on a raised dais and knelt at his feet.

'Come Jane, get up and rest with us for a while. You have delighted us with your singing and the Queen wishes to reward you.'

Queen Jane came over to where Jane was kneeling and raised her to her feet. Then, taking off the necklace from around her own neck, she fastened it round Jane's, to the delighted applause of the onlookers. Jane was stunned. She looked at the necklace which was an intricate setting of pearls and sapphires and worth a king's ransom. Never having possessed any jewels of value, this gift was beyond her wildest dreams. She stammered her thanks, but the Queen stopped her.

'It is we who have to thank you, Jane. You are our precious jewel because you bring happiness to my lord and me. Now be so good as to summon my ladies as I must be away to bed.'

'I, too, will retire early,' said King Henry, rising to his feet. 'We must do nothing to upset the precious burden you carry,' he said, leaning over to pat Queen Jane's round belly, tightly restrained under her stiff-fronted dress.

As Jane went to gather the Queen's ladies together, Daffyd came up to her. His dark eyes were glowing with enthusiasm, and his Welsh accent was more pronounced than ever.

'Jane, I must speak to you,' he said, taking hold of her arm. 'Why do you keep avoiding me? Can't you see I'm mad with love for you? Look, girl, in two days' time, the King has his birthday. We could declare our betrothal that night. You are my heart's delight; no one else could ever take your place. Say you'll marry me, Jane, my darling love. Don't keep me in suspense any longer, or else I shall die of love, just like lovers do in the songs we sing.'

'Daffyd, Daffyd, calm yourself,' said Jane, trying to back away from his embrace. 'I have to see to the Queen and what with all the rehearsals we are having tomorrow and the next day for the King's birthday performance, how can I think of being wed? Be sensible. Talk to me later, when there's not so much on our minds.'

'Why do you always run away from me, Jane? Why are you so hard on me? Do you love someone else? Is that it? Surely you can't still be hankering after that clodhopper Peverell? Oh, I see, that's the way the wind blows, is it? So you do have a regard for him?' he said, as Jane blushed at the mention of his name.

'Now look you, my girl,' he said with

mounting excitement, 'you'd best forget him. He's a lost cause. Rumour has it that he's been sent on a mission to Porchester Castle, and he's not carrying out the King's instructions. It seems he amuses himself with the custodian— he's Sir Charles Neville, you know—and his beautiful wife, instead of doing what he should do. It will end in trouble, lass, so don't waste your time on him.'

Jane felt the world come to an abrupt halt. All around her people were laughing and congratulating her, wanting to see her necklace, but all she could think of was Nicholas in danger. She was aware that the Queen had left the hall and she knew her place was by her side, so she pushed Daffyd away and tried to collect her thoughts.

'Lord Nicholas knows what he's doing. He saved the King's life, remember? The King trusts him completely. Now let me pass. I've got to attend to the Queen.'

Daffyd, seething with frustration, had to let her go; even he could see that the Queen could not be kept waiting. Jane, her mind in turmoil, went to get the Queen ready for bed.

* * *

That night, Jane slept fitfully, her tired brain refusing to relinquish the image of Nicholas. They had once been so close, working together to thwart the King's enemies. Why shouldn't

136

they work together again, this time to save Nicholas himself. She knew how easy it was to fall from favour in this Court. Many people had seen the King favour him; many would be delighted to witness his fall. Maybe she could be of use to him now. But first, she would have to know what was going on.

Fortunately, on the following day, the Queen had a lot to occupy her mind with the preparations for the King's birthday celebrations and Jane found herself freed from her duties. It was time to make some enquiries. But the problem was that she had few friends at Court, preferring to keep herself to herself. She was friendly with the Master of the Revels, but he was far too busy that day to bother with her. She knew and liked the happy band of royal dwarves who entertained the King and the Court with their tumbling, but they were not known for their discretion and loved gossip. Her favourite was Simon, known as Simple Simon because he pretended not to understand what was going on, but Jane knew he was one of the shrewdest people at Court. But he was rehearsing a special acrobatic act with the others and could only wave to her from the top of a pile of bodies.

Then she remembered Lady Isabel Hardwicke, one of the Queen's elderly ladies-in-waiting. Lady Isabel had always taken a motherly interest in Jane from the moment she had arrived at Court because she realised that a young, good-looking girl with no aristocratic friends at Court would need guidance in Court etiquette. They had become friends and it was to Lady Isabel that Jane turned that morning. She was told she'd find her in the royal gardens choosing roses for the King's table. Jane found her there, and went up to her, dropping a curtsey before she spoke.

Lady Isabel had been a widow now for ten years, but she was still slim and elegant despite being in her sixtieth year. Her face was unlined, her expression kind, and her grey hair carefully concealed under her head-dress. She was much respected and the Queen relied on her experience. She gave her basket of roses to one of the under-gardeners and greeted Jane warmly.

'Why Jane, what brings you here? Surely you ought to be rehearsing with that handsome Welshman of yours? No? Well, I'm glad to see you. Just look at these flowers, all perfect, all just ready for gathering. This sunshine has brought them all out. The timing couldn't be better. Now, how's the Queen this morning?'

'In good health, thanks be to God. She's excited over the King's birthday celebrations, which is only to be expected. But why I've come to see you is to consult you about a certain person who's not at Court at the moment, but as you know everybody and their family histories, I thought you might know something about him.'

Isabel laughed. 'You do know how to cheer a person up, Jane, my dear. I feel as if I've just stepped out of the Ark. But come and sit down over here, away from the servants. This Court has ears, as I expect you've found out.'

They walked over to a stone seat by the central fountain where water spurted out of the mouths of plump cherubs and sat down in full view of anybody who was watching, but out of earshot.

'Now what's the name of this person who interests you so much, Jane?'

'His name is Sir Charles Neville. I believe he is custodian of Porchester Castle. Do you know him?'

'I know of him; but why does he interest you?'

'Because . . .' And here Jane looked away and studied the cherubs. Isabel waited. 'Because Lord Nicholas Peverell has gone there and there is a rumour that . . .'

'Don't tell me. I know,' said Isabel laughing merrily like a young girl. 'Someone's told you that Neville has a beautiful wife. Now don't you worry yourself, my dear. If you are interested in Lord Nicholas, and he has any regard for you, Ursula Neville is no threat. Who told you about Neville, may I ask?'

'Oh, it was Daffyd Owen. He mentioned him last night after the masque. He said Nicholas had gone to Porchester on a mission and seems to be wasting time.'

'If Daffyd told you that, then think no more about it. Daffyd's jealous of Lord Nicholas, don't you see? He wants you to think less of him and more of Daffyd. From the little I've seen of Lord Nicholas, I know he is a man of honour and the King trusts him. But I can see that Neville's situation has changed since the Duke of Richmond's death last summer.'

'Why should that affect him?'

'Don't you know? How ignorant you girls are! Richmond was the King's official royal bastard. I can remember when he came to Court; yes, my dear, I am as old as that, yet it seems only yesterday. Richmond, Henry Fitzroy he was called, was the child of Bessie Blount who enjoyed the King's favours when he was married to Queen Catherine who didn't bear him a son. Fitzroy was a splendid son and the King loved him, treated him like a prince, and rumour had it that he was going to make him his heir. And all this was gall to Neville. You see he's the older bastard, born some twenty-eight years ago when Henry had just married Queen Catherine. He was born from a casual liaison with one of the serving girls when the Court was in progress up north, but the King never recognised him. Oh yes, he was found a place in the household of one of the northern earls, and when he came of age he was given a knighthood and a marriage was arranged for him to a wealthy heiress. The

King would never see him go in want. But, somehow, the King never liked him; Richmond was the son he wanted, and Neville was never invited to Court. The King doesn't trust him and the reason why he was put in charge of Porchester Castle was because the King wanted him away from the north which was in a state of rebellion last year. If Neville told the rebels he was the King's son, he could become a powerful rallying point.

'Now, I expect Neville is seething with resentment. Richmond is no longer here and still he hasn't been invited to Court. His wife is probably furious because her husband hasn't been given the recognition he deserves. Resentment leads to trouble, Jane. And when the stakes are high, Neville could be tempted into causing trouble in the south of England. And that's where Nicholas comes in. He's been sent to Porchester to keep an eye on Neville, I'm sure. Let's hope he keeps his wits about him because, mark my words, Neville will want him out of the way. He could try to implicate Nicholas in some treasonable activity, and remember, my dear, that the treason law has been extended to cover nearly every contingency; even we are at risk talking together like this. If we have enemies, and if they should be watching us at this moment, it's possible we could be arrested on a charge of conspiracy. Come, let's walk back to the roses, and try to laugh, Jane, look cheerful. It seems

141

that conspirators are expected to have doleful faces. But don't worry about Nicholas. He's the King's spy; he'll be aware of the danger he's in. He'll be back soon, and I'm sure that the reports he'll bring back with him will not be favourable to Neville. Nicholas Peverell would never be guilty of treason. Loyalty is his family's motto.'

Hoping that Isabel's optimism was well founded, Jane left her in the garden busily telling the gardeners which roses to pick. She was grateful to her friend for giving her so much information, but she would not have any peace of mind until she saw Nicholas again.

*   *   *

The preparations for the King's birthday celebrations took up the rest of that day and the following. At the last minute, Henry decided he wanted to play the part of Zeus, the king of the gods, in the production, and insisted on writing his own script. It wasn't until the following day that Jane had any time to herself.

There was still no news of Nicholas. But there was one person who would know where he was, and because of her unusual status at Court, a lady-in-waiting to the Queen, but also an entertainer, a nobody, Jane knew she wouldn't be taken seriously as she presented no threat. The one person who could help her was Thomas Cromwell.

She asked to see him and was admitted straight away to his room next to the royal apartments. He was seated at his desk busily writing letters. If he was surprised to see her he didn't show it. He merely glanced up from the pile of papers, told her to be seated and he would give her his attention shortly.

As usual she felt uneasy in his presence. His heavy, peasant face never registered any emotion. He was an efficient machine, able to demolish administrative affairs, but he never seemed to relax. Even when he was jovial his eyes remained suspicious. As she sat there waiting for him to put down his pen, the thought came to her that Cromwell was no more than one of the King's servants, and as such he was just as vulnerable to the King's displeasure as the rest of the courtiers. He couldn't afford to make a single mistake. And he also liked pretty women, she realised, as his face relaxed into a fleeting smile when, at last, he looked up and saw her sitting there demurely. There was even a suspicion of a twinkle in his small, puffy eyes.

'Well, well, if it isn't Mistress Warrener; or can I call you Jane?'

She nodded, biting back the obvious retort. This was no time to be assertive.

'I suppose you've come to see me about that Welsh fellow of yours. He wants to marry you, lucky fellow, and you want to know if the King

143

will approve. Well, put your mind at rest. The King loves romance and he'll give his blessing, rest assured. He'll let you use the Chapel Royal and he'll probably endow you with a couple of manors. A wedding will cheer the Queen up. I might even be persuaded to give you away as I can't see that curmudgeonly old devil of a father of yours travelling up here for the ceremony.'

'No, Baron Cromwell, that's not why I've come to see you. I have no intention of marrying Daffyd Owen. I like him and we are good partners in music, but that's all. I've really come about Lord Nicholas Peverell. You see we were once good friends and he is the lord of the manor in that part of Sussex we both come from, but I am worried about him and wondered if you had any news of his whereabouts.'

Suddenly, Cromwell's good humour vanished and his face darkened. 'So that's what this is all about,' he said, looking so severely at Jane that she felt her heart beat faster with fear. 'Now stay away from that quarter, my girl; don't give him another thought. He's about the King's business, and that's all I can say. He's not for you, Jane Warrener. Go back to your Queen and practise your songs and marry Daffyd Owen. Peverell is out of bounds.'

It was useless to ask any more questions. Cromwell had ended the interview. He picked up another piece of paper and summoned his secretary to take some dictation. Jane left the room.

Why had Cromwell become so angry when she'd mentioned Nicholas's name? Where was he? What was he supposed to have done? Frantic with worry, she had to wait until the following day to find the answer to these questions. Nicholas was in the Tower on a charge of high treason.

CHAPTER ELEVEN

'I never thought I should live to see the day when a member of the Peverell family is brought to the Tower on a charge of high treason,' said Sir Philip Digby, Constable of the Tower. 'But there it is; and it saddens me to say this, Lord Nicholas, but I must ask you to accompany me to your lodgings.'

Nicholas looked up at the elderly, upright figure standing to receive him at the top of the watergate steps, and felt some sympathy for him. It couldn't be pleasant to receive as prisoners those people he had been used to calling his friends. It had only been two years ago that he had dined with Sir Philip in the Constable's house and he had been given a comfortable room and treated like an honoured guest. Nicholas had been on a visit to the Tower for the purpose of trying to persuade Sir Roger Mortimer, who had been put to the rack, to reveal the names of his fellow conspirators. Now he, Nicholas, was following in Mortimer's footsteps along with all the other people who had been brought here. In most cases they had stayed here, their headless bodies buried in the church of St Peter ad Vincula which stood close to the place of the scaffold.

'I am sorry to put you to the trouble of looking after me,' said Nicholas formally, 'but I would like to say one thing before I leave these steps and follow you to my prison cell. Not once have I spoken against the King or done anything which might endanger his life or threaten the stability of this realm. Two years ago I saved his life. Since then he has trusted me implicitly. Treason is not a word in my vocabulary. My family's motto is "Toujours Loyal" and I will remain loyal to our lawfully crowned King for the rest of my life.'

Digby turned and looked at Nicholas. His soldier's face, scarred by sword cuts received in many battles, looked drawn and weary. 'They all say that,' he said sadly. 'But I do believe you, my Lord; and I also know you must have many enemies. But my job is to guard you, not to try you. Please follow me.'

Nicholas was lodged in the Bell Tower, above the room where Sir Thomas More had been incarcerated. His room was not uncomfortable. It was large and airy, the tiny slit windows letting in fresh air and a modicum of light. There was a wooden bed with no mattress, a large table with writing materials on it, a comfortable chair and two other chairs. The rug on the floor was tolerably clean, and on a small table in one corner was a bowl and a pewter jug. Digby stood aside to let him enter the room first.

'You will not be too uncomfortable, my Lord, and you have some privileges. Food will be brought to you and you can arrange for any delicacies you require to be brought in from outside. Your washing water and your laundry will be brought to you and collected from you daily by one of our own laundresses, someone who has worked for us for years and who looked after Sir Thomas More when he was here. Her name is Hannah Bidgood and she is completely loyal to me. Should you attempt to bribe the servants or try to escape, which I'm sure you would never consider, Lord Nicholas, all these privileges will be taken away and you will be confined to a dungeon. Any visitors will have to report to me first and I will bring them to you and see they leave the premises. I hope that, for both our sakes, your sojourn here will be brief and you will soon be walking as a free man across the bridge and out of this place. God be with you, my Lord.'

Sir Philip Digby left the room, the door closed and the key turned smoothly in its well-oiled lock. Nicholas was alone.

Still feeling numb with shock, he walked over to one of the tiny windows. Looking out, he was just able to see the Thames where boats were making their way upstream on the incoming tide. The other window looked towards the west, over the moat that surrounded the inner walls of the Tower and he could see people walking across the drawbridge towards the main gate. Outside, life was going on as normal, whereas his life had come to an abrupt halt. He was grateful to Digby for giving him such a light and airy room, but the fact remained that there was no way for him to escape. The windows were too narrow to let a body squeeze through. And even if it were possible, he had no rope to lower himself down. He was at the top of the Tower so it wasn't possible to dig a tunnel even if he had the wherewithal to do so. The door was massive, the lock unbreakable. The walls were as thick as his arm and he had no tools to break through them.

Giving way to despair, he sank down on the edge of his bed clasping his head in his hands. How long, he thought, would he have to wait for his trial? How long before he was confronted by a series of trumped-up charges? How long before he was taken to the scaffold to suffer the same fate as Sir Thomas More and Queen Anne Boleyn? And, above all, what was he supposed to have done to get him into this predicament?

He heard the sound of the key in the lock and a guard entered bringing in a plateful of bread and cheese and a jug of ale. He was a burly soldier doing his duty. His face was expressionless and he said nothing. Nicholas couldn't face the thought of food. He felt sick with fear and powerless to do anything.

Just before nightfall, the door opened again, and a huge woman came in with a jug of water. She was dressed in the clothes of a working woman, a long, thick skirt, the front covered by an apron, a loose-fitting shirt with a shawl knotted across her chest. Her hair and most of her face were covered by a grey linen bonnet. She glanced at Nicholas as she went across to fill the jug by the bowl on the table, and he was repelled by her ugliness. The heavy, coarse face was covered with warts which seemed to cluster most profusely around her bulbous nose. Her eyes were red-rimmed and one was discharging yellow pus which had coagulated on her cheek.

'Mistress Bidgood?' he said.

She nodded as she filled the jug and glanced at the bucket in the corner of the room. She had a linen bag slung over one shoulder which she took off and shook at Nicholas.

'Have your linen ready for the next time I come. I charge one penny a load.'

She went over to the door and Nicholas noticed she walked with a pronounced limp as if one leg was shorter than the other. She opened the door and went out, banging it behind her.

As darkness fell, he lay down on his bed and tried to sleep. His first night in prison. How many more days and nights would he have to endure?

*   *   *

The next morning, Sir Philip Digby ushered in a visitor. To Nicholas's astonishment he saw, standing in front of him, the stocky figure of Thomas Cromwell. Nicholas jumped up, hope surging through him. Cromwell knew he was innocent. Cromwell had come to release him.

Cromwell stood there, rubbing his hands together as if he were at a loss for words. He stared impassively round the room.

'I trust your accommodation is satisfactory, Lord Nicholas,' he said. 'It's the best we have available.'

'I should prefer my own room in my house in Dean Peverell, Baron Cromwell.'

'Quite, quite, but there are some things we have to sort out first. May I sit down?'

'Of course. Be my guest. The chair behind the table would suit you best, I think.'

Cromwell, if he sensed the irony, chose to ignore it. He sat down in the chair behind the table, drew the paper and pens towards him as if they had been put there for his benefit, and then looked thoughtfully at Nicholas. Nicholas

150

stood up, and faced his inquisitor. He knew Cromwell. How long before he came to the point?

'May I know of what I am accused, and who is my accuser?' Nicholas began.

'All in good time. You will have a fair trial, rest assured.'

'A trial, you say?' said Nicholas, aghast. 'On what charge?'

'I thought you'd been told. The charge is one of high treason.'

'What evidence have you to substantiate this charge?'

'All will be revealed in due course. Don't fret so. We pride ourselves on our sense of justice in this country. Thank God we're in England, not France. You know that here you are presumed innocent until proved guilty. You've got rights, you know.'

'I also know that things can get twisted to suit someone's personal vendetta. May I ask who has brought these accusations against me?'

'Let me just say that we have received information that gave us no choice but to order your arrest. For instance we had reports that you said things against the King's Majesty.'

'What things, for God's sake,' said Nicholas with mounting anger.

'You were overheard talking to Lord Southampton when you visited him on . . . let me see now—' and here Cromwell referred to his notes, 'on June the twenty-fourth, at the site of the castle which he is building to the east of Portsmouth. You were heard to say that the time had come to get rid of the King. Now that sounds like treason to me and it's enough to send you to the scaffold.'

'Whoever said that is lying. Who is this person?'

'He's unknown, but his report was handed in to the Sheriff of Portsmouth.'

'Did it never occur to you that this man was saying what he'd been paid to say? Surely you know about false witnesses? And why haven't you spoken to Southampton? He'll remember the conversation. He asked me if I was loyal, and I said that I had always served the King and would continue to do so until the end of my days.'

'We did speak to Southampton and he says he can't recall the conversation as there were too many other things on his mind.'

'Of course he can't, because it never happened. Don't you see that someone wants me out of the way?'

'Maybe, but we have to go into it. This is a serious accusation. There's also the question of Bartholomew Tyler's box of papers which you say was stolen from your room at the Master Mariner's tavern in Portsmouth on the night of the twenty-fourth of June. It hasn't been found and it could be because you have the box in your own possession. Maybe it wasn't stolen at all.'

'Wasn't stolen?' roared Nicholas advancing towards Cromwell who was glad to have a desk between them. 'Don't be so ridiculous. Do you actually think I broke into my own room and knocked myself out in order to pretend that someone had attacked me and made off with the box?'

'Calm yourself, Lord Nicholas, or else I shall have to summon the guard. If you think about it, it's not so ridiculous. It's possible to give oneself a blow on the head to make it look as if one's been attacked by another person.'

'Then the world's gone mad and I am the only sane person left. The landlord of the Mariner's will confirm that someone came asking for me that day and he pointed out my room. The serving girl will also say the same thing.'

'I'm sorry, Lord Nicholas, the landlord denies hearing any disturbance in the night and certainly denies that he had any visitors that day, and certainly no one came asking for you.'

'Then the man's lying. I don't blame the serving wench—she'd say what she'd been told to say. Someone's bribed the landlord to bear false witness against me. By God, just you wait till I get my hands on that scoundrel! But the Sheriff? Have you spoken to the Sheriff? He knows the box was stolen. I reported it to him. He knows I was trying to find who had stolen

153

the key off Tyler's body.'

'The Sheriff doesn't deny this. He says you reported the theft, but theoretically that doesn't prove you haven't got the box. You could have made up the whole incident. Until the box is found, you are under suspicion.'

'This is utterly absurd. Why are you so interested in Tyler and his infernal box?'

'Because Tyler was one of my agents and gave me good service for several years. We have been receiving regular reports from him. Now this last report would have given me what we need to know, the timing of the threatened invasion from the continent.'

Suddenly Nicholas's anger evaporated. Now the truth was emerging. He sat down on one of the chairs and looked at Cromwell in horror. 'But the box contained only a list of his customers.'

'Maybe, but underneath the papers, Lord Nicholas, there was a false bottom in which Tyler put his despatches to me.'

'Then I am beginning to understand. I was a blind man in a maze, and no one gave me one clue how to find the way out. I expected to help the Sheriff of Portsmouth investigate the murder of a harmless wool trader and didn't know that I was dealing with the death of one of your spies. It would have helped if I'd known the facts before I embarked on this mission.'

'It was better that you shouldn't know, my

Lord. It's dangerous to know too much in the world of espionage. But I'm sorry that you let the box slip out of your hands, if that is what has happened. You know that in order to clear your name you will have to produce that box. We must have that information concealed in it.'

'And just tell me how I am to find it when I am incarcerated in here?'

'Just tell us where we can find it and we'll deal with the rest.'

'I've told you, I don't know where it is.'

'Then, my Lord, I'm afraid you'll have to stay here until you remember where it is. And I'm sure you don't want us to resort to force to help you to remember.'

Nicholas felt his legs giving way and he groped for a chair and collapsed on it. A vision of Sir Roger Mortimer flashed across his brain; Mortimer, his body torn by the rack gasping out his life in a welter of pain.

'You talk of justice, Baron Cromwell, but is it just to condemn a man to prison without one jot of solid evidence of his guilt? At the moment what I am being accused of is just hearsay. Witnesses can only be believed if they can be shown to be without prejudice. I haven't got Tyler's box; and even if you keep me here for years and put me to torture, I cannot tell you where it is, because I don't know. What I do know is that someone is spreading lies about me; someone whose

155

motives I can only guess at.'

'That's what all prisoners say, Lord Nicholas. As it stands at the moment, there is no one prepared to come forward and say a good word for you.'

'Surely the Earl of Southampton?'

'He remains silent.'

'The Sheriff?'

'Says he knows nothing.'

'The landlord of the Mariner's?'

'Denies everything.'

'Sir Charles Neville? I was his guest, remember.'

'And he's complained bitterly about you. He says you talked about using the guard and the artillery to assist foreign mercenaries; moreover, he accuses you of adultery with his wife.'

Then the world had gone mad, and Cromwell, whom he had never liked, but respected, had to be the most gullible man on earth.

'Neville! Has it never occurred to you that it's he who should be in this room, not me? My God, Cromwell, I now see it all. Here you have your traitor, ensconced in a fortified castle, plotting God knows what, and you arrest me, whose only crime was extreme naivety.'

'Sir Charles has many faults, but he has no stomach for treason. He's a weak, pathetic creature, and terrified of incurring the King's disapproval.'

'That's as maybe, but you've overlooked one thing in this character description—ambition.'

'He has no ambition, Lord Nicholas. He knows his limitations.'

'Then you've forgotten someone else—his wife!'

Now it was Cromwell's turn to look startled. 'His wife? Since when has a wife had any influence over her husband?'

'I can't answer that, but I do know that Ursula Neville is a formidable, manipulative woman, and Neville is terrified of her. She'll stop at nothing to get Neville the recognition she thinks he deserves; even if it means removing King Henry off his throne.'

There was silence as Cromwell continued to study Nicholas, all the time rubbing his hands together as if deliberating his next move.

'How did you know Neville is the King's bastard?' he said, after a long pause.

If Nicholas felt any surprise, he didn't show it. It needed two people and a cool head to play this game.

'I'm not obliged to reveal my sources of information at this stage, but let's say that now Richmond is dead, Neville has ambitions to step into his shoes, aided and abetted by his wife.'

Suddenly, all the confusion and uncertainties dispersed like early morning mist being dissolved by the sun's warmth. Cromwell had given him the one piece of information he

157

needed. Now he no longer had to guess at motives. It was blindingly obvious. Neville wanted the place Richmond had enjoyed at Court. There had been a strong rumour that the King had intended to make Richmond his heir. Neville wanted the throne. To what lengths was he prepared to go? Remembering Ursula's greedy, pitiless behaviour, he knew she was capable of risking all. But how was he to convince Cromwell?

'We have absolutely no evidence that Neville aspires to the throne,' said Cromwell.

'You had no evidence against me, but you arrested me all the same.'

'That's different. We received reports incriminating you. We have no reports against Neville.'

'And you took no steps to check where these reports against me came from?'

'Your conversation with Southampton was overheard. The informant did what he considered his duty by reporting what he'd heard to the Sheriff.'

'And it was all lies. It means that Neville has an agent, maybe several, who has been watching me and distorting the facts to build up a case against me.'

Suddenly Nicholas remembered how he'd thought someone was following him the first time he went to see Southampton. Probably he'd been followed all the time he was in Portsmouth.

'Can you give us the name of this agent, Lord Nicholas?'

'Of course not. If I knew his name I'd have given it to you by now.'

Cromwell seemed to make up his mind and he rose to his feet. 'I must get back to the King and make my report. There is much here that we must consider. But I beg you to think carefully about the whereabouts of Tyler's box. He was bringing us vital information and we must know what it is. Unfortunately, someone knew who Tyler was and killed him before he could reveal that information.'

'And I tell you I had nothing to do with his murder, nor with the theft of his box.'

'And you, Lord Nicholas, will have to prove that. After all, you did have it in your possession and as far as I know you could have read the contents and been tempted to use the information the box contained for your own treasonable purpose. At the moment, I don't believe the box was stolen. I think you know where it is. And until you tell us, you will remain here. Good day to you.'

Cromwell walked across to the door and knocked twice. It was opened and he turned to look at Nicholas before he left the room.

'Remember, my Lord, in the game of statecraft it pays to trust no one. It's a lesson that can only be learned through bitter experience. Let's hope you learn quickly before you run out of time.'

159

CHAPTER TWELVE

Jane decided she had to see Nicholas. She had been goaded beyond endurance by Daffyd's taunts over Nicholas's disgrace. There was no doubt in her mind that he had been set up by his enemies for their own purposes. And after the conversation she had had with Isabel Hardwicke in the garden she knew that Nicholas's main enemy could only be Charles Neville. He alone had sufficient motive to set up an elaborate plot; he alone had the means, a castle, guards, guns, to implement it. She also realised that, if she was to help Nicholas, then she would have to be as subtle as a serpent.

She had an ally in Queen Jane, who was compassionate towards people in trouble; especially when she suspected romance was involved. She was also resting as the weather had turned hot and humid and she tired easily. So when Jane was preparing her for bed, she felt bold enough to ask the Queen a favour. Queen Jane, who had sensed that Jane was not her normal self, looked at her in surprise.

'What is it, Jane? What's wrong?'

'Forgive me, madam, I have just received some bad news.'

'Then share it with me; that's what friends are for.'

'You are very kind. I don't know anybody I would rather turn to than yourself.'

'Then don't waste any more time and tell me how I can help you.'

'Madam, it concerns Nicholas Peverell.'

The Queen looked sharply at Jane and put up her hand to stop Jane brushing her hair. 'I hear he's in the Tower on a charge of treason. You'd best keep right away from politics, Jane; it's dangerous to meddle in these matters.'

'And I know he's the last person on earth to speak or act against the King's Majesty. Didn't he save the King's life only a short time ago? I think he has enemies who want him out of the way for a reason which we can only guess at.'

'Jane, everyone who goes to the Tower believes that he is innocent and it is his enemies that have put him there. It's the nature of those in captivity to blame others for their predicament,' said the Queen gently. 'You asked for my advice, Jane, so let me say that you should forget Nicholas Peverell. Leave him to the King's mercy. Unless . . . oh, I see how it is,' she said as the colour rose in Jane's face. 'You have tender feelings for him. Then, in that case, you must stifle those feelings, and turn your thoughts towards more suitable lovers. Daffyd spends all his days sighing for your favours. He would make a most suitable husband and we would grant you both an honourable position at Court which you would have for life, and we would endow you with a fine house in which you could bring up your children. But I can see this doesn't meet with your approval. You have that inflexible look on your face, and it doesn't suit you. You are cursed with a stubbornness, Jane, which will be your downfall.'

'I would like nothing better than to stay here at Court and entertain you and his Majesty, but I feel so sorry for Nicholas. My father, as you know, is one of his tenants and I have known him since I was a child. All I want to do is to see him and take him something to give him comfort in that horrible place. And I shall tell him that I shall pray for him every day until he's released. That's all. I beg of you, madam, to release me for one day so that I can go and see him.'

There was a long pause as the Queen studied Jane's anxious face. Finally, she indicated that Jane should continue brushing her hair.

'Of course you can visit him. Prisoners of his rank have that privilege. I can also order you some delicacies from the kitchen, and you can use one of my boats to take you to the Tower. I cannot have you riding off on your own through the streets of London; not now when the plague kills many people daily and the air will be rank with infection. But if I do this, then you must promise me on the holy scriptures that you will not stay for more than half an hour at the Tower and that you will return here immediately as soon as the tide turns. I shall expect you back here by dusk. You will have to leave by first light tomorrow morning to catch the ebb. Remember, Jane, that I have only granted your request on compassionate grounds. You are not to get involved in Nicholas Peverell's affairs and the guard will be watching you all the time to see that you offer him no help. If you get involved in his case, then you, too, will be arrested and I shall lose a dear friend and the Court will lose a gifted musician.'

Jane fell on her knees in front of the Queen, her heart filled with gratitude. 'Madam, you are most merciful and very understanding. I only want to see Nicholas to give him some comforts to ease his stay in that place, and to assure him that I am praying for his release. That's all. There will be no talk of helping him in any other way.'

The Queen bent down and helped Jane gently to her feet. 'Get up, Jane, you are my beloved friend, remember. We must all have our friends' happiness at heart. Now, let me give you another piece of advice—tell no one. I will say you are unwell. Dress soberly and cover your head. Don't draw attention to yourself in any way. Now come with me and swear on this holy Bible that you will do nothing to interfere with the King's justice. Nicholas Peverell will have a fair hearing, you may count on that. I hope for your sake he will be acquitted.'

* * *

The next day, Jane rose early and dressed in a plain linen dress and covered her head in a white bonnet. She went to the kitchen where a basket containing some cold chickens, some jars of preserves and some sweetmeats had been prepared for her. Then she went out of the palace, and crossed the courtyard just as the sun was trying to penetrate the dark lowering clouds which covered it. A boatman was waiting for her at the steps leading down to the river. He helped her into the boat and told her where to sit. She put the basket on the seat next to her and the boatman pushed off from the bank and began the long journey downstream to the City of London and the Tower.

It was hours later before they reached one of the watergates of the Tower and the boatman tied the boat up to one of the mooring posts. Jane, stiff from sitting in a cramped position for so long, climbed out on to the shore. She felt oppressed by the sultry atmosphere and the huge walls of the Tower which loomed ominously above her. One of the guards came over to see what she wanted and she explained her mission to him. He nodded and asked her to follow him.

Outside the Constable's house, he told her

to wait. When he returned, he had a second guard with him. He ordered her to uncover her basket and together they checked the contents. Then he told her to follow him. With a guard on either side, Jane was escorted to the Bell Tower. She followed them up the stairs and waited whilst they unlocked the door. Then they pushed it open and Jane came face to face with Nicholas.

*   *   *

For a moment, Nicholas didn't recognise her. She was dressed as a servant girl, her hair covered by her tight-fitting bonnet. He was sitting at the desk trying to write and he jumped up and would have come rushing over to her, but he stopped when Jane gave him a warning look. The guards retreated two paces but the door was left open.

'Lord Nicholas,' she said formally, 'I've brought you some delicacies from the Queen who ordered them to ease your stay here. She hopes they will bring you some comfort in these distressing times. Here, let me put them on the table.'

The two guards watched impassively as she opened the basket and took out the provisions. She couldn't look at Nicholas. The sight of his dejected appearance filled her with misery and she had to fight hard to control her tears.

'Nicholas, I am so sorry,' she whispered.

Nicholas could restrain himself no longer. He took hold of her arm and turned her round to face him.

'Jane, you must believe me. I am innocent. I don't know what's going on, but I've been set up as a scapegoat and I fear the worst.'

Jane put a warning finger to her lips and tried to back away from him; but Nicholas held on as if he was frightened she would vanish at any minute. One of the guards approached and dragged Jane away.

'There's to be no contact, my Lord, and you have only two minutes left. You are not to discuss your case.'

'Let me have time just to tell him that the Queen agreed to my coming, and that she is kind and merciful.'

'Then be quick,' he said gruffly. He was a kindly man and had a soft spot for attractive female servants.

'I must just say this,' she said. 'I know you are innocent and I know other people want you out of the way. I shall pray for you every day, and will do my utmost to help you in any way I can.'

Time had run out. She looked significantly at the piece of paper on the desk. He picked up the pen to write a message but the guard stopped him.

'That's all, lass. You'll have to leave. Orders is orders and you don't want to get into trouble now, do you?'

'You'll come again?' said Nicholas gazing at her intensely so as to remember every detail of her appearance.

'If the Queen allows it—but it won't be for a day or two. Maybe she'll let me travel by night so that I can get back to see to her during the day. Be ready for me,' she said, looking again at the sheet of paper.

'Jane, my love . . .'

'That's enough, sir. No endearments, if you please,' said the guard, taking hold of Jane's arm and propelling her towards the door. She turned her head just as she was leaving.

'The Lord of Porchester waits news of you, Lord Nicholas,' she said.

Nicholas rushed towards her, but the guard pushed her out of the room and slammed the door. Nicholas was stunned. He fought back the desire to bang on the door and scream for her to come back. But he knew that it would be futile. He stared at the collection of delicacies on the table and tried to collect his thoughts which were whirling away out of control. Jane! Why hadn't he realised she would come to see him? Jane, part of his life, had risked everything to bring him some comforts. He cursed his own stupidity that he hadn't been ready for her. Of course, he could have written a message on the sheet of paper, and she could have read it whilst she unpacked her basket. He prayed desperately that she would come again. But it seemed unlikely. The

167

Queen could not risk antagonising the King by sending one of her ladies-in-waiting to see him too often.

He thought back over every detail of this short visit. She had taken a risk by that last remark—the Lord of Porchester waits news of you. But he thanked God she had said it. Now he realised Jane knew about Neville. She also knew it was he who had engineered this whole sorry situation.

The realisation that Jane believed in him filled him with enormous relief. He felt the resurgence of hope and with that, a fierce determination that, impossible as it seemed, he had to get out of this place and return to Porchester. There he wouldn't rest until he had the proof he needed to clear his name and see Neville thrown into one of the Tower's dungeons.

*　　　*　　　*

That evening, the King summoned Thomas Cromwell to his private ante-room to take a glass of Bordeaux with him before dinner. They stood together in front of the fire which burnt all the year round in that cold room. The King was in a jovial mood, Cromwell, wary.

'So, Peverell's cooling his heels in the Tower, eh Thomas?'

'He is indeed, your Majesty.'

'I hope he's contrite.'

'That's not his nature. He protests his innocence and demands to be released.'

'Just as they all do. I hope you told him why we've decided to lodge him there?'

'Of course. But I am afraid that the evidence against him, as it stands at this moment, will not stand up in a court of law. It's mostly circumstantial and based on evidence from unreliable witnesses. I think we both know, your Majesty, that Peverell has been falsely implicated.'

'I'm not so sure. Remember there's no smoke without fire, Thomas. I've always thought Peverell a decent man, above reproach. But I also know everyone is capable of risking everything to realise his ambitions. Follow my example; trust no one. And, by God, Thomas that includes you too.'

The King threw back his head and roared with laughter. Cromwell, used to the King's pleasantries, stared at him stonily. Sometimes, he thought, the King's sense of humour could be infuriating.

'I hope I serve your Majesty to the best of my limited ability. I pride myself on being your loyal and obedient servant.'

'Oh yes, oh yes, Thomas. Relax man, your post's secure for a few more years. The trouble with you is that you have a limited sense of humour. Drink up man, and cheer up. I don't like sanctimonious fellows around me at dinner time.'

Cromwell reached for the flagon and filled both their glasses. He was perplexed. What was the King trying to say? And why was he finding it so difficult? He knew that when the King was most jovial he was also at his most devious.

'This evidence against Peverell, Thomas,' said the King, looking thoughtfully at Cromwell. 'You say that it won't stand up to scrutiny in our court of law?'

'I don't think so, your Majesty. As I said, it's based on reports from unreliable witnesses. We both know witnesses can be bribed and intimidated. Every man has his price, as the saying goes.'

'Very true, Thomas. I didn't know you were a philosopher. But Peverell, Thomas, I never thought he would stoop to treachery. Why should he? He's a lazy sort of fellow. He knows I like him. Why should he suddenly embark upon a treasonable career?'

'He could have been tempted. It happens. In any case we can get him to tell us why.'

'Perhaps. But what if he hasn't a motive? What if he is innocent? Remember most people will confess to anything you want them to when put to the rack. I want incontrovertible evidence against Peverell before we try him.'

'May I ask what sort of evidence that would be, your Majesty?'

'Oh, you know—a letter written to a known

170

enemy, proof of joining a conspiracy, or engaging in a treasonable action such as trying to raise an army against myself.'

'I agree, that would simplify matters enormously. But Peverell, as far as we know, hasn't done any of these things.'

'Exactly. Let's face it, Thomas, we both know that it's highly unlikely that Peverell has had a single treasonable thought in his head. And whilst we tie ourselves in knots trying to compile evidence against him, the real traitor, the one who's responsible for these rumours is still at large.'

'So you think, your Majesty, we've got the wrong bird?'

'I'm almost certain; but I also know we have no reason to arrest any other bird. Yet. But, think about it, Thomas, one bird could lead us to the other, eh?'

'Possibly. But Peverell can't lead us anywhere whilst he's in a prison cell.'

'Knowing Peverell as I do, Thomas, I am quite sure he'll try to escape.'

'He won't be that stupid. No one's escaped from the Tower.'

'There's always a first time. Now, come closer, Thomas and let me tell you something.'

Here it comes, thought Cromwell; the King at his most devious. Reluctantly, Cromwell drew closer to the King, a position he found uncomfortable. He liked to maintain a distance between himself and another person, preferably the distance marked by a desk, and with himself sitting behind it.

The King put an arm round him and drew him closer to the fire. 'You know Thomas, he had a visitor today—Mistress Warrener. My Queen, being of a compassionate disposition, God be thanked, granted her leave to go. She took him some delicacies from our kitchen to comfort him in his trouble.'

Cromwell, wondering where this was all leading to, remained silent.

'Now Jane Warrener is a clever girl; too clever for my taste. She is also in love with Peverell and is, at this moment, I am quite sure, plotting his escape.'

'And you want me to allow this to happen?'

'Oh no, nothing as obvious as that. Just tell Digby to turn the occasional blind eye. Let him relax the guards; nothing more, mind. Let's see if Peverell has any initiative. He's desperate to escape, I presume?'

'Oh yes. He'll want to escape in order to clear his name. He's proud of his family motto.'

'And where will he go?'

'To find the other bird.'

'Exactly. So why don't we lead Peverell to take us to the other traitor. He knows we'll need positive proof of treachery. He'll be a man with a mission, Thomas. And we need such people.'

'Most likely he'll get killed.'

172

'That's a risk he'll have to take. Now forget this conversation ever took place. We don't want to appear to be manipulative.'

'Of course not, your Majesty. That would never do. Your Majesty is the fount of all justice.'

'Thank you, Thomas. Now I must be away to the Queen and I shall compliment her on her merciful nature. I think she should send Mistress Warrener on another errand of mercy. Come Thomas, drink up. We must be away to dinner. The Imperial ambassador dines with us tonight.'

Cromwell followed the King into the Great Hall and took his place at the far end of the high table. As he watched the King greet Queen Jane with great ceremony he thought that no one understood human nature with all its strengths and weaknesses as well as King Henry. Probably he'd had to learn it the hard way. His father had won the throne through victory in battle and his son had had to be ruthless to keep it. There were too many Yorkists around who had a better claim to the throne than Henry Tudor. Some had pursued their claim; and had paid the price for failure.

As a statesman, Cromwell knew that success depended on a dispassionate assessment of a person's character and a ruthless elimination of those who had to be got rid of. All very necessary. But as he settled back in his chair to allow the servant to spoon soup into the bowl in front of him, he knew that the King would not hesitate to manipulate him, Cromwell, just as he was manipulating Peverell. The King had no friends. Everyone, however, had his use. And when he was no longer useful, then the King didn't hesitate to discard him like an old cloak; even his Queen; even Thomas Cromwell.

CHAPTER THIRTEEN

Next morning, Jane went down to the kitchens where 'Simple' Simon held court. She felt at ease with the underworld of the King's entertainers. They were a motley collection whose origins were obscure and in some cases unknown. The dwarves constituted a special group of small people whose job was to entertain the King and his Court with tumbling and juggling acts. Some of them had been given to the King by visiting ambassadors, some had caught the King's eye when he had been on tour and he'd offered them posts at the royal Court; some of them had been at Court so long that they couldn't remember any previous existence. As a group they were well liked. During the long dark evenings of winter their cavortings and comic sketches were particularly popular.

That morning, Simon, the 'king' of the

dwarves, was relaxing on his 'throne' in one of the cupboards which had been given to him for his own special use. The King had also given him a chair. It was an ornate piece of furniture carved out of solid oak and decorated with intricate carvings of foliage and mythical beasts picked out in gold leaf. The unicorn, carved on the head of the chair, sported a brilliant golden horn, a suitable heraldic crest, the King had said, for someone like Simon, who, although small of stature, nevertheless was very popular with the ladies of the court.

Simon's room was a cupboard where spices, not needed for immediate use, were kept. When he was ready to receive visitors, he opened the door wide so that everyone could see him. When he wanted to be left alone, he left the door ajar. That morning, it was open, and a crowd had gathered round Simon and, judging by the amount of mead being drunk, he was in fine humour. Jane stood in the background, waiting her moment to approach him.

Perhaps because she had been brought to Court at the King's request, and having no experience in the ways of the nobility, Jane had turned to the kindly dwarves for friendship and guidance. She had grown especially fond of Simon. He'd made her laugh when she had felt homesick for her friends back home in the village of Dean Peverell. He'd taught her the songs and jingles of the ordinary people of the streets of London, and he'd shown her how to dance the reels and jigs of the country people. And, of course, he had amused her by his tumbling acts with his fellow dwarves and he'd taught her how to juggle with brightly coloured balls and how to play tricks with cards. Above all, he'd encouraged her to sing, and had kept a benevolent eye on her so that no one had dared to take advantage of her because they knew they would incur the wrath of the little people who were both loved and feared because they themselves were fearless. They knew that as long as they amused the King they were safe. And they made certain that the King had no cause for complaint.

It had been a source of amusement to the King that Simon resembled him physically, and Simon had cultivated this, and today, seated on his throne, with his red-gold hair neatly combed, his bristling red beard so similar to the King's, his ruddy complexion and his corpulent body, the resemblance was very striking. He was, thought Jane, King Henry in miniature. His expression was different, though. King Henry could never relax his guard and his eyes were always wary, whereas Simon's lit up with pleasure when he saw Jane. He told the others to leave him and good naturedly endured their ribald remarks as they went away.

'Well, here's my little song bird,' he said

when the others had gone. 'What brings you here, Jane?'

'To see you of course. It's been a long time since we've had a talk. And how well you look today in the doublet and silken hose. You only need a crown on your head and I would address you as your Majesty.'

'I'll see if the King will lend me his. He gave me these clothes, so he might find me an old crown which he no longer has use for. I believe there's a bishop's mitre going begging, and there is always the papal crown.'

'Don't get too ambitious. It's a long way to fall when things go wrong. The King doesn't take too kindly to Popes these days.'

'I could excommunicate him.'

'That's been done. No point in rubbing salt into the wound.'

'Then I'll stay as I am, the King's shadow. But come closer, Mistress Jane and help yourself to the sweetmeats. Dame Sarah, the queen of the pastry cooks, has brought me some which she made at first light this morning.'

On the table which stood by the side of the throne there were bowls of sweetmeats and grapes and little cakes—offerings which people put there as if he were a god and had to be placated. There was also a pewter jug of mead, and Jane, as a specially favoured friend, was handed a goblet of the sweet, pungent liquid which she sniffed and drank appreciatively. Only when she had nibbled at a little cake and eaten some walnuts covered in marzipan did she sit down on the floor at Simon's feet and wait for him to invite her to speak.

She felt comfortable near him and found the silence companionable.

'Now Jane, tell me everything. How can I help you? Surely you don't want a love potion? Master Daffyd has more than enough Cupid's darts in his body. To add a love potion would be like piling coals on fire. I've never seen a man so inflamed by passion. You're a cruel woman, Jane, to resist his advances. Do you want the man to die of love?'

'It's of no interest to me what Daffyd does. I hope his passion will die down and he will direct his attentions elsewhere. I find his attentions unwelcome, to say the least.'

'I fear Daffyd's passion will burn for ever. It will only need a tiny puff on the bellows to fan his flame into action when you decide to give way to him. You can't remain a maid for ever, Jane.'

'But surely, you, of all people, wouldn't want me to marry someone I don't love?'

'Now you're being old-fashioned, and it doesn't become you. You're not suited to being so prim and proper. Now why don't you let me warm you up a bit? I'm a bit of an expert when it comes to breaking in young mares.'

178

'You don't have to tell me that. You've got a bit of a reputation, you know. But I haven't come here to discuss affairs of the heart.'

'But what else is there to interest a maid?'

'Let's just say that I've come to ask your advice for a friend of mine who's in trouble.'

'Then why doesn't he come here himself—if "he" is a he, that is? I shouldn't have thought you, of all people, would be at anyone's beck and call.'

'Because he's under lock and key. He has been wronged, Simon. He has to prove his innocence. To do this he has to get out of his prison. Now how can he do this? What's the best way to escape? You've done everything in your life, Simon. You know all sorts of people. You know every trick in the books. How can he slip away unseen?'

'I don't like the sound of this, Jane. It seems to me that you are treading on treacherous ground. This smacks of politics. Now politics is for fools; not for the song birds. Stick to what you know, girl; sing your songs and look after the Queen and be nice to that Welshman of yours. That way you'll live to be as old as me and richer than anyone at Court. Kings and queens come and go but entertainers go on for ever; but only if they steer clear of politics.'

'I only want to help a friend. I'm not interested in intrigue.'

'If your friend is who I think he is, this is a very political matter. You have a very pretty

179

head, Jane, with hair the colour of chestnut leaves in autumn. Keep it where it is—sitting tightly on your neck. It won't look half so pretty stuck on a spike on London Bridge.'

'It won't come to that. The Queen gave me permission to see my friend, so there can't be any danger in trying to help him.'

'Then the Queen ought to be more careful. But she's safe until her child is born. But after that happy event, she should steer clear of helping other people's friends. Not even Queen's heads are safe, as you know only too well, Jane.

'However, you are my friend and very special you are, too. There's no harm in telling you what I do when I am in a tricky situation and have to disappear for a bit; usually it's when the King's kicked me once too often, or when my Lord of Monmouth sets his dogs on me because his wife fancies a tumble with Simple Simon between the sheets when her lord and master's away on military service. That's when I disguise myself. It's as simple as that. I haven't been called Simple Simon for nothing, you know.'

'What disguises do you use?' Jane asked, looking up at him with increasing excitement.

'Well, it's best if a man becomes a maid, and vice versa. Now as the Almighty has caused me to stop growing as soon as I reached the height of other men's thighs, I can dress as a girl. I shave my face, of course, put on some petticoats, collect a goose or two and make for the common pastures. I then become accepted as the new goose girl. Mind you, I'm just a bit robust now for that sort of disguise. Next time I disappear, I shall have to use my ingenuity a bit more.'

He patted his stomach and grinned down at Jane. 'Now tell me about this friend of yours. He's a bit bigger than me, I expect?'

'He's tall. Too tall to play the part of a woman.'

'Nonsense. He's only got to stoop down like this.'

He got off his throne, pulled his neck down into his hunched shoulders, picked up Jane's cloak and wrapped it round himself. Then he picked up one of the sticks lying by the fire, and in a moment the royal Simon had been replaced by a poor old woman whose bones were bent and twisted with age.

Despite the seriousness of the situation, Jane couldn't restrain a laugh. 'My friend hasn't got your actor's gifts.'

'Then he'll have to learn. Necessity is a powerful teacher. But let me make it easy for him. Dame Sarah will do anything for me. She'll even give me her petticoat—and not ask any questions either. I'll get you a petticoat or two. You find a bonnet big enough for this friend of yours to hide his face in. I can't help him with shoes. He'll have to manage in his bare feet like most of the ordinary people do.

181

He'll need a shirt to cover his chest. So there we are. He'll not be recognised dressed as a woman. It's the easiest disguise. With any luck he'll be able to walk out of this prison. Mind he removes his beard. Bearded ladies have a tendency to attract attention. Come and see me this evening and I'll try and get Sarah to remove her petticoats for me during the day. She'll think I need them for some comedy turn we're putting on in the evening. She's lent me them before.

'Now I'd not do this for anyone but you, my political Jane, but because you and I have always been good friends, and because I can see that your days at Court are numbered I'll get you a petticoat or two. I only risk getting a beating should anyone find out what I've done. But this doesn't mean that I approve of what you're doing. Take my advice, keep clear of gentlemen locked away in prison cells and stick to making music.'

* * *

It was Queen Jane who suggested that Jane should pay another visit to Nicholas—a blessed errand of mercy, she called it—and the same boat was made ready for her use and the same large basket of provisions was waiting for her in the kitchens. It was easy to fold up the petticoat and shirt and flatten them down under the cakes and pies. Then she put on the large bonnet, which she'd managed to obtain from one of her friends, over her own neat-fitting cap. That night, when everyone was asleep, she crept downstairs to where a guard was slumbering on duty. He'd dined too well, and drunk more than his fill of wine. Quickly, she removed his dagger from his belt and crept silently upstairs.

Early next morning, the boat took her down to the Tower. This time the security was more relaxed. There was only one guard on duty who didn't bother to look in her basket and who escorted her to Nicholas's room. This time, he opened the door, told her to go in, and shut the door behind her. He said he'd come for her after ten minutes to escort her off the premises. She couldn't believe her luck. It was so easy; anyone would think that the authorities wanted Nicholas to escape.

*　　　*　　　*

Nicholas, too, had noticed the relaxation in the prison routine. Mistress Bidgood had taken her time in changing his water and seeing to his personal needs. He'd been offered the services of a barber and in the interest of keeping himself clean he'd had his hair cut short and his beard removed. The man hadn't been unfriendly and the thought entered Nicholas's head that it would be easy to knock him out with a chair and walk out of the room because as far as he could tell, the door hadn't been locked. Next time, he thought, he'd risk it.

But then Jane arrived, and the guard left them alone and he was able to take her in his arms and hold her close.

'How did you get permission to come here, Jane?' he said as he breathed in the scent of her hair and relished the feel of her body so close to his own.

'It couldn't be easier,' she said, drawing away from him at last. They couldn't expect the guard to leave them alone for long. 'The Queen suggested I come again. A compassionate visit, she called it. But look what I have here.'

She put the basket on his desk, and began to unpack the provisions. Then she took out the petticoat and held it up to show him. 'Be quick, put this under your coverlet. And this.' And she shook out the shirt. 'Now this.' And she took off the bonnet she'd been wearing and handed it to him.

After a moment's surprise, Nicholas quickly put the clothes under the coverlet on his bed. The bonnet was more difficult but he stuffed it behind the bed and grinned at Jane.

'What makes you think I'll be able to play the lady's part? But I'll do my best. But where did you get these clothes from?'

'Sh, I'll tell you later. This is one way of leaving this place, disguise yourself in women's clothes. How you set about it, I don't know.'

'I think I know of a way. But, quickly, Jane, before the guard returns, I shall need a horse. Harry is at the post house in Putney, but I can't ride him. He's too well known. If I can escape from here I shall need a sturdy cob, the sort farmers would ride to market. I shall have to change my clothes again once I'm out of here, but that shouldn't be difficult.'

'I can get you a horse. My own horse, Melissa, is at the royal stables and I often used to ride out with the Queen. The grooms will gladly lend me a working horse in exchange for letting them ride Melissa. I can say that the Queen is sending me into the country on a charitable mission and I need a working horse to carry the baskets. There will be a horse waiting for you at Putney. You can call yourself Master Warrener, and you've come to collect your sister's horse. And see, I've even brought you something you might find useful.' And she handed him the dagger, concealed in the bottom of the basket.

'Jane, how can I thank you? You are taking a terrible risk helping me.'

'I only do this because I know you're innocent and I know you'll not rest until you catch the person who's behind all this. I know that you'll see to it that he's brought to justice.'

'That I shall do even if I die in the attempt. But listen, my Jane, I shall be gone for a long time. Nicholas Peverell will disappear; Master

185

Warrener will take his place. I must find irrefutable evidence against this traitor whose lies were responsible for putting me in here. There must be no loopholes, no doubt in the King's mind. And this will not be easy. But when it is all over, I shall come to Court and find you. You are my inspiration, Jane. I shall think of you every hour of the day and when I have succeeded in landing this big fish I shall ask for your hand in marriage. Because, without you, life would be meaningless. I can't ask you to marry me now because it wouldn't be right to impose such a promise upon you. But tell me one thing, will you ever be able to love me? Is it possible that you could think of me as a lover, a suitor, a husband?'

There was a loud knocking on the door. Time had run out. She faced Nicholas and looked at him intently.

'Come back soon, my love. I shall be waiting for you.'

As Nicholas took her in his arms, the guard opened the door with a bang and glared at Jane.

'Come along, Mistress. That's not allowed, as you know. Next time I'll not be so soft. As for you, sir, keep your kissing to yourself, or at least until your time comes to kiss the executioner's block.'

He hustled Jane out of the room and left Nicholas to his thoughts. He was stunned by the sudden reversal of his fortunes. He now had clothes for a disguise, and the heady certainty that Jane loved him and had faith in him. And all that was needed now was the opportunity for his escape to present itself.

*　　*　　*

He didn't have long to wait. The next day, Hannah Bidgood came as usual to fill up his water jug and take away the pail of dirty water. She, too, looked more relaxed. She walked over to the window and peered down at the river.

'King's on the river today, they say. He's bringing musicians with him and maybe the Queen'll be with him. The fresh air will do her good, poor soul. Shut up in Hampton Court's no place for a lady drawing near her time.'

Nicholas walked across to her. She was standing on tiptoe and far too interested in the scene below her to notice that Nicholas had picked up a chair. With a sudden movement, he raised it and brought it down on Mistress Bidgood's head. She fell to the floor and Nicholas, suddenly feeling a pang of remorse, bent down to see if she was still breathing. All was well. She was only stunned.

Quickly he put on the petticoat which Jane had brought him, and fastened it over his trousers. Then he put on the shirt, a bit tight, but he took off Hannah Bidgood's shawl and tied it across his chest. No shoes. With a quiet

187

apology to Hannah, he took off her shoes, large leather boots, tied with laces, and put them on. They fitted perfectly. Hannah Bidgood had big, peasant's feet, and her shoes were well-worn and comfortable. Then he put on Jane's bonnet, hid the dagger under the shawl, picked up the pail of water by his washing table, and walked out of the room. It was as simple as that.

He walked down the stairs and out into the yard. One of the guards glanced at him, but didn't challenge him. He crossed the drawbridge which went over the moat and brought him to the main street gate of the Tower. The man in the gatehouse nodded to him, and he went out into the streets of London. He was a free man. It was a heady feeling and he could hardly stop himself from flinging away the pail and running as far as possible away from that horrible fortress.

Once he'd left the Tower behind him, he plunged into the maze of streets which constituted the City of London. The air was hot and sultry and he was conscious of an all-pervading sweetly cloying smell which he recognised as the stench of death. London was in the grip of an outbreak of plague and the sweating sickness which often broke out at this time of the year. Keeping his head lowered, ignoring the ribald shouts of the passers-by who regarded unescorted women as fair game, he made his way through the piles of filth

188

which cluttered the narrow streets walking
west towards the fields of Westminster.

It was late in the day when he reached an
alehouse frequented by carriers. He found a
farmer who was returning to Surrey after
delivering a gaggle of geese to the Smithfield
butchers, and was only too pleased to take
Nicholas to Putney for a fee. The driver of the
wagon was a taciturn man who wanted to get
home as soon as possible, away from the City
folk with their foul air, dirt and disease. He
told Nicholas to travel in the back of the
wagon as he didn't want to risk contaminating
himself with someone who had come from the
City, and, curled up on some coarse sacking,
Nicholas fell asleep.

CHAPTER FOURTEEN

At the first light of the new day, Nicholas
awoke to the gentle sound of the oxen
crunching their oats and blowing the chaff
away. A man cleared his throat enthusiastically
and spat out the contents. Then the ox cart
rocked as the man jumped down and walked
round to the back of the cart. He raised the
tarpaulin and stared at Nicholas.

'Wake up, mistress. This is as far as I can
take you. You've had enough sleep, mind. Like
a corpse you were last night. I've been here

most of the night and not a sound from you. Well, on your feet. Putney's no more than a mile down the road.'

His rough voice brought Nicholas to his senses. He sat up, rearranged the bonnet Jane had given him so that his face was partly concealed. Then he stood up and shook down his petticoat, conscious that the carter was staring at him curiously. However, the man said nothing, and Nicholas gave him sixpence for his trouble and the man's manner changed from truculence to obsequiousness.

'Why, thank you, mistress. God go with you.'

Nicholas set off in the direction the man had pointed out and he very soon found the post house where he'd left Harry, and with any luck, another horse would be waiting for him. But first, he had to rid himself of his petticoat.

There was a barn behind the post house and it was too early for anyone to be working there. He took off his shawl, bonnet and petticoat and stuffed them under a pile of old straw in one of the dark corners of the barn. Outside there was a pump with a bucket standing beside it. He filled the bucket, drank some water and tipped the rest over his face and shoulders. Then he shook himself dry.

Inside the post house, breakfast was being prepared by a sleepy servant girl who gave him a jug of ale, some cold meat and a loaf of bread. The inn keeper shuffled into the room where Nicholas was eating the food and nodded in his direction.

'Morning, master. Everything all right?'

'Thank you, sir. In a moment I shall need a horse and a hat. I left mine in the cart which brought me here and the man's a mile away now.'

'A horse I can provide. But a hat . . . You'll have to wait till you get to a market. But wait, you can have one of mine if you've money to pay for it.'

He went out and returned with a wide-brimmed hat, made of leather, the sort farmers wore to shield their heads from the sun. It was old and worn, and was just what Nicholas needed. Pulled well down it would practically cover his face. He paid the man and told him his name. Jack Warrener. The man nodded and said he was expecting him. A horse, by name of Oswald, had been delivered yesterday for the use of a Jack Warrener.

'A great sturdy beast, master. Looks as if he's used to doing a day's work.'

Oswald turned out to be a sixteen-hand farm horse with strong legs and hairy fetlocks. Not built for speed, Nicholas thought ruefully, but he would have great stamina and would go unnoticed in a crowd. Suppressing a desire to see if Harry was all right, Nicholas mounted Oswald, nodded to the inn keeper and set off west along the Guildford and Farnham road.

Just five days, he thought, since he'd been

191

taken to the Tower. Now Peverell had vanished. In his place was Jack Warrener, yeoman. His mind had changed along with his identity. He was no longer a reluctant spy chasing shadows. Jack Warrener was a man with a mission; one he was prepared to die for. Two things he had to do and do quickly. The first was to clear the name of Nicholas Peverell from the ignominious smear of treason. The other was to hunt out the real traitor who had spread lies about him. That man, he knew, could only be Charles Neville. He wanted him caught red-handed. The evidence against him had to be overwhelmingly conclusive. There was to be no slip-up.

*   *   *

As Oswald settled down into a comfortable, ambling gait, the miles passed and the sun grew higher in the sky. At noon, he stopped at a wayside inn and ordered food for himself and Oswald. As he set off once more, he began to consider the events of the past fortnight in the light of the new information he'd been given during his stay in the Tower.

It was obvious from his conversation with Thomas Cromwell that Tyler had been murdered because of the information he was carrying to Cromwell. Someone knew about Tyler's activities. Someone had wanted to stop that information from ever reaching London.

It was also obvious that whoever had murdered Tyler knew about his box and what it contained and had stolen it. The same person had also stolen the key to that box from Tyler's dead body. There was only one person who would have wanted the information contained in Tyler's box. There was only one person rich enough to pay his own agent and bribe landlords and the Sheriff to distort the truth. That person, thought Nicholas, had to be Sir Charles Neville.

As he jogged along the main road leading down to the coast, Oswald skilfully avoiding the potholes and deep ruts made by the carts in the winter months, he thought back to his brief stay in Porchester in the light of what he now knew about Neville. He was the only person with a strong enough motive to contemplate high treason. He was Henry's bastard. Cromwell had told him that. The Duke of Richmond, the King's official bastard, the royal favourite and regarded as the probable heir to the throne, had died last year. Neville had not been invited to take his place. That gave him a grudge against the King. Neville also had an ambitious wife. She would spur him on to do anything he could to fulfil her own ambitions. If the King would not come to Neville, then Neville would have to go to the King—with an army behind him, if necessary.

An army. Where would Neville find an

army? Admittedly there were still several dissatisfied Yorkist claimants around. Lord Montague had estates on the Hampshire border and the King had never trusted him. But Montague would not be able to raise a sufficiently large enough army to take on the King's troops. Not on his own. No, he'd need another source. And there was one near at hand. The Emperor Charles V and Francis I, King of France, were both declared enemies of King Henry. Especially now the Pope had excommunicated the King and given his blessing to anyone who removed him from his throne. If Neville had joined forces with the continental powers who were planning to invade England, then certainly he would not want that information to reach the King. If Tyler had gathered enough information whilst he was spying for Cromwell in France and Flanders and the box he carried contained information about an impending invasion, then Neville would most certainly want him out of the way.

But Neville would have to have his own spy network. Someone well known to the Sheriff of Portsmouth and the landlords of the various inns and alehouses of the area. Someone who could bribe and intimidate possible witnesses to do what Neville wanted them to do. He thought back to the horsemen who had come to Porchester in the middle of the night. Neville had obviously been expecting them.

And he'd been evasive when he, Nicholas, had asked who they were. How long had they been coming to Neville and making their reports? How far had the plotting advanced? How many agents had Neville in the field? And which one of them had murdered Tyler?

One man had known Tyler, had talked to him on the boat from Le Havre, had known where he was staying in Portsmouth. That man was Jacques Gallimard, the Frenchman. He was the most likely suspect and almost certainly one of Neville's agents. He had probably lain in wait for Tyler, murdered him when he returned to his sister's house from the Mariner's, robbed him and taken the key, and later returned to steal the box. Jacques Gallimard. Neville's agent. Now the box was almost certainly in Neville's hands. He would have read its contents. He would now know the date of the proposed invasion and would be making plans to assist his continental allies to overthrow King Henry and, in return, become the King of England, sustained by the might of the King of France and the Emperor of Germany. A formidable combination.

And the worst part of all, thought Nicholas, as ahead of him he caught sight of the first glimmer of the sea, it was up to him to produce, single-handed, irrefutable evidence of this plot and Neville's involvement in it. No use going to the Earl of Southampton and telling him all this. Southampton would have him re-arrested immediately and escorted back to the Tower, this time in fetters. No use trying to see Cromwell and the King. Neither would believe him. Only when it was too late and Charles and Francis had sent over their invasion fleet and landed troops at Porchester where Neville would allow them full use of the castle, would the authorities realise they'd made a terrible mistake and arrested the wrong man. And by then it would be too late for Nicholas Peverell. His head would be decorating London Bridge on top of an iron spike.

There was only one thing in his favour, Nicholas thought grimly. Neville still thought he was in the Tower. He, Peverell, would be the last person he would ever expect to see again. And now, Peverell had disappeared. Jack Warrener, farmer, had taken his place. But how was this Jack Warrener to get into Porchester Castle and remain there as the King's spy—and without anyone noticing?

By the time he reached the outskirts of Portsmouth, the daylight was going. He stopped for the night at a modest inn which offered him a mattress on the floor of a room shared with twenty other travellers, and a stall for Oswald. By the next day, a plan was forming in his mind.

*   *   *

The next morning, he made arrangements with the landlord to leave Oswald at the inn for the time being. Then he walked into Portsmouth, stopping to buy a leather bag at one of the stalls set up in front of the Domus Dei, the scene of the attempted assassination of King Henry two years ago. Today, no one took any notice of him. After a night spent on a dirty straw mattress he looked no different from all the other townsfolk and countrymen who thronged round the stalls. He then bought some dried sausages and a loaf of bread which he put in his bag, and drank down a jug of ale. From then on he would have to steal what food he needed because where he was going there were no stalls and no inns. Then he went down to the Point and looked across at the Isle of Wight towards the King's ships which were anchored at Spithead. He recognised Henry's flagship, *Henri Grace à Dieu*, floating like a swan asleep, with sails furled and only a single flag, the cross of St George, hanging limply at the masthead.

There was an air of festivity at the Point that day. The sun was shining, the sultry air had cleared away and people were out and about prepared to enjoy themselves. All round the King's ships—Nicholas counted ten—small boats were carrying on a good trade with the soldiers and sailors on board. The sailors, when idle, made small objects which they carved out of wood and sometimes ivory—

figureheads, toys for children, wooden tops and whips, models of boats. These they exchanged for fresh food and liquor. This practice was encouraged in peacetime when it was necessary to keep everyone busy, but discouraged when there was a possibility of action. Today, the prospect of danger seemed the last thing on people's minds. The sound of laughter and raucous singing drifted across the still water and added to the holiday atmosphere.

Sitting cross-legged by the wall of the Point was a small man, a seaman, Nicholas guessed, judging by his greased pigtail, his loosely fitting trousers and tight jacket, and the woollen hat covering his head as if it were a cold day. He was playing a penny whistle and a crowd had gathered around him and threw him coins. Nicholas walked over to him and stood watching him. The man finished the jig he was playing and put down his whistle.

'Are you from one of the King's ships?' Nicholas asked.

'What's that got to do with you?'

'Nothing at all; except I would have thought there was enough work to do on board ship without you coming ashore and entertaining the citizens of Portsmouth.'

'Well, there's nothing going on aboard ship at the moment. The Admiral's too busy building forts along the coast, and the officers have all taken leave ashore. So I got a lift in one of the small boats and here I am earning myself a few pence if folk feel fit to give me any.'

Nicholas dropped a few pence into the tin bowl placed on the ground in front of the man who grinned his thanks.

'Which ship are you from?'

'The *Pelican.* She's a good enough ship, but I can't abide being idle.'

'Are they taking on more hands?'

'Lord no. What's the point when we've got more than enough already. Maybe things'll change if the Frenchies come sneaking up on us.'

'Let's hope that day's a long way away. Good day to you.'

'Good day to you, master. Let me send you on your way with a jig.'

He picked up his whistle and Nicholas walked away with the shrill sounds of the whistle piercing the clear air. For some reason, the chirpy, cocky music filled Nicholas with foreboding. Discipline in the fleet was lax if common seamen could come ashore unrebuked. It could only mean that the Earl of Southampton was not taking seriously any rumours of a foreign invasion. Southampton should be more vigilant.

One of the small fishing boats which had been swarming round the King's ships was returning to harbour. Nicholas watched it come in and lower its sail. It gave him the idea he was waiting for. If he was to infiltrate Porchester Castle then the best way to approach it was by sea, just when the tide was turning so that the sentries would have lowered their guard as no ships could land at low tide. And it would have to be by night. He could be landed along the coast and he'd have to make his way to the castle on foot. Then he'd have to climb the wall and, once inside, he'd have to rely on his wits.

For a fee, one of the fishermen agreed to take him up to the top end of Portsmouth Harbour and land him on the western shore. The wind was slight so it would take a long time to get Nicholas as far up the harbour as he required. If they waited for the tide to turn and timed it right, they could sail up on the last of the incoming tide, Nicholas could go ashore wherever he wanted and the fisherman could return on the ebb. In that way he could keep his oars for emergencies only. This seemed a good plan, because, if things worked out properly, landing at the height of high water would mean that, once the tide had turned, the sentries in the bastions would be off guard. No ships could sail up against the ebb.

They would have to wait for early evening to start their journey. Nicholas ate his last proper meal down on the Point and watched the remnant of the King's ships rock gently on the slight swell. No sight could appear more peaceful. But he knew that, if he was right and invasion plans were under way and Neville was plotting rebellion, then these ships, England's main defence against an invader, should not be lulled into a false sense of security. They should be taking on provisions, making sure they had their full complement of sailors and soldiers. The King's flagship, he knew, carried three hundred and forty-nine soldiers and three hundred and one sailors. There should be fifty gunners to man the one hundred and eighty guns. And more ships should be brought round to Spithead. The King's fleet consisted of eighty-five warships as well as the thirteen twenty-ton row-barges he'd commissioned to sail amongst the enemy ships with guns blazing. They were very effective when the wind dropped and sails were useless. Southampton had told him that there were nearly eight thousand men serving the King in his fleet, of which two thousand were soldiers and five thousand were sailors and a thousand were gunners. Where were all these people now? Things had got so lax that sailors were allowed to come ashore and beg for money on Portsmouth Point when they should be on the alert. He prayed that he could get positive proof of Neville's treachery, and soon, so that he could instil some sense of urgency into the Earl of Southampton. And he also prayed that there was still time to bring the other ships round to Spithead. For all he knew,

201

Tyler could have been about to send to Cromwell the expected date of an impending invasion. And now that knowledge would be in enemy hands. Everything depended on his successful infiltration into Neville's stronghold.

At last the conditions were right for a night sail to Porchester. As the sun was setting he went down to the inner harbour where the small boats were moored. The man was waiting for him and anxious to be off. He stepped aboard the small clinker-built boat with its single, tan-coloured sail, and they set off. The wind had freshened into a stiff south-westerly and they made good progress. The man dropped him off on a shingle spit which provided firm footing across the mud. He paid the man and watched him turn his boat and proceed back to Portsmouth on the opposite tack. Then Nicholas went ashore scrambling through the coarse grass up on to firmer ground, where, sheltered by a thornbush, he could survey the walls of the castle looming up in front of him.

As night fell, the waning moon rose and shed an eerie light across the mudflats which now lined the harbour as the tide fell. All around him the night creatures began to emerge. A hunting owl hooted. A nightjar, perched in a nearby bush, shattered the silence with its rasping call. From the marsh pool behind him a chorus of toads set up a monotonous croaking.

The moonlight was just enough to see by and, cautiously, he approached the walls of the castle, making use of the cover of the thornbushes as much as possible. The watergate, as expected, was shut. He gazed up at the bastions but could see no signs of life. The sentries had gone off duty. Then he began to climb the castle wall at a place furthest away from the southernmost bastion. The flint stones, used for building the wall, were sharp but gave plenty of footholds, especially in the places where the wall had crumbled through neglect. Soon, Nicholas was at the top. He pulled himself up and over the top of the wall and slithered down the inside, landing gently on his feet. All was quiet. No one, as far as he could tell, had seen him.

Creeping along in the shadows of the wall, he stopped when he saw ahead of him the jagged outlines of the ruined nave of the old priory church whose monks had long since departed for less remote parts, long before King Henry had abolished the abbeys and convents. Nicholas stopped and drew a deep breath. He'd made it. He was inside the castle. So far, so good.

CHAPTER FIFTEEN

Daffyd watched her all the time these days; not with the languishing looks of a lover but with the suspicious stare of a jealous man. He knew she had been down to the royal stables. He'd watched her return as if he were timing her. He also resented her friendship with Simon and sneered at his diminutive size.

Jane did all she could to avoid meeting Daffyd. Fortunately, the Queen required her services more and more frequently and she could avoid him at meal times when the Queen wanted Jane to wait on her. But she couldn't avoid him all the time. The music drove them together. The King liked their particular combination of voices and, as the Court was settling down to await the birth of the royal child, the King wanted to hear soothing music about the triumph of true love. He commanded the Master of the Royal Music to stop putting on entertainments about war and knightly exploits; instead, Jane was required to put on the costume of the god of love who lulled everyone he encountered into a state of tranquillity. Because Jane's voice had the bell-like quality of a boy soprano, with the emotional overtones of a woman, she was chosen for the part, and with her slim figure and long legs she made a ravishingly attractive boy. Only when he was accompanying her in these performances did Daffyd put aside his ugly, suspicious expression and gaze at her with an intensity which she found cloying and oppressive.

At the end of one of these performances, when she had successfully soothed into submission one of the fierce satyrs of Greek mythology, Daffyd came to see her in the small room which had been set aside for her own personal use because, sometimes, she had to make several changes of costume in one evening. Usually, one of the Queen's ladies-in-waiting was there to help her, but this evening she was alone. When Daffyd came in without knocking, she had her back to him and was slipping a petticoat over her head, having removed the short Grecian tunic she'd worn as Eros. She turned her head and scowled when she saw who had come in.

'Go away, Daffyd—at once, do you hear me? This is my room. You have no business to be here.'

'I must see you alone, Jane. You are always surrounded by people. Why have you been avoiding me?'

'What nonsense. We've just sung two duets together.'

'That's different. I can't talk to you when we're performing together. I want to talk about us. Jane and Daffyd. Not Eros and that stupid satyr.'

'There's nothing to say. Just go away and let me get dressed.'

She'd dropped the petticoat over her head but it had got caught up round her shoulders in her haste to cover her nakedness. Quickly Daffyd came up to her and cupped his hands over her bare breasts, holding her fast.

'Get out,' she shouted, praying that one of the Queen's ladies would remember to come to see if she was all right. But the strong oak door was firmly shut and there was no escape.

Daffyd pulled her to him and covered her back and shoulders with passionate kisses. She could feel his excitement and suddenly realised the danger she was in. Trying not to panic, as she knew that would only make matters worse, she struggled to get away from him but he was too strong and very aroused and beyond reasoning.

He turned her round to face him and she clawed at his face with her sharp nails, drawing blood which trickled down his cheek, splattering the front of the white tunic he was wearing. The pain seemed to inflame him even more and he pressed his face down on to hers and she felt his lips on hers. Then roughly he pushed her back towards the bed in the corner of the room which had been provided for her to rest on during performances when she wasn't on stage. She fought every inch of the way. He had pinned down her arms but she could still kick out with her feet but she wasn't wearing shoes as she had kicked off the gold sandals she'd worn during the performance. Her small feet made no impression on Daffyd. He only grunted and propelled her more forcefully towards the bed. She couldn't stop him. Suddenly, he picked her up and threw her down on the bed and then collapsed on top of her, muffling her screams.

'Daffyd, stop, you fool,' she shouted when, for a moment, she was able to turn her head away from him. 'Don't you see that this will get you nowhere at all? I'll hate you for ever after this.'

'Better this way than let that traitor Peverell have you. Why do you bother with him? He had a fine gallop with Neville's wife so why don't we do the same?'

He'd relaxed his grip when he said this and, with a twist of her body, she was able to spring up off the bed and, quick as lightning, she darted over to the corner of the room where she kept the quiverful of arrows she'd used during that night's entertainment. The arrows were only made of painted wood but they had sharp points and could inflict considerable damage if used with force. She seized hold of one and turned to face Daffyd.

It didn't stop him. He rushed at her, grasped her raised arm and forced her to drop the arrow. The pain was excruciating and she fought back like a wild thing, kicking and screaming at him to stop.

'My, my, you love birds,' said a quiet, level voice behind her. 'This is a strange billing and cooing. Are you all right, my dear?'

Jane knew that voice only too well. How often it had comforted her in the past when she'd been upset and lonely. Lady Isabel Hardwicke had opened the door to the dressing room and come in quietly. With a silent prayer to her guardian angel, Jane broke away from Daffyd and angrily rearranged her petticoat.

'This is no lovemaking, Lady Isabel,' she said. 'Master Owen is just leaving. He has no business to be here.'

'Indeed he hasn't. This room is solely for Jane's use,' said Lady Isabel severely. 'You'd better leave quickly before the King hears about this.'

There was no arguing with Isabel when she used that tone of voice. She stood there, stiff with disapproval, and Daffyd slunk out, flashing a look at Jane which told her everything. By fair means or foul, he was going to have her.

When he'd gone, Jane's control slipped. She collapsed on the bed and burst into tears. Isabel sat down next to her and held her hand.

'There, there, my dear, no harm done, I hope. Just a few bruises. Young Daffyd's a passionate man. He's inflamed with lust, I fear. You'll either have to give in to him and hope his ardour cools or become properly engaged to him. It's surprising how men change once they know they are going to be married. The King will be pleased—I'm sure he'll give you a dowry—and the Court will approve. So why not save yourself all this unpleasantness and agree to become his wife. He'll soon become possessive, proud to be promised to you, and he'll get himself under control when he knows he'll soon get what he wants.

'But one practical piece of advice, my dear,' Isabel went on as she could see Jane was calming down under the influence of her quiet voice. 'Don't come in here alone after a performance. Our Court is full of men like Daffyd and you are very attractive. They also think the boy's costume is provocative and will expect you to welcome their advances. It is the way of the world, and men are so full of their self-importance and so sure of their overwhelming allure that they think every woman is panting for them; especially woman who sing and act in public. They are regarded as easy game.

'You could do worse than marry Daffyd. At least you will have a protector and he'll be no trouble once you've tamed him. But I see that is not to be. You've got that stubborn look on your face, Jane. You still think you will wait for the man you think you love. Don't be foolish. Nicholas Peverell is a doomed man. He's escaped from the Tower, God knows how, and they haven't caught him yet. But when they do, he'll return in fetters with his reputation in tatters. What use will he be to you then?'

'I'm glad Nicholas has escaped, and I'm certain he'll prove his innocence. Meanwhile I'll have none of Daffyd. But thank you for your advice, Lady Isabel. I know you have my interests at heart.'

'Indeed I do, Jane, and I hate to see a beautiful and talented girl, who has to fend for herself in a man's world, being taken advantage of. Sooner or later, you will have to find protection in marriage. As it is, you have no status and no family to help you. But use your brains, child. If Daffyd doesn't appeal to you, then look around for some elderly widower who will look after you. How else do you think women survive at Court? We attach ourselves to some doting man—wise ones marry him; stupid ones become his mistress; astute ones become his mistress if he's already married, and save up all the jewels and houses he will heap upon them out of gratitude. In that way, at least they have something to fall back on when the time comes, which it does, inevitably, when beauty fades and the man moves on.

'Come, my dear, dry your tears, put on a dress and come with me. The Queen wants you and you must not keep her waiting. And, if I might give you yet one more piece of advice, say nothing to anyone about Daffyd's advances. People will only laugh at you and say you got what you deserved. Everyone knows Daffyd loves you and everyone thinks you're foolish to resist him. I sympathise with you but think you have no choice. Better to marry than to be regarded as everyone's harlot.'

Jane finished dressing and went with Lady Isabel to assist the Queen. As she left, she looked at her rescuer with a look of quiet determination.

'Thank you, Lady Isabel, for spelling out my position here at Court. Rest assured, I will give you no more trouble in future.'

'That's my girl,' said Isabel cheerfully, giving Jane a playful push out of the room. 'We all have to come to it sooner or later. We women must stick together, though. Men are such fools, my dear, as you'll soon learn. Play your cards right, and you'll end up like me, grey haired, undesirable, but respected because my dear husband left me enough jewels and manors to see me through comfortably to the grave.'

Thinking that nothing on earth would make her follow Isabel's advice, she followed her to join the other ladies-in-waiting who thronged round the Queen.

*   *   *

The next morning, Jane went to see Simon again. He was in the kitchen, holding court as

211

usual, and he ordered the others to leave when he saw Jane. They all left, except one, a woman with a mop of red hair as bright as rowan berries. She was stoutly built with the trace of a hump on her back. Jane knew her well; and knew she loved Simon. If he was the king in miniature, she was his queen. She dressed as a queen in a series of beautiful dresses, many of them encrusted with jewels, the gift of King Henry and his queens when they were in indulgent mood. She was the same height as Simon and Jane often thought that these little people who graced the King's Court were treated like toys, the royal playthings of a bored Court. They were like dolls, to be dressed up and played with, but not to be regarded as real people. But Jane knew otherwise. She had seen the real Simon, and knew that he had the brains and worldly wisdom of any one at Court. And Molly Doyle's intelligence equalled her own. She also had the same emotions as any other woman and her love for Simon made her resent Jane. That morning, she hung back when the others left and scowled at Jane.

'So, you've rejected Daffyd again! It's a hard woman you are, Jane Warrener, to be sure. Many would say that you've been spoilt here at Court and now you're giving yourself the airs and graces of a real lady. But you're heading for a fall, my darling. The likes of you and I can't afford to ride the high horse too often.

212

It's a nasty long way to fall when the time comes.'

'Oh stop your blathering, woman,' said Simon impatiently. 'Mistress Jane has every right to choose her own husband. If she doesn't want Daffyd Owen then he'll have to take no for an answer and look elsewhere. Now, be off, woman, you've got to play the Queen tonight and remember Mistress Joan Waters wants to fit you up with a crown this morning. It'll take a long time to fix a crown on that mop of hair of yours, so better get off and see she does it properly.'

The shot went home. Molly, thoroughly alarmed, scampered off. Jane went up to Simon who sighed lugubriously and rolled his eyes.

'Women! Heaven protect me from them! Once they've got their claws in you . . . But enough of this, what can I do for you, my dear? I've heard about your contretemps with Daffyd last night. It's only to be expected. The man's besotted with you, and I must say you look very fetching in that Cupid's outfit of yours. No wonder the man's mad with lust. You're a pretty woman, alone at Court, Jane, and you need a protector. But don't go looking at me. No one takes me seriously. Besides, I'm not totally indifferent to your charms, you know. I'm not a bad fellow when it comes to pleasing the ladies, as I'm sure you've heard.'

'I know all about your noctural activities,

213

but, as it happens, I do take you seriously. I know you have an astute brain in that head of yours. Now can I make use of it today and ask for your advice?'

'If you've come to consult me about your love life, then you've come to the wrong person. My advice to everyone is follow your heart when it comes to love, but stop and think for a second or two about where it's all going to lead to. If Mistress Anne Boleyn had only listened to me, she would still be here with us wearing her crown on that pretty head of hers.'

'No, I've come to see you about another matter. You see, that friend of mine followed your advice and has escaped from his prison dressed as a woman. Now I've decided I must get away from this Court and I want to know, what's the best way to set about it?'

'If you really mean what you say, and I think you're making a terrible mistake, then I can only say that you looked fine as Cupid last night and I think you'd look equally convincing in a doublet and hose. I'd have to find you a codpiece, though.' And he roared with laughter at his own joke. However, he soon calmed down when he saw how serious Jane was.

'You're not serious, are you Jane? Leave Court? Leave all this luxury and fine living? Go out into the unknown? You've no friends out there. No family. I suppose you want to go after this fellow of yours. Stop him

214

philandering with anyone else. I'll give you full marks for courage, Jane, but no marks at all for common sense. Do you actually think Nicholas Peverell—yes I know all about him—wants you tagging along behind him? Of course he doesn't. You'd be a mighty millstone round his neck. If he has any regard for you, he'd want you to stay here even if you do have to teach young Daffyd a lesson or two. And another thing—by God, you look as fetching as a boy as you do as a girl. How far do you think you'll get on your own dressed as a pretty boy?'

'I have my own horse, remember? Melissa. I brought her with me from my father's house. She goes like the wind when I tell her to. Now, I want you to cut off my hair, Simon. I'm not needed in tonight's entertainment so we could do it after dinner.'

'You forget Molly and I play the King and Queen tonight. Are you suggesting King Hal gets down from his throne and cuts off the hair of one of his wife's ladies-in-waiting?'

'As soon as the performance is over, I could come to your room.'

'And be murdered by Molly Doyle? She guards me like a watchdog, and is just as ferocious.'

'Then you must give her the slip and meet me somewhere else. I can't cut off my own hair, and you're the only person I can trust.'

'Jane, get away with you, and don't come

bothering me again with your stupid ideas. I'll not consent to you gallivanting around the countryside on a beautiful grey mare dressed as a boy. I won't have anything to do with such a stupid scheme.'

'And I've quite made up my mind. So, it seems I must make my own arrangements. However, I shall be in the royal stables at midnight and I hope to see you there. If you don't come, then I shall leave just the same, and cut my own hair off later on. I didn't expect you to be a coward, Simon.'

'Then you misjudged me. I won't risk my position here; and I value my head staying where God put it. It's the only bit of this body of mine which I'm proud of.'

'Then I'll bid you goodbye, Simon. Perhaps we shall meet again one of these days.'

Simon saw that Jane was deadly serious and he stared at her in consternation.

'My God, girl, you do mean it. And where the Devil do you think you'll go?'

'To Portsmouth. Then to Porchester.'

'Of course. I see now what you have in mind. You think you're going to save this fellow, Peverell. It's time he learnt to stand on his own feet, you know.'

'I've got to get away from Court. Daffyd's made my life intolerable and I want to be with Nicholas even if I follow him to the gallows.'

'Then I have misunderstood you, Jane. I thought you were above the rest of womankind

216

who are ruled by their passions. You've got a brain in that pretty head of yours; it's time you started to use it. Stop being foolish and follow my example. Know when you're well off, and don't go looking for trouble. Only fools fight lost causes; and you're no fool, Jane Warrener. Well, go if you must, and I'll be there when you lay that pretty head of yours next to Peverell's on the block on Tower Green.'

'And I shall be standing next to you when another person lays his head on that block; someone who has blackened Nicholas's name and is the real traitor.'

'Well, one thing's for sure, Mistress Jane, you'll never see my head stretched out on that block!'

*   *   *

That same morning, Daffyd Owen went to see Thomas Cromwell. He'd spent the night restlessly tossing and turning reliving in his mind every detail of the scene with Jane in her dressing room. He knew he'd been foolish. Women like Jane didn't respond to rough wooing. He should have treated her more gently, taking time to arouse her and then fan her fire into a blaze with a delicacy of touch which she would appreciate. But, once alight, he knew instinctively that Jane's passion would burn with an intense flame that would completely satisfy him. Then he would have

217

achieved all he wanted from life; a place at Court, and Jane by his side. Jane, his heart's desire, his dearest love. Why wouldn't she agree to become his dearest possession?

He couldn't help it if he felt so strongly. He was only made of flesh and blood, like any other man. She had played with him as Anne Boleyn had played with the King, but he had not the patience of a king and there were too many other contenders for her hand. It was these shadowy rivals that drove him to see Cromwell. If he wasn't to have Jane, then he'd see to it that no one else would have her. If she was put under house arrest then he would be able to see her as much as he liked, and gradually, over the days, weeks, years, as long as it took, he'd woo her gently until she came to value his friendship and, maybe, that friendship would turn to love. He and Jane were one. Hadn't they been singing night after night about Cupid's darts and people dying of love? Hadn't she looked at him with glowing eyes and deep sighs when she sang such words? How could she communicate such passion when she was on stage and become so hostile when they were alone? As that long night wore on, he'd felt sure that Jane really loved him, her body longed for him, but she would not trust her instincts. At the thought of her body, the small, firm breasts, her smooth, silky body and long, graceful legs, he became more and more excited, and as the dawn broke, he knew he would have to have her, by force, if not by consent. And he also knew he would murder anyone else who came near her. But before it came to that, he would try to have her put out of the way of other suitors; and he saw how it could be done.

Surprisingly, Cromwell agreed to see him straight away. He was busy at his desk, as usual, his secretary working hard beside him. Cromwell scrutinised Daffyd's face, noticed his haggard appearance, and felt a surge of impatience. What was the world coming to if he was acquiring the reputation of helping young men sort out their love life? The Court was a hard place and women at Court were notoriously hard to get, if that was the way they wanted to play it. He didn't invite Daffyd to sit down. Nor did he dismiss his secretary.

'Master Owen, what can I do for you? You don't want me to interfere with your marital expectations, I hope. I'm no use to you there.'

'No, I can manage my own personal affairs, thank you. I've come to talk to you about Nicholas Peverell. It's common knowledge that he's escaped from the Tower.'

Cromwell looked at him sharply and dismissed his secretary. 'The bird's flown, I have to admit that. Foolish man; but we'll catch him and bring him back. The King's safety is our prime concern. But what has this got to do with you?'

'I think I know who helped him escape.'

219

Cromwell sat back in his chair and looked at Daffyd thoughtfully. 'Do you now? Then tell me your suspicions.'

'Mistress Warrener has been acting strangely of late. She has disappeared twice for long stretches of time and I've seen her in the royal stables talking to the grooms.'

'She has every right to do that. I understand we stable her horse. As to her disappearances from Court, I expect the Queen sent her on some charitable mission. I can't see how Mistress Warrener has anything to do with Lord Nicholas's escape from prison.'

'I believe she thinks she has some affection for him.'

'I daresay. And has none for you, I suppose. But why, in God's name, are you denouncing her as being involved in treasonable activities? Do you seriously imagine this will help you to win her affection? I don't understand your reasoning, Master Owen.'

'I have the King's safety at heart.'

'Highly commendable. But that's not the real reason, is it? Do you want to see her in prison alongside Lord Nicholas? Is this the idea? Do you want to punish her for not loving you? This is a strange wooing, Master Owen.'

'No, Jane has no treasonable thoughts whatsoever. She believes Lord Nicholas is innocent, stupid girl. And I'm sure she'll go to any length to prove he's innocent. I want you to stop her from doing anything foolish. Put her under guard, at least until Peverell is caught.'

'I thank you for your advice, but I believe you are making a mistake. Mistress Warrener has more sense than to go rushing off on a fool's errand after a traitor. But thank you again for your warning. I shall take note. Now go and relax, man. Go and have some fun with the ladies who are not so particular as Mistress Warrener. There's plenty who'll not say no to a good-looking young man like you who sings so divinely. Now, be off with you, man, and let me get on with more important matters.'

It was no use arguing with Thomas Cromwell. The interview was at an end. Daffyd was dismissed. As he went back to his apartment, he felt that he'd made a fool of himself. Cromwell would never believe Jane had anything to do with Peverell's escape. Of course not. Now, his real fear was that Jane would take the law into her own hands and run after the traitor. She was quite capable of doing that. And he, Daffyd Owen, had forced the issue.

*　　　*　　　*

When he'd gone, Cromwell scribbled a note on a piece of paper.

'Your Majesty, Daffyd Owen informs me that Jane Warrener is likely to go after Peverell. He wants her put under guard. His motive? To keep her out of harm's way—from other suitors—that is. The man's mad, but this could cause complications. What action should I take? My advice is to do nothing. She can't do any harm. She might possibly get herself killed.'

He signed it, recalled his secretary and told him to take the note to the King. Then he sat back and waited for the reply. It wasn't long in coming.

'Let Mistress Warrener be. She's a fool, and dispensable. Pity to lose a good singer, though. Let Owen be placed under guard. He's more likely to give us trouble. There's no greater fool than a man in love. Peverell must not be interfered with in any way. Let him get on with his work. He'll be hot for the kill by now.'

Cromwell nodded his agreement and gave the necessary order. Daffyd, to his astonishment, found himself under house arrest.

*   *   *

At midnight, Jane, dressed in a plain doublet and hose and wearing a short cloak with a man's cap holding up her long hair which she'd coiled round her head, went to the stables. Melissa, her fine, pure-white Arab mare, which Nicholas had given her for her sixteenth birthday, greeted her with enthusiasm, whinnying her pleasure at the touch of Jane's

222

hand on her face. She stroked the long nose and spoke gently to her.

'Are you ready for a long ride, my pet? Can you take me all the way to Porchester?'

'And she'll have to carry me as well,' said a deep voice behind her. She turned round and saw Simon, dressed in a working man's clothes, a lute and a bag slung over one shoulder.

'Simon! You've changed your mind. You've come to cut my hair?'

'Later, girl, later. If you've a mind for night riding, then I'll come with you. I won't let you go alone. That horse of yours looks strong enough to take us both. We'll be a couple of travelling entertainers. You'll sing; I'll tumble and juggle and accompany you on this lute. We'll call ourselves Simon and Roderick King. You'd better be my nephew. No one will believe you're my son.

'Now, let's get one thing straight. I don't approve of what you're doing. You're as headstrong as Daffyd Owen, but I know there's no stopping you and I can't let you go alone. Besides,' he said with a grin, 'I can't stand any more of Queen Molly. I can't abide the woman. Come, let's be off if we're going. We'll need to be a long way away from here by daylight. The King's not going to be too pleased when he learns that we've flown the nest.'

CHAPTER SIXTEEN

Creeping along the outer wall of the castle, Nicholas made his way towards the church which was situated in the south-western part of the castle enclosure. He remembered Neville telling him that the church was not used nowadays. The monks had long ago left for a safer place inland, and the people of Porchester worshipped elsewhere. Maybe it could be a suitable base for his spying activities.

When he was near the church, he darted across the open space to the west door. He pushed it open, the hinges creaking alarmingly, and went in. Then Nicholas shrank back against the inside wall of the nave and waited. Nothing happened. The only sound was the rustling of tiny creatures all around him, and the flapping of wings of a night owl which the noise of the opening door had disturbed.

The roof of the nave was in a ruinous state and through one of the gaping holes the moonlight streamed in. Looking around, he saw the reason for the rustlings and squeakings. The floor of the nave was covered with straw. He picked up a handful and sniffed it. It was fresh and clean, only recently laid, he reckoned, but long enough for the field mice to discover it and start making their nests. So, he thought, someone was expecting visitors, and a lot of them, judging by the extent of the straw which carpeted the nave and extended up into the chancel, as far as he could see.

Cautiously, he made his way up the nave and into the chancel, where there stood the remains of the high altar, now just a chipped and cracked stone, resting on four stone pillars. Looking round he saw there was a chapel to the west of the chancel. It had its own altar and he also noticed there was a small, wooden door in the west wall of the chapel. He went over to it. It was a narrow door, suitable for only one person at a time to go through, and it was so low that he would have to crouch down when he went in. It was very solidly built, made of oak, and unlocked. He pushed it open and saw the outline of stone steps leading down into a dark void. The moonlight didn't reach as far as this corner of the church. Feeling his way, he went down the steps into what felt like a small room. He raised his hands above his head and touched a vaulted, stone ceiling. He was in a crypt of some kind. Groping his way round the room, he realised it was very small, and there was an altar at one end. The floor under his feet was made of stone and was dry. The air, too, smelt musty but with no hint of damp or mildew. Realising he couldn't do much more until daylight, he decided to bed down for the night.

Tomorrow he would have to find some tallow candles which he'd stupidly forgotten to bring with him. He had brought his flint with him as he always carried that on his person, but somewhere in the castle he would find candles. Meanwhile the night was well advanced. He went back up the steps, helped himself to a bundle of straw and shaped it into a bed by the side of the altar. Then he closed the door, finding, to his relief, that it could be bolted on the inside, and threw himself down on the straw for a few hours' sleep.

He awoke, hours later, to the sound of voices above him. He got up and groped his way up to the door. The voices were clearer now. There were two men, as far as he could judge. He could hear the clanking of their swords against their armour as they moved around, and by placing himself by the door he could just get the gist of what they were saying.

'It's good enough for them,' one man said.

'Too good for that rabble,' said the other.

Then they must have moved away because he could hear no more.

He waited for a few moments, then cautiously opened the door. The church was flooded with sunlight. He'd slept longer than he'd realised. The men's words floated across his mind. Too good for whom? he thought. What sort of 'rabble' was coming to invade this church? He felt hungry and realised he hadn't eaten for a long time. Then he remembered the food which he'd bought in Portsmouth and he looked round for signs of stores in the church. If people were being brought here, then they would have to be provided for. He noticed a wooden box by the altar, and he went over to it and opened the lid. It was packed with rough, tallow candles. Of course, he thought, whoever was coming would need light. He couldn't believe his luck. He helped himself to as many as he could carry and went back down into the crypt. He lit one from his flint and saw his surroundings for the first time. Had it not been for the altar he could have been in a prison cell. The ceiling was vaulted, as he'd discovered last night, and there were no windows. There were a couple of wooden benches placed along the far wall and he thought the place had once upon a time housed a relic or an image of a saint, and Masses had been said there on its feast days. Now there was an atmosphere of neglect and disuse as if the place hadn't been visited for centuries.

He ate some of the food he'd brought with him, and began to scrutinise the flagstones on the floor. He knew that a church inside a castle was often a place of refuge for the surrounding inhabitants when fighting broke out in their neighbourhood. The monks, too, whose church he was in, would also want to hide in dangerous times; especially in a place such as Porchester where attack could come from the sea and the church could be very vulnerable. Could there be a tunnel to the castle? He remembered there was a tunnel from the keep to Neville's house. Maybe there were other tunnels.

He felt each stone carefully looking for any which seemed unstable. All of them were well worn and hadn't been disturbed for centuries. But in the corner by the side of the altar, he found a slab that wasn't as stable as the others. Using his knife he was able to raise the slab a few inches. Then he could lift it with both hands. Below it was a trapdoor, made of wood, with a ring on top. He heaved it up and saw that there were steps leading down into a deep hole. Holding his lighted candle, he climbed down the steps and stood on the earth floor at the bottom of the hole. He felt he was very near sea level. The castle was built on a hill, but the sea was all around them and this place now smelt of damp and mildew. Ahead of him he saw the entrance to a tunnel. He wondered if his candle would hold out long enough for him to see where the tunnel led to but he knew no tunnel within the castle precinct would be too long and he decided to risk exploring it.

The tunnel had a barrel ceiling lined with stone bricks, and trouble had been taken over its construction. Bent almost double because the ceiling was very low, Nicholas, feeling like a mole burrowing underground, crept along it.

It appeared to go in a straight line and he

thought it quite likely that it would lead to the inner bailey where the keep was and the Constable's house where anyone fleeing from an enemy would want to find shelter. After he'd been creeping along for about fifteen minutes, he came to a part of the tunnel where it forked to the right and the left. Taking the right-hand fork because he thought that might lead to the castle, he crept along it, pushing aside the bits of fallen stone and earth as the tunnel seemed to deteriorate as he proceeded. Sometimes there was only just enough room for him to squeeze past the piles of earth and he began to fear that his candle would not last much longer if the air, which was foul, became worse. He had just made up his mind to turn back when he heard voices above him. This time there seemed to be several people speaking all at once so that it was impossible to hear what anyone was saying. Proceeding cautiously, the noises grew louder and he heard the clatter of metal objects and the commanding voices of what he thought sounded like cooks giving orders to the scullions. He was under the keep. Above him were the kitchens.

The tunnel now began to slope upwards and the going got easier. Suddenly the end of the tunnel was ahead of him, and above his head was a trapdoor. There was no point in trying to open it in broad daylight, but he'd found what he wanted: a safe place to hide, and a way in to the castle. But this wasn't the time for stupid heroics. He wanted to see Neville dead, that was certain, but he wanted him brought to justice first and declared a traitor. Then and then only would his own name be cleared.

Backing away from the trapdoor he made his way back to the crypt. Bartholomew Tyler, he thought, had been the King's spy and he'd been murdered in the King's service. Now Tyler's mantle had fallen on him. He, Nicholas, was no longer a reluctant spy. He was now fully committed to the work Tyler had been unable to complete. Now he needed incontrovertible proof of Neville's treason.

*   *   *

He hadn't long to wait. Later that day, just as the sun was setting, he heard a commotion above his head. Listening at the locked door of the crypt, he heard the noise of a company of men arriving, tramping around the church, discarding their swords and dropping their metal breastplates on the floor. Quarrels soon broke out over the best places to camp down, then laughter and orders being given. The place was swarming with men and, by the sounds he could hear, they were soldiers. Probably foot soldiers, he thought as there was no indication that horses were being stabled with them. And these men, he realised, weren't English. The voices he heard were speaking French. As he retreated down into the crypt he thought ruefully that he was trapped by a contingent of French soldiers, settling down for the night. They would indeed provide him with the irrefutable evidence he needed to prove Neville's treachery. But one thing more was needed. The information contained in Tyler's box. According to Cromwell, this gave the date of the continental invasion. He would need that to warn the King and allow time, if that was possible, to bring up ships for the defence of the south coast. What he had seen at Portsmouth Point made him realise that the Admiral of the Fleet, the Earl of Southampton, had no sense of urgency about the dangers he would be facing. Pray God, he thought, that there was still time to raise a fighting force and alert the fleet. As the night wore on and the sounds above him grew quieter as the men settled down to sleep he began to see a way of gaining this information. The risk was considerable. It could all go wrong and he could expect no mercy from Neville if he was caught. But he had to take that risk.

*   *   *

Nicholas spent a restless night listening to the sounds of the sleeping men above him: the snoring that provided a continuous ground bass to his thoughts, the occasional shout of someone having a nightmare, the curse, as someone turned over and encountered the body next to him. Finally, he got up and went over to the store over the trapdoor. A plan was forming in his mind, just a tiny spark of inspiration. He knew it had little chance of success, but he had to give it a try. He couldn't remain a mole in a tunnel for ever.

He pulled open the trapdoor and entered the tunnel, taking a bundle of candles with him. He checked his dagger was secured in his belt. Then he lit a candle and pulled down the trapdoor. He felt that he wouldn't spend another night in that crypt. Where he was going there was no return.

He made his way along the tunnel until he reached the place where it forked. This time he took the left-hand fork as he knew the right-hand fork led to the keep. If he was lucky and his sense of direction hadn't let him down, then by taking the left-hand fork he should arrive at the outer wall of the castle, with luck by one of the bastions. That would suit him very well. Also, he thought he'd noticed, on his previous visit, a sally port by one of the bastions, with steps leading down to the sea on the western side of the castle. He knew the monks would have had a reredorter on that side of the castle complex, by their church and sleeping quarters. These latrines would be in the form of alcoves containing seats and a drain which would lead straight down into the sea when the tide was in and the mudflats when it was out. A contingent of infantry would need these latrines and would need them especially when they woke up.

He continued along the left-hand fork which, as it turned out, wasn't very long. Ahead of him he saw another trapdoor which he pushed open with difficulty. This time there were only two steps up, then a gap, so he had to leap up and grasp the edge of the hole with both hands and haul himself out. The breath of sweet sea air which greeted him as he climbed out of the tunnel made him gasp with relief after the stale air in the tunnels and in the crypt.

He had, as he hoped, come up in one of the bastions. But he couldn't stay there long. A cannon had been positioned there with its muzzle pointing out to sea and soon men would come to service it and maybe put in some artillery practice. Outside the bastion, he looked along the strong defensive walls. Sure enough, to his left was a row of small alcoves, the monks' latrines. He went over and looked down into the harbour mud. The tide was coming in, but had not yet covered all the mud which creaked and crackled at the approach of the sea. By the side of the latrines was an opening in the wall and steps led down to the shore. This was one of the sally ports where the inhabitants of the castle could leave if they had to evacuate the place in a hurry. He glanced over to the east and saw red streaks staining the sky. Dawn was coming. Very soon the soldiers in the church would be stirring.

He hid himself inside the bastion and waited, dagger in hand, praying that the soldiers would not all rush to the latrines together. Sure enough, as he waited, he saw the west door of the church open and a soldier came stumbling out clutching his stomach. He'd put on his corslet of armour but hadn't fastened it. He also had tucked his burgonet under his arm probably to prevent anyone stealing it whilst he was outside. As he rushed for the first alcove and went inside, for a second, his back was exposed. It was enough. Nicholas darted out of his hiding place, grasped the man round his neck and heaved back his head until the man's terror-stricken eyes seemed to bulge out of his head. Then, with one slash of his dagger, Nicholas slit the man's throat as if he was killing a pig in the slaughterhouse.

As the man fell, Nicholas caught him and dragged him over to the sally port where he pushed him down on to the shore. He went down after him and stripped him of his corslet and jerkin which was embroidered on the collar with the fleur-de-lys of France. Then he dragged off the man's boots which were stronger than his own, picked up the man's burgonet which he'd tossed down the steps after the body, and looked round for a piece of driftwood in order to dig the man a shallow grave.

It was a race against the tide and the appearance of the other soldiers. There was no time for feelings of remorse over killing a man who'd done him no harm. Things had to be done and done quickly when so much was at stake. He found a suitable piece of driftwood and he scratched out a shallow grave in the soft mud. Then he tied four pieces of masonry which had fallen off the wall on to the man's legs and chest, laid the man in the grave and piled the mud on top of him, using the piece of driftwood as a shovel. Then he put on the man's boots, his armour, and, much to his relief, the burgonet was on the big side so he could drag it down over his face. He climbed back into the castle, and looked down on to the shore. Soon the sea would reach the castle walls and cover the grave of the French mercenary.

Nicholas then wiped the blood off his dagger, fastened it to his belt, and went back to the church. He hoped the man he'd just killed wouldn't have any friends who would miss him. He knew mercenaries were an independent band with neither time nor inclination to form attachments but, all the same, someone might spot the difference between the person who'd rushed outside and the person who'd come back.

Back in the church, the other soldiers were

waking up and making for the latrines. One of them grinned at Nicholas and he gave a sigh of relief. At least his appearance had passed muster. Tables had been set up at the back of the church and Nicholas joined the queue for the bread and ale which was provided for the infantry. A burly Frenchman pushed past him and said in French:

'Out of my way, you dog. Make way for the men of Paris. And what's your name?' he added as he seized hold of a jug of ale which he drained in one go.

'Philibert d'Artois,' said Nicholas, helping himself to bread. And then he added, 'From Ypres.' He knew his French was fluent—his father had insisted on that—but his accent could have betrayed him. Ypres was a flash of inspiration because most people there were Flemish and spoke with a strong accent.

The man grunted. 'A Flamand, then. Well, you can't help that, I suppose, and no doubt you can wield a pike as well as we can. Let's hope this little fracas will soon be over and we can all get paid and go home. The ale's good, though. That's one thing the English can do, make strong ale.'

Nicholas began to relax. He'd passed the first challenge. Now he prayed to God that there weren't too many pikemen from Ypres in this contingent of mercenaries.

CHAPTER SEVENTEEN

Simon cut off Jane's hair in a barn where they had stopped for a few hours' rest before daylight. He snipped away at her long, copper-coloured tresses muttering curses at her folly in sacrificing her most beautiful adornment for the sake of that wretched fellow Nicholas Peverell, a traitor. When he'd finished he handed Jane a comb and said there was no mirror so she couldn't see what he'd done.

'I never set out to be a hairdresser so I'll not be held responsible for the massacre of your hair,' he grumbled, as she smoothed the ends of her hair down and combed the rest into some sort of order.

'Don't take on so; it'll soon grow again when the time comes. There's no harm in having a haircut once in a while. You should see a barber yourself and get that beard of yours trimmed. It could do with it.'

'Not on your life. The King and I are uncommonly attached to our beards. As for your head, my dear, by the way you're going, it's only a matter of time before someone stronger than me hacks it off. But come now, eat some food and let's rest a while. Don't say Simon doesn't look after you.'

He'd brought bread and meat with him and a bottle of ale. Melissa munched contentedly at a pile of hay they'd found in the corner of the barn, and there was clean straw on the floor. Outside, the first sounds of the dawn chorus warned them that the sun was rising. Jane curled up on the straw and Simon covered her with his cloak. Then he sat down beside her with his back resting against a beam and waited. He hadn't slept that night. He would always watch over her, he knew that, whatever happened to her. He wanted nothing more. He realised Nicholas Peverell had her heart and, much as he regretted this, he was glad for her sake that she had experienced the consuming passion of real love. He knew his task was to keep her safe, and if things went well, then he would tumble for her at her wedding and watch over her first-born child.

He let her sleep on until the sun was high overhead. He prepared some breakfast and brought her fresh water in a leather bucket from a trough outside in the yard. If they left now, they would reach Portsmouth by late evening. This would mean they would avoid those people who might ask awkward questions. Also, if the King was to send guards after them, they would be well ahead of them by now.

'Come on, lass, he said gruffly as she tipped water over her head and flattened down her hair, 'We've got a show to prepare, remember? We're a team, uncle and nephew, and we'll have to sing for our supper tonight. That means learning some songs of the taverns, wench. None of your fancy court songs. Between now and nightfall I'll have to coarsen you up a bit or else we'll be laughed out of town. We'll have to rehearse on the broad back of Melissa, not that she'll mind. She's a real trooper, that mare of yours.'

*   *   *

They reached Portsmouth by nightfall and found a small alehouse in one of the warren of streets just off the Point. It went by the name of the Lobster Pot and, judging by the sounds of laughter coming through the open door, it was popular. Leaving Jane outside with Melissa, Simon went in, reappearing a few minutes later and telling her there was a stable at the back where they could stable their horse and bed down for the night. They could also have a bowl of soup each and a cut off the pig turning on the spit, in return for a few songs.

They went into the room which was full of seamen out to enjoy themselves whilst they were in port. Simon was greeted with good-natured laughter, but he took everything with good humour and they soon stopped and handed him a pot of ale.

'And what about the lad, master?' said one fierce-looking seaman, his pock-marked face criss-crossed with battle scars. 'He looks as if he wants nothing stronger than his mother's

239

milk. Did you bring her with you? Hidden her somewhere?'

Simon waited for the laughter to subside. 'He's not my son. He's my nephew and he's called Roderick and he's older than he looks. Give him a jug of ale now and he'll sing for you. He's got the voice of a nightingale.'

They earned their supper that night in that rough tavern cheered on by seamen who loved a good song. Simon had taught Jane the songs of the people as they went along, and Jane had been a quick pupil. She had a good sense of rhythm and a quick memory and she discovered that she, like Simon, had a talent for mimicry. She had no difficulty in picking up the Hampshire dialect and she enjoyed the robust songs which had the same themes as the courtly songs, unrequited love, grief, and the joys of courtship and weddings. Simon had a robust, bass voice and with his actor's gifts he could mime the actions and soon the company settled down and called for more ale and more songs. In any other circumstances, Jane would have enjoyed herself.

It was late before the drinkers tottered out into the night to find their homes or bed down for the night on the Point. Out at Spithead, the ships had lit their lanterns and the points of light glowed like fireflies in the summer night. In the inner harbour the fishermen waited for the dawn.

'Well, masters, you've earned your supper

240

tonight,' the landlord said. 'You're welcome to stay here as long as you please. It's been a long time since I've enjoyed myself so much and we'll be having a full house tomorrow night. You, Master Roderick, can help us in the kitchen tomorrow, if you like. We need someone to turn the spit for us and it'll keep you out of mischief. Better to do some honest work than waste your time roistering round the town where you'll come to no good. But get some sleep now, both of you; you'll be comfortable in the stables and won't be disturbed. Now don't sleep too long, boy. We'll be needing you soon after first light.'

They settled down for the night in the straw next to Melissa. As she drifted off to sleep, Jane felt Simon shaking with laughter.

'What's so funny, Simon?'

'Everything, Master Roderick. If only the King could see us now. And Lord Nicholas. He'd not look twice at you tonight. But I'm proud of you, lass. I always thought you were a bit of a prude, too clever by half, and a bit disapproving of the goings-on of ordinary folk. But I was wrong. I have to admit it. You just needed someone to liven you up, that's all. And that's my job. We're a good team, you and I. We'll survive.'

He stopped speaking, as he realised Jane had fallen into a deep sleep.

*   *   *

241

The next day Jane prepared the pig for the day's meals and cleared away the previous night's debris. Then she was told to put down fresh straw on the floor and keep the fire going, ready for the pig. Rushing from one job to the other she cursed Simon who had sidled away into the town. However, she was glad of one thing. She had been accepted as a boy. Although several of the men had eyed her lecherously the previous evening, there had been no trouble as it was obvious that any over-enthusiastic admirer would have Simon to contend with and he, although short in size, was well endowed with powerful muscles and a nimbleness of his feet that would run rings round a prize fighter, let alone a drunken seaman.

Simon, however, was not wasting his time. Leaving Jane to her kitchen work, he went down to the Point where there seemed to be a great deal of activity that morning. He stood looking out to sea, absorbed by the big ships anchored out there. He was fascinated by everything to do with the sea. This was the first time he'd seen it because for the last twenty years he had been at the King's Court and, before that, everything was just a distant memory. At first, he didn't want to risk mingling with the crowd, but after a while he realised that no one was taking any notice of him. The reason for this was, he thought, that he might be small in stature, but otherwise he looked quite normal; not like some of the people he saw around him on the Point with deformed limbs and faces scarred by smallpox or slashed in fights.

He perched himself up on the seawall near the place where small boats were coming and going, picking up boxes of goods for the ships and bringing back men to the shore. He saw whole sheep and pigs being lowered into the boats and a man stood there ticking off items on a list. He looked up and saw Simon's interest.

'Hungry buggers, the King's seamen. Fussy, too. Like things fresh. Still, fighting men needed fighting rations. Can't expect them to fight on empty stomachs.'

'Are they expecting a fight soon?'

'Who knows? We've got our orders to start provisioning the ships so someone, somewhere, must expect action soon. They don't feed sailors to be idle, that's for sure. Butchers are happy, though. Takes a lot of pork to feed a shipload of fighting men. More ships on their way too, I hear. Coming round from Woolwich where they've been fitted out with guns. It's all guns these days. Shan't need soldiers on board soon. No chance of hand-to-hand fighting when cannons can blast the ships out of the water. The *Mary Rose* will be here soon, I'm told—if this wind holds. Now there's a ship, master, that will put paid to the

Frenchies. She's got new guns that'll blow them out of the Channel once and for all.'

'When do we expect visitors?'

'Don't know that, master. I'm not the Lord Admiral. Rumour has it that there's a build-up of ships over in Honfleur and Le Havre. Mind you, the Frenchies are always puffing and blowing about coming over to get us. All wind they are. Hopeless when it comes to action. Still, it pays to keep alert.'

The man was distracted by the arrival of a cartload of pigs and Simon slid down from the wall. So something was going on, he thought. It was worth asking a few more questions.

The fishermen brought their boats back at sunset. They landed their catch and, leaving their wives and other members of their families to clean and gut the fish, they rushed to the Lobster Pot to get down a few jugs of ale before the show. Simon winked at Jane who looked hot and ill tempered after a day's work in the kitchen. She glared at him as she laboriously turned the handle of the spit on which the pig was roasting. He passed her a tankard of ale and took one for himself, then he perched up on a high stool near the counter, and rested his lute across his knees. People grinned at him. He was a novelty, a good-humoured fellow who spoke their language and livened things up a bit.

'Quite a bit going on down here,' he said to a fisherman who was gulping down his ale as if his life depended on it. 'Place is full of people. Not many strangers, though. Apart from the likes of me and Roderick.'

'Strangers?' said the man, wiping the froth off his mouth. 'Place is full of them. All come to see the *Mary Rose*. Supposed to be here tomorrow. Mind you, I'll believe that when I see it. There's been not much wind today, and a ship like that needs a good wind to get her moving. Even if they get the sweeps out I doubt if she'll be in sight tomorrow. Still, folks always live in hope and want to gawp at something.'

'Bad luck for fishermen, though. No one would want to gawp at you.'

'Oh don't you be too sure of that, master. We've got our uses. We catch the fish, don't we?' he said to the circle of men standing round him. 'And we sell it to his Majesty's fleet. Salt pork, salt fish; that turns a man into a mariner.'

'And some of us goes night sailing with the gentry, isn't that right, Joshua?' said one of the company addressing the man next to him, who grinned and looked self-conscious.

'Now don't be shy,' said the man who had brought Joshua into the conversation, 'we all know you made a bit out of that trip, but there's no need to be shy about it. Luck comes to all of us from time to time, we all know that. Tell us what happened. Simon here wants to hear about your adventure, don't you Simon?'

'I like a good tale, yes,' said Simon nonchalantly. 'It could be worth a jug of ale if it's well told.'

'There you go, Joshua, tell Simon your story. There's ale at the end of it, so your luck's still in.'

'Well, this man comes up to me. Wants to get up to Porchester. Couple of nights ago, it were. I tell him he'll have to wait. The tide's not right until late afternoon. Moon's on the wane so tides are not high. We'd have to be quick if I'm to get back again. So I tells him to come back later and I'll see what I can do.'

'What did this man look like?' said Simon.

'Oh, tall fellow. Had to bend his legs a bit to sit down in my boat. Countryman, but talked like the gentry, right? Not like us. But then I didn't think he was local. None of us would want to go to Porchester after night. Not with that she-devil up there.'

'Who might that be?' said Jane quietly, suddenly stopping turning the spit to give the man her full attention.

'Don't you go burning that pig, lad,' said Joshua turning round to look at her in concern. 'I can't abide burnt pig. The she-devil's called Lady Neville, and she'd eat you for breakfast. Don't you go near her, lad. She's not for you. Anyway, this man took out his purse and we agreed on a price . . .'

'Tell us, tell us,' shouted the company, much to Joshua's annoyance.

246

'Now you can stop that, friends. You know that's my business. I don't ask you how much you got for your mackerel; you don't ask me how much I charge passengers. Anyway, this man got into my boat, I set sail, and we went up the harbour. I got the sail up and we pushed along at a right good speed. We got as near as we could before I had to turn back, and I dumped him on a spit of land sticking out of the shore. I didn't want to risk getting stuck on the mud and had to get home before the water ran out. That's what I did. That's the end of my tale, and now I want my reward.'

Simon called for the ale, and glanced across at Jane. She had heard everything. He cursed silently to himself. Now she'd want to go to Porchester tomorrow, that was certain. And that meant the end to the good life, once again.

'Some of us get all the luck,' one of the men said. 'Gadding around the harbour at night and getting paid a month's wages for the trouble.'

The men fell silent at the thought of so much wealth until the smell of burning pork brought them back to the present.

'Here, get turning that spit, boy,' shouted the landlord, coming in to the room and noticing Jane's negligence for the first time. 'Burnt pork is no use to us. Get back to work or you'll feel the weight of my belt on that pretty bum of yours.'

Simon winced and struck a chord on his lute. 'Well, it was a good tale even though we don't know who the man was. Could've been the Lord Admiral wanting to see how good you are at getting a boat up to Porchester, Joshua, but most likely it was someone up to no good with someone else's wife. Maybe he had a tryst with this Lady Neville. You didn't stop to see where he went after you'd landed him?'

'Lord, no, master. Tide had turned, see. I had to get back or I'd be in right trouble with the missus. Besides, it was none of my business where he went after I dumped him on that spit.'

'If he went after the she-devil he'll not be seen again,' said one of the men. 'Rumour has it she uses her lovers then kills them and has them served up for dinner. No man yet has lived to tell the tale.'

'Someone'll come along one day and satisfy her and she'll be as sweet as a cooing dove. Women, they're all the same,' said Simon.

And then he struck some opening chords on his lute, and broke into a ribald song about a farmer and his wife and the wife's lover who was a priest called Edmund.

Later that night, as they settled down to sleep, it was Jane who nudged Simon awake.

'We leave for Porchester tomorrow, Simon, I'm sure Nicholas is there.'

Simon grunted and pulled his cloak over his

ears.

'Go to sleep, lass. Tomorrow's tomorrow. Let's enjoy this moment; a warm barn, clean straw, a bellyful of over-cooked pig, and a contented horse.'

*　　　*　　　*

'Ah there you are, Thomas,' said King Henry glancing up from the pile of papers on his desk. 'I want to speak to you about matters of national security. Well, sit down, man,' he said irritably as Thomas Cromwell remained standing in front of the desk nervously rubbing his hands together as he always did when he was trying to judge the King's mood. He didn't know which King Henry he distrusted most: the bluff King Hal, everyman's friend, or the ruthless manipulator of statesmen, men he had chosen and paid well in return for their loyalty, but whom he never trusted. Usually it only took one glance at those pale, flickering eyes for Cromwell to know what he was up against, but that morning he could read nothing in the King's unsmiling face. Cromwell drew up a chair and sat down.

'I have a letter here from the Lord Admiral of my fleet. It seems that he has become so besotted with building forts that he has neglected to read intelligence reports. Tyler might be dead but there are other men in the field who have reported that there is a steady build-up of French and Flemish ships in the French ports along the Channel coast. Now this mustn't be dismissed lightly just because it's happened before, and will, most likely, happen again. But since the Bishop of Rome has seen fit to excommunicate me, the King of France and the Emperor seem to think it their mission in life to declare a crusade against me to remove me from my throne. No, don't look so shocked, Thomas, it doesn't suit you. You know as well as I do that when we broke from Rome most of Europe condemned us. What these papal supporters can't quite decide on is, when I've been turned off my throne, who will be the next king of England. Unfortunately, my Yorkist cousins whom I have always treated with great leniency are much favoured as my successors. We've dealt with one of them, Reginald Pole, and he can't get up to much in exile on the continent. Besides, I don't think he has the stomach for treason.

'But his brother, Lord Montague, causes me much disquiet, Thomas, as his estate is in Sussex and I fear he could be tempted to join forces with the French King. We've already warned his mother, the Countess of Salisbury, and I regret that I can't trust her either. It grieves me, Thomas, to have to watch members of my own family, but there it is, I can't trust them.'

'Where does Sir Charles Neville fit in with all of this, your Majesty? Surely he has the best claim to the throne as he is directly of the blood royal.'

'Damn you, Thomas, surely you don't believe those lies? I admit to one bastard, my beloved Richmond, but I utterly reject all those rogues who keep telling me that I am their father. There's nothing of me in Neville. He's lucky to be the Constable of Porchester Castle. Let him stay there. The man's a fool and a weakling. He's no more capable of treason than you, Thomas. King Francis would make minced meat of him.'

'I agree, your Majesty. Neville, on his own, hasn't the brains to plot a coup d'état. But his wife . . .'

'No, Thomas, his wife is a whore but she likes her comforts too much to risk everything. She might play with the idea of treason, but she'd he the first person to throw her husband to the wolves when the going gets rough.'

'Then why send Peverell to Porchester in the first place, your Majesty?'

'Because if Neville is tempted to join forces with the King of France, Peverell will be the first person to tell me. His honour is at stake, Thomas, and the Peverells have always prided themselves on their loyalty. The trouble is that Peverell seems to have disappeared, sunk without trace. I need him, Thomas, to report back on these great lords who will plague me to my grave. There's so much we don't know now that we haven't got enough spies.

251

Rumours of ships assembling at Le Havre and Honfleur, and we've no idea when they intend to sail. And there's Southampton still building our fort at Southsea and our fleet in disarray at Spithead. At least I've told him to start victualling the ships that are there. Damn it, man, I think I shall have to go down there myself and hurry things along. I would, if the Queen weren't in a delicate condition.'

'Do you want me to go down to Portsmouth, your Majesty?'

'No I don't,' roared King Henry, who sometimes found Cromwell intensely irritating. 'You're not a soldier, nor a spy. Your place is here with me, helping me with all these petitions, dealing with my correspondence. But I need to know where Peverell is and what, if anything, he's found out in the course of his investigations. And I also want to know where that fool Simon has got to. Also there's the Queen asking about Jane Warrener and I haven't any idea where she is, either. By God, Thomas, the Court's falling apart. What's the use of a spy if he won't communicate, and what's the use of entertainers if they go rushing off round the country. Now don't you go telling me that the girl and my fool have gone to find Peverell.'

'I think it's quite possible,' said Cromwell evenly. 'The girl seems inordinately fond of Lord Nicholas.'

The King got up and walked over to the

window where he gazed out into the garden where the roses were drooping in the sultry July heat.

'I'm losing touch, Thomas,' he said, still with his back to Cromwell. 'I must be getting old. It's almost a month since Tyler was killed in the back streets of Portsmouth. I despatched Peverell there to find out who did it, and why, and then he was reported speaking treasonable matters to the Earl of Southampton. We arrest him, and he escapes from the Tower. Then, silence. We don't know for sure that he's with Neville. He might have drawn a blank and decided to conduct his investigations elsewhere. God's teeth, Thomas,' he said, turning round to face him, 'we might have misjudged the man and he could have gone over to join the ranks of the King of France's invasion force.'

'Lord Nicholas? Never. It's not in his nature.'

'Who knows what men are made of or what they are capable of doing. There's many a good man seduced by the offer of lands and riches. Lord Nicholas isn't the only man who's been tempted by the offer of great wealth.'

'He only wants to clear his name.'

'Then let's hope he succeeds and gives us the names of the real traitor in the process. But this all leads to one thing, Thomas, we must get England alerted to a threat of war. I've given orders for the *Mary Rose* to be brought round from Woolwich to Portsmouth, but I've now heard she lies becalmed at Dover.'

'At least that means that the French fleet cannot sail, for the same reason,' said Cromwell calmly.

'Don't start telling me my business. I'm not entirely ignorant of nautical matters, but I want my ships in place before the French arrive, not after.'

'Your Majesty, I wasn't questioning . . .'

'Oh stop blathering, man. You do try my patience. Now get a message down to Southampton telling him to prepare the fleet for action. We mustn't be caught napping.'

'There've been no reports of troops landing, your Majesty.'

'Troops? Of course not. The King of France won't risk landing an army on our shores. No, the attack will come from the sea. We'll raise the musters, of course. Notify the Lords Lieutenant, Thomas. Let's hope to God they're loyal. We had enough trouble from the northern lords last year. Let's hope the southern lords have more sense. I don't like this, Thomas. Things are building up and I don't yet know what we're up against. We need more intelligence officers. As it is we're groping in the dark. Anything can happen and we're not prepared. Well, go for it, man,' he yelled. 'God damn you, let's see some action.'

Thomas Cromwell bowed and left the room.

Sometimes he hated his job. He had been well rewarded by the King but sometimes he felt the price he'd paid was too high. Whatever he did, whatever he suggested could be misconstrued by the King. And now, it seemed, he was to be blamed for the build-up of foreign ships in continental ports when he himself had only learnt of it that morning.

As he went back into his own room he was wondering how long it would take to bring the war ships to Portsmouth. And then, he thought, one crucial piece of information was missing. And that was, when was this suspected invasion to take place?

CHAPTER EIGHTEEN

'Heh Flamand, move that fat arse of yours! There's work to do.'

Nicholas cursed his luck. The burly Frenchman who had pushed him out of the way that morning had not forgotten him. He'd been watching him all the time, and Nicholas, sensing trouble, had kept out of his way. He learnt that the man's name was Gilbert, and, although he took it upon himself to be their leader, the men didn't like him. In fact, they resented all authority, which was not surprising in such a motley bunch of men coming from all over France, used to fighting wherever the pay

255

was good and not particular whom they fought against.

However, Gilbert was a giant of a man, and that was enough to make the men wary of him. He had hands on him that could fell an ox with one blow and ring the neck of a fowl as effortlessly as if he were shelling peas. His face was coarse and weather-beaten and partly concealed by a straggling mane of black hair which merged into the thick, black mat which constituted his beard. He'd watched Nicholas all the morning whilst the men played cards or bet on the throw of a dice, and Nicholas had withdrawn to the wall of the church where he'd sat with his back to a pillar and feigned sleep.

However, he got to his feet at Gilbert's summons, and reluctantly went over to him.

'Get the tables cleared and be quick about it. The men get bored in this heat with nothing to do and will soon want to feed their bellies.'

Nicholas did as he was told. This was not the time to draw attention to himself by telling the man he wasn't paid to be a kitchen hand. After he'd pushed aside the remains of the breakfast bread, he went over to the kitchen where bowls of stew had been prepared. The cook scowled at him as he went in and spat on the floor.

'Hungry already? It's like feeding a pack of wolves,' he said in English, and when Nicholas pretended not to understand he contemptuously pushed one of the bowls

256

towards him.

'Come on then, pick up that bowl of pig swill. Anything's good enough for frog-eaters. I suppose you'll be wanting ale, although I'd give you water if I had anything to do with it, and I wouldn't be too fussy where I got it from either.'

This was accompanied by a series of rude gestures which could be understood in any language, much to the mirth of the other kitchen servants who stood by watching and who refused to help Nicholas when he picked up the bowl of stew and staggered out of the door. He had to make several journeys and each time he returned to the kitchen he glanced round to see where the trapdoor to Neville's house was. He remembered that on his previous visit, Neville had told him that he didn't like food prepared in his own house but had it cooked in the kitchen on the ground floor of the keep and had it carried over to his house through a connecting tunnel.

Then, when he was making his final trip for another jug of ale, he noticed one of the servants go to the corner of the kitchen where he bent down and raised one of the flagstones. Underneath was a trapdoor which he opened and disappeared down a flight of stairs. Nicholas went back to the church and carried on with his menial tasks until the men had eaten their fill and were settling down to finish off the ale. Still Gilbert watched him.

'Clear that muck away now, Flamand,' he roared, his huge face much inflamed by drink. 'It's what you're good at. All Flamands are pigs, and live like pigs so clean out this sty. Look, I'll give you a hand.'

And he picked up one of the bowls which had the dregs of the stew in it, and poured it over Nicholas's head, roaring with laughter as the greasy mess dribbled down Nicholas's face on to his jacket. The men roared their approval and rushed up, glad of the diversion. Suddenly, Nicholas was conscious that all eyes were on him, waiting to see how he would react. He knew that one false move could be disastrous. Taking his time, he wiped the mess off his face with a handful of straw, then he lifted one of the jugs of ale and dashed it into Gilbert's face. The men cheered and rapidly cleared a space.

'Pigs we may be, but pigs can fight,' said Nicholas evenly. 'Let's see what a French sewer rat can do against a fine Flemish boar.'

The two men faced each other, Gilbert's face dark-red with fury, his breathing laboured. Nicholas, on the other hand, was angry but controlled. He knew that what needed to be done had to be done quickly or else the men would turn on him and kick him to pieces. He could expect no mercy from a bunch of bored mercenaries.

Gilbert looked round for a sword but Nicholas knew that this was not the time for

258

serious bloodshed.

'No weapons, sewer rat. Come and fight with bare fists. Those great hams of yours look strong enough to kill a hundred pigs.'

'No weapons, no weapons,' screamed the men delightedly. Gilbert was much hated and Nicholas could sense he had the men's support.

Gilbert didn't wait to argue. With head lowered like a bull in the ring, he charged at Nicholas. Nicholas was ready for him. He knew if Gilbert landed a blow it would be all over for him. Without his helmet, which he'd taken off, Gilbert could crack his skull open with those fists of his. But Gilbert was big and clumsy, with a belly like a bag of oats strapped round his middle, and his brain was confused by too much drink. Nicholas stood his ground, then, almost at the moment of impact, he stepped nimbly aside. Gilbert, not expecting his target to move, rushed straight into one of the wooden stools which stood by the table. He knocked it over, lost his balance and with a roar of rage, fell flat on his face on to the stone floor of the nave.

The men howled with delight and clapped Nicholas on the back. Nicholas gave a sigh of relief and with great satisfaction aimed a vicious kick at the Frenchman's backside.

'Give it him! Bash his head in!' roared the men, dancing with glee.

Gilbert staggered to his feet and stood there

for a moment trying to get his wits together. Then, once more he rushed at Nicholas who, this time, stood his ground. As Gilbert came lumbering up to him, Nicholas punched him full in the face and he heard the scrunch of breaking bone and saw blood begin to stream out of his nose and down on to his beard. Again the men roared their appreciation and Nicholas, not waiting for Gilbert to rally, landed another blow on the man's head. For a second Gilbert swayed on his feet like a stricken bull, then fell on the floor, out cold.

The soldiers showed Gilbert no mercy. Like a pack of hounds at the kill, they fell on Gilbert kicking and punching his recumbent body until Nicholas, fearing lest someone should come and see what all the noise was about, intervened and ordered the men off.

He was not alone in trying to stop the fight. One of the men, with an air of authority about him which made Nicholas think that, in normal life, he could have been an officer, took command. His voice did the trick. The men backed off Gilbert and obeyed the order to drag him away and douse his face with water. Then the man turned to Nicholas and held out his hand.

'That was well fought, Flamand. You have a cool head. We value that when it comes to real action.'

'How long do we have to wait for that?' said Nicholas.

'God knows. We're waiting for the German troops to arrive. Then there will be fights enough. Pray God they won't be billeted here with us. By the way, I'm Jacques. I know who you are.'

'Jacques who?'

'Just Jacques. Best not to tell too much in this game. Now come with me and show us how you wield a pike. We could do with some practice and we need to keep the men occupied.'

Nicholas was familiar with the weapon because he had taken part in jousts at Hampton Court. The French pike was heavier than the ones he'd used at Court but he was able to acquit himself well. By nightfall the men had accepted him and treated him with the respect they afforded Jacques.

As they ate their evening meal, one of the soldiers who had wielded a pike with Nicholas came and sat with him and began to talk companionably.

'He's all right, is Jacques,' he said. 'He's a vicomte, by the way, a great lord. The Vicomte de Crèvecoeur. Rumour has it that he fell out with his father over a girl. The old man married her and banished his son from the ancestral estates. So he went off to fight for France.

'Then what's he doing here with this rabble?'

'Because there's a lot in it for him, I

261

suppose. The King has promised us all rich pickings when we defeat the English. We've beaten the dogs once before and we'll beat them again if they'll let us get at them. We don't need the help of German soldiers, bloody cabbage eaters.'

* * *

Night fell, and the men were comatose after an evening's heavy drinking. Nicholas couldn't sleep. His instincts were telling him that he should go at once to the Earl of Southampton and tell him of Neville's treachery. There was more than enough evidence here, all around him. But there were several factors which made him hesitate. In the first place there was the practical one of how to get away from the castle without a boat, and he couldn't risk getting lost over the mudflats if he left at low tide. Also he still had to find answers to the questions which Southampton would undoubtedly ask him. Who else was involved in the conspiracy? When were the German mercenaries due to arrive? And when was the invasion expected to take place? The answer to the last question was in Tyler's box, and that was almost certainly somewhere in Neville's house. There was nothing for it, he would have to penetrate Neville's stronghold and find out the extent of his treachery. Only then could he leave the castle and report to Southampton.

And then, he thought, would any one believe him? After all, he had been arrested on a charge of treason, and as far as the authorities were concerned, that charge had not been withdrawn. No, there was no other way. He would have to pay a visit to Neville's house. And go now, when everyone was asleep.

He got up and quietly crept out of the church, opening the door carefully so that the squeaking hinge didn't wake anyone up. Then he walked over to the bastion by the latrines and pulled up the trapdoor to the tunnel. This time, he knew where he was going and didn't need a light. He groped his way along the tunnel to where it divided. He took the right-hand fork which he knew led to the castle keep. It wasn't far. Ahead of him was the trapdoor which, this time, he raised and found himself in the kitchen. Two of the scullions were curled up on the floor sleeping the sleep of the damned. Creeping along the wall of the keep in the shadows cast by the light of the flickering torches on the wall, he went over to where he'd seen the man disappear down the steps into a tunnel. The trapdoor was well used and easy to raise, and the tunnel was high enough for him to stand upright. Groping his way in the dark, he hadn't far to go. He bumped into the steps and climbed up to another trapdoor which opened easily to only a slight pressure. He climbed out into what was the cellar of Neville's house. He paused, trying to get his bearings. This was where Neville had his bath house, and he winced at the memory of the night when he'd warded off the advances of Ursula Neville. It seemed years ago that he'd first visited the castle and had been lulled into a false sense of security by the beauty of the setting and the fairy-tale qualities of Neville and his seductive wife. But it was only two weeks ago that he'd left the castle under arrest and now the fairy tale had turned into a nightmare. The prince had turned into an arch-traitor and his wife his accomplice.

He went up to the first floor, the stairs lit by torches attached to the wall. Here, he knew, Neville had his dining room, and there were other rooms which Nicholas hadn't visited. Above were the bedrooms. He was standing at one end of a long corridor, dimly lit by flickering rush lights. Suddenly, he heard a sound, or sounds, coming from the far end of the corridor where there was a door. And men's voices were coming from the other side of that door. He crept forward, praying that the door would remain closed. Next to it, there stood a tall cupboard, and he was able to squeeze between it and the outside wall of the house. It was a very good hiding place, but the voices were too faint for him to hear what was being said. However, he could make out that there were two people speaking, and one of them was Neville. He would recognise that clipped, rapid speech anywhere, and that light, melodic tone. The other voice was deeper and slower. He would have to listen at the door and hoped that he'd get enough warning to retreat into his hiding place when the meeting broke up. Nicholas remembered the night visitors he'd seen when he'd stayed here before. It appeared that Neville was accustomed to conducting his affairs under cover of darkness.

'Have they landed yet?' he heard Neville say.

'Not yet. They're becalmed the other side of the channel,' said the other man.

'How will they get here?'

'By covered wagon, at night, of course. It's not far from Dorset.'

Then the voices became indistinct and Nicholas flattened himself closer to the door. Finally there was an outburst from Neville.

'My God, I detest all this waiting. The place is full of Frenchmen, all getting restless, because there's nothing for them to do except eat and drink and fight one another. Where the devil am I going to hide a hundred German soldiers? Just think, one visit from Southampton and we're finished.'

'Damn it, Charles,' said the deeper voice. 'I can't be held responsible for the weather. You're getting as jittery as a maid on her wedding night.'

'We've everything to lose.'

'And everything to gain. Don't fret, Gallimard will tell us when the ships leave port.'

'Gallimard? He's already given us one useless date.'

'It can't be helped. Things have changed since Tyler's death. He didn't take the weather into consideration. Next week should see the ships off Portsmouth.'

'And I'll be rid of the troops. I can't tell you what a relief that'll be, Henry.'

'Just hold fast and don't worry. And above all, don't be precipitous. We can't fail. With Southampton fighting his sea battle, he'll be stabbed in the back. We've got enough troops to sack Portsmouth and march on London long before he can rally his land forces.'

'With a couple of hundred foreign mercenaries?'

'And the muster, Charles. Don't forget the muster. I've been ordered to raise a force and that I shall do. The only thing is that Southampton won't know they'll be fighting for me against Henry Tudor and not for him. Men will follow us to London, you'll see. Henry Tudor has outlived his popularity and everyone wants to see the old religion restored and the rightful King on the throne.'

'And who will that be?' said Neville.

'Me, Charles, of course. King Henry the Ninth. I have as strong a claim to the throne as the present Henry. My grandmother and his mother were sisters. I have a son and heir and Henry hasn't. People like the idea of a stable dynasty. It's time the Yorkists were reinstated.'

Nicholas, appalled at what he'd heard, crept back to his hiding place between the cupboard and the wall. This was treason beyond his wildest imaginings. What he'd just heard amounted to a full-blown conspiracy. Sir Charles Neville and the man he called Henry. He knew who he was. Henry Polc, Baron Montague of Montacute, eldest son of the Countess of Salisbury whose estates at Midhurst in Sussex were near his own manor of Dean Peverell. The last time Nicholas had seen him was at Hampton Court where the King was standing talking to Queen Jane with one arm draped affectionately around Montague's shoulders. And now he had just heard him plotting with Neville to be the next King of England.

Suddenly, the door opened and the two men came out. He watched them go down the corridor and mount the stairs to the first floor. He'd heard enough for one night. The scene was set. Porchester Castle had become a nest of vipers. Foreign mercenaries were about to sack Portsmouth and march on London. And Southampton suspected nothing. However, the foreign ships hadn't yet left port, and the Germans were becalmed somewhere off the coast of Dorset. But the *Mary Rose,* the pride of the English fleet, was also becalmed and all

267

the other ships which would come with her. It was stalemate. All it needed was the weather to break and a strong wind to blow from the south or east and all hell would break out.

Creeping back to his place on the straw in the nave, Nicholas lay still thinking over the full horror of what he'd heard. For too long Southampton had been staring in the wrong direction. He had ignored the fact that the enemy could be within the realm. Although the King trusted no one and especially not his Yorkist relatives, not for one moment would he have expected them to embark on treason of such magnitude. The conspiracy had all the elements of the northern rising of the previous year when rebels had marched on London supported by the great northern earls. They, too, had wanted to see the old faith restored. But this southern rising could be even more serious. The march from Portsmouth to London was nothing compared to the march from Doncaster to London during which many of the rebels had become discontented and gone home. He wondered how many would rally round Montague when he told them what he had in store for them. It would depend on how much he offered them, and how many others joined them on the march. And London! Would the apprentices join forces with Neville and Montague? They were always a volatile bunch and he wouldn't like to vouchsafe for their loyalty. On the whole, the burghers of London liked peace and stability, but the apprentices had always been fickle.

It was stiflingly hot in the church and the sleeping men stank abominably. Outside, there was no whisper of a breeze. It was as if all nature was waiting in hushed expectancy for the action to begin. When, he thought, would the wind start to blow? And from which direction?

CHAPTER NINETEEN

At noon the following day they arrived at Porchester. The ten-mile ride from Portsmouth had been uneventful; the road clear of farmers' carts. Melissa had carried her double burden with ease, Jane sitting astride with Simon in front of her, his lute strapped across his chest. As they turned off the main coastal road, they saw, ahead of them, the great walls of the castle and Jane immediately fell under the spell of its magical beauty. She saw it as a fortress from a bygone age, an age of chivalry and romance. She could smell the sea and felt the hot, sultry air press down upon them. Sunbeams shimmered over the massive walls of the keep and lit up the gatehouse and danced on the water of the moat. The heat began to make her feel giddy and disorientated. There was no sound except the twittering of a lark way up in the sky and the eerie cry of a curlew out on the mudflats.

She reined in Melissa, uncertain what to do next. The castle seemed like a mirage and she half expected it to fade away as she drew closer to it. Then, suddenly, the gate opened and a cavalcade came riding across the drawbridge led by a lady of dazzling beauty which intensified the feeling of unreality which had descended on her at the first sight of the castle. The lady was wearing a dark blue hunting dress which emphasised every curve of her body, and her pale skin and full red lips contrasted spectacularly with her dark hair which was only partially concealed under a small hat decorated with swan's feathers. She was riding side-saddle on a powerful bay gelding with a slender neck and delicate head. A beautiful horse, Jane thought, with Arab blood in it.

Behind her rode two huntsmen, both mounted on stocky horses, bred for strength and stamina, and one of the men was leading on a chain a huge mastiff with a coat of coarse black hair and a large, ugly head which seemed to have been designed solely as a vehicle for its massive jaws. Jane shuddered. She had once seen a dog like this in action against a poor, defeated bull which had no strength left, but would not give in to its tormentor. She had watched horrified when one of the dogs had despatched the poor creature with a single snap of its jaws.

The lady saw them and raised her whip to stop the other riders. Then she rode slowly towards them, appraising them. She reined in her horse and stood there staring at Simon after giving Jane only a cursory glance. He, in turn, returned her gaze, treating her to one of his most engaging grins.

'Get down from your horse, dwarf,' she said, 'and let me take a look at you.'

She might look like a goddess, Jane thought, but she's got the manners of a fishwife. Simon didn't seem to care. Insults were run-of-the-mill to him. He slid down from Melissa and stood in front of the lady's horse, bowing profusely, with not a trace of mockery. Only Jane knew what was in his mind. She knew that he was sufficiently used to the ways of the Court not to be overawed by an arrogant woman, however beautiful she might be.

'Your name, dwarf?'

'Simon King, your Highness.'

'Mind your tongue, Simon King, or Gaston here will bite it off for you.'

'That would be a pity, Highness. You'd never hear me sing if I lost my tongue. I sing well, so I've been told, and I tumble and turn somersaults, and I've made a king laugh and several queens and innumerable ambassadors. And I have to say that my nephew up there sings even better than I do. Together, we can entertain you for as long as it pleases you and I

271

will guarantee that we will not give you one dull moment.'

The lady looked from one to the other and then went back to staring at Simon, taking in every detail of his appearance.

'Is that all you can do? I've heard that dwarves possess other talents besides tumbling.'

Simon bowed. 'I will do whatever your Highness requires me to do.'

'Is that so? Then you can entertain us for a day or two and I look forward to enjoying your performance. But please don't call me "Highness". My name is Lady Neville, Ursula to you, dwarf.'

'I am deeply honoured,' said Simon grinning knowingly at her. Jane felt a ripple of irritation. There was no need for Simon to be so ingratiating, she thought.

The porter from the gatehouse had come out to see what was going on, and Ursula Neville pointed to Jane and Simon.

'Put them in Ashton's tower,' she said. 'There's plenty of room there for the horse as well. See they have everything they want. I shall expect you this evening,' she said, turning back to look at Simon. 'You will be sent for.'

Then she struck her horse with her whip and signalled the others to ride after her.

Simon watched her go with a look of satisfaction on her face that Jane thought revolting. 'A fine woman, that,' he said to the porter, an old man, bent with the weight of years.

'You keep away from her, master, if you'll take an old man's advice. I can see she's taken a fancy to you. Best if you leave now and go back to where you came from.'

'I've never been frightened of a wench, yet,' said Simon, taking hold of Melissa's bridle and following the porter into the castle.

'They do say she's no ordinary wench, master. They say that when she tires of her lovers she takes them out into the forest and sets that hellhound of hers on them and watches him rip the poor sods to death just like he rips up them boars.'

'And what makes you think she'll tire of me, old man?'

'Because that's the way she is. Mind you, she's never had a little fellow like you before, as far as I know, so you might be able to keep her happy.'

'Well I'll give it a go and maybe get some fun out of it.'

'Simon!' said Jane primly from her perch on Melissa's back. 'You forget yourself. This is no time to talk of fun.'

'Sorry, nephew, my imagination's getting the better of me. Well, show us where this tower is, my good fellow,' he said to the porter, 'and we'll prepare our entertainment for this evening.'

The porter took them into the inner

courtyard and pointed out the tower which a previous Constable of the castle had built as part of the fortifications. It was next to Neville's house in the corner of the inner bailey, and the door was open. An old man, small and bent like a gnome, stood in the doorway watching them arrive. He came forward to greet them, a smile creasing his small face, which was fringed by wisps of grey hair.

'Welcome, masters. We are very glad to see you. This place needs cheering up.'

Other servants came rushing out of the keep and stood at a respectful distance curious to find out who the newcomers were. Jane jumped off Melissa, and led her towards the tower and the old man ushered them in with elaborate courtesy.

It was dark and gloomy inside the tower, the only light filtering in through tiny slits of windows. Coming in from the sunshine, the place felt chill and it took them a few moments to become accustomed to the gloom. A colony of jackdaws had taken over the top floor and old nesting material and their droppings had fallen down into the great fireplace which hadn't seen a fire for years. Jane, having tied Melissa to a ring in the wall, asked the man if hay and straw could be brought to make her comfortable.

'Of course, of course, master,' said the old man, bowing low. 'Anything you ask for we can

274

get for you. Just ask for me. I'm called old Hugh and there's not much going on in this place that I don't know. Upstairs there are some beds. Nothing fancy, mind, but they have been used recently to put up some visitors. I'll send over some blankets and get fresh straw on the floor, and I expect you'd like some hot water to wash off the dust of the journey before you perform this evening. Sir Charles likes everything clean and sweet smelling around him. So wait here and I'll send some servants over. I should stay inside, if I were you,' he went on, giving them a meaningful look. 'Don't go wandering off. These are unsettled times and you, master, will attract a lot of attention. No offence meant, mind you. I've every sympathy with you little fellows. From what I've learnt, you've more brains than the rest of us put together. And as for you, young master,' he said, glancing at Jane, 'you're a bit too . . .' He paused, unable to find the word he wanted. 'Too delicate,' he continued. 'With that face of yours you could be mistaken for a girl. Well, I've things to see to. Good luck, masters. Make yourselves comfortable. Come and get some dinner when you've cleaned up. There's always food over in the keep.'

He bowed again and scuttled back to the keep, shooing the crowd of people that had gathered round the door back into the kitchen. Jane looked at Simon.

275

'Well sir, we're here and so far so good. And you can take that look off your face. I know you've been asked to perform extra duties, but they're not going to start right now. We're here to find Lord Nicholas, remember?'

'Ho, so it's hoity-toity madam we've become suddenly. Now you mind your manners, wench, and don't take that tone to me.'

He had a look on his face that Jane had never seen before, a defiant, triumphant look, and she didn't like it at all.

'Don't speak to me like that, sir. Remember your place. Just because someone's taken a fancy to you doesn't mean that you can order me around.'

'Who's ordering whom, madam? Just leave me alone. I'm not here to find Nicholas Peverell, remember? I don't care where he is or what he's doing. I'm here to look after you, that's all. Nothing more. And what I care to do with my free time is none of your business. Now stop nagging me, and let's get on with making ourselves comfortable. Here comes the straw for Melissa and some for us, so, cheer up, and let's get down to work.'

A steady stream of servants brought over blankets and provisions to make them comfortable. Everyone seemed willing to do whatever was asked of them and smiled and grinned their approval. Simon was in his element clowning around, ignoring Jane, and playing to his new audience. Because of his size, the servants felt they could take liberties and began to tug at his beard and push him over in order to see him bounce up again. Jane, getting angrier by the minute, sorted out Melissa's food and bedding, and told the servants where to put the jugs of hot water. She began to feel dispirited. She thought Simon was on her side, but she'd been mistaken. He was treating the whole episode as a holiday, an opportunity to get away from Court and enjoy country life. Maybe it was all a horrible mistake. What on earth had made her think she could just walk into Neville's castle and find Nicholas? They'd had no news of him for days. They didn't even know he was here. Maybe he'd just given up his hunt for the real traitor and was in hiding. Maybe he'd left the country. And now here was Simon, her dear and loyal friend, happily playing the fool with Neville's servants and looking forward to pleasuring Lady Neville at the first opportunity.

The servants had brought over bread and hot meat pies, and Simon sat down on the floor and began to eat heartily.

'Come on, Roderick, old fellow,' he said with his mouth full. 'Don't waste all this food. It's free and, with any luck, we might get paid well for tonight's entertainment. It's no good moping because Peverell hasn't put in an appearance. I hope to God he doesn't. He'll only spoil everything. I think life in the country's going to suit me fine. It'll be easier to serve a lady than the King. He's never satisfied.'

*   *   *

That same morning, Jacques, Vicomte de Crèvecoeur, who had taken command of the French soldiers now that the former, self-appointed commander, Gilbert, was recovering in a side chapel, came up to Nicholas as he stood on the castle wall looking out across the harbour. Nicholas was deep in thought wondering how he could escape from the castle without being noticed and warn Southampton about Neville's treachery. He was looking for Neville's boat which he knew Neville kept for his own personal use, but there was no sign of it that morning. It was impossible to get away from the men in broad daylight, and if he left by night, he would need a boat. He was surprised to see Crèvecoeur and cursed his luck at the prospect of an unexpected complication.

'The weather's unfortunate, Philibert,' said Jacques, evenly. 'We are in stalemate. Nothing moves. Reinforcements are still stuck off the Dorset coast, I hear. We can't attack the English with a handful of soldiers and no back-up from the sea.'

'Then let us at least be grateful that the English are also becalmed.'

'Quite right. And we should also be grateful for the English King who has been so imprudent as to have most of his fleet in the wrong place at the wrong time.'

'I agree. He's a fool and lives in a fool's paradise. Not only is his fleet in disarray, but he has no idea that we're here, waiting for orders to attack his kingdom.'

'A king should be ready for every eventuality. But you seem an intelligent fellow, Philibert, for someone coming from Ypres.'

'It's just common sense, that's all. I like to think things out.'

'And that's more than can be said for those dogs in there. They think with their bellies. If we don't have action soon I can see trouble. If the Germans do manage to get here, there will be fighting. You can't feed soldiers and keep them in idleness. I'm going to need your help, Philibert, in keeping the dogs occupied. I'll have to get permission to exercise them out in the open. Pike practice, hand-to-hand fighting and unarmed combat, that's what they'll need. You can teach them to fight with bare hands; you've shown them you're good at that. I want them to exercise until they drop otherwise they'll be fit for nothing when the order comes for them to start behaving like real soldiers.'

'They'll soon pull themselves together when they know they can sack Portsmouth.'

Jacques looked keenly at Nicholas. 'How do you know that?'

279

'It makes sense,' said Nicholas with a shrug, 'it's what I would do if I was planning to remove the King. No use marching on London and leaving your back exposed.'

'Then you are a thinker. I knew we were two of a kind. We must work together and see that nothing goes wrong with this little adventure. We need cool heads and I don't trust Lord Neville and that other English lord. Neither of them have had any military experience. They're ambitious, but that's not enough to unseat a king. King Francis warned me about them. He could see that we were going to need leaders and that's why he told me to take over the troops when action was imminent. These men might be mercenaries, but they are paid for by our King and he doesn't want to waste his money.'

Nicholas bowed. 'I didn't realise you are a friend of our King, my Lord.'

'You must call me Jacques. We are equals now. Yes, I know King Francis well and I know what he wants. He wants this heretic off the throne of England, and I know he's got his own idea about who will take his place.'

'Any idea who that will be?'

'Let's just say that it won't be Neville, nor the English lord, Montague; but neither of them know that. There will be trouble, of course. I've travelled a lot and been to the court of the Emperor Charles, and I know he, too, will have his own ideas who sits on the

English throne when the heretic is overthrown. You know how much he hates the English king, especially as he rejected Queen Catherine, the Emperor's own aunt; rejecting her for that whore Anne Boleyn. And he resents the King's treatment of Catherine's daughter, Mary, preferring his bastard daughter, Elizabeth, the whore's child. You know, in the end, the battle will be fought between the Emperor and our King. England will be the battlefield.'

'Well, with any luck, we shall be needed again to fight the Emperor when we've finished with the English. You know, I'm beginning to feel sorry for these unfortunate English who have had enough of war and have only just got used to living in peace.'

Jacques looked across the harbour to Portsmouth, his face inscrutable. 'They're just pawns in this international game of chess. It's unfortunate but it's the way of the world. Our King and the Emperor Charles will never be friends. At the moment they are allies against the heretic because it suits them. The Emperor wants to avenge his aunt, and Francis wants to get his own back on the English who used to own so much of France and still have Calais. He wants it returned to France. But this friendship between the two rulers is unnatural. Both hate each other. Once the heretic is removed the two armies will battle it out here on English soil. And I agree with you,

281

Philibert, I feel sorry for the English. I hate to see innocent people suffer.'

'And Neville and this man Montague? What will happen to them?'

'They're just puppets, Philibert. After they've served their purpose, they'll be disposed of. No king wants discontented subjects around him. Their estates will be divided up between the victor's friends. If we win, then I have expectations of getting some English land. It has been promised me, by the way; not that I attach too much importance to the promises of kings.'

'You seem knowledgeable in the ways of kings, Jacques?'

'I've made a study of them, that's all. I told you I've travelled a good bit, mostly in embassies. I was ambassador to the Emperor, and to his sister Queen Mary in Brussels. I am to go to Constantinople after this is all over and study the customs of the Grand Turk.'

'But, in the meantime, here you are commanding 'a handful of lazy dogs and expected to get them fighting fit in a matter of days, hours even, if the wind gets up.'

Jacques laughed. 'I'm very adaptable. I've had to be. Life's never predictable. But what about you, Philibert? You seem too much of a philosopher to be a soldier.'

Nicholas laughed. 'I, too have been in Brussels. I studied law there years ago.'

'So why are you not practising the law in the

regent's courts?'

'I killed a man,' said Nicholas quietly, amazed at his own inventiveness. 'It was in a brawl, outside a tavern. I was a student, you know what students are like. I'd drunk too much wine and this fellow came up to me and spat in my face. We fought without weapons but I punched him too hard and he never recovered. My father thought it best that I abandon my legal studies and become a soldier.'

'So you, too, have a past, one not unlike my own. However, I lost the girl I loved, and your experience has stood you in good stead when it comes to dealing with pigs like Gilbert. But come now,' he said, putting an arm round Nicholas's shoulders. 'Let's get these dogs working until they drop. I have to eat dinner with my Lord Neville tonight and with his charming wife who looks at me with those inviting eyes of hers. I don't know how long I shall be able to resist their invitation, but I shall have to control myself. It would be a disaster if I gave in to her blandishments, and King Francis would never forgive me. It doesn't do to fall into disgrace a second time.'

* * *

The day seemed interminable to Nicholas. The men resented exercising in that heat and needed frequent rests during which they drank vast quantities of ale. All plans of leaving the castle had to be abandoned. Maybe, after dark, Nicholas thought he could slip away and make a dash for it across the mudflats, but he knew this could be highly dangerous for anyone without local knowledge.

The soldiers were exhausted after the exercise and the ale and settled down to sleep straight after supper. Nicholas retired to the side chapel which he shared with Jacques who had turned it into the officers' quarters. The tide was coming in and he would have to wait until it turned before he could consider crossing the mudflats to the shore. Besides he wanted to know if Jacques had anything to report after his dinner with Neville.

When everyone was fast asleep, Jacques returned and threw himself down on the straw mattress which served as a bed.

'What happened?' whispered Nicholas.

'Nothing happened. Neville eats and drinks and enjoys himself as if he hasn't a care in the world. Anyone would think that the invasion was over and he was King of England. His wife drove me wild with her flirtatious glances and then abandoned me for a lecherous dwarf who seems to be part of the household. God knows where he came from. But he's got a good voice, I have to admit that, and a muscular body that can perform every acrobatic trick there is. He's got a boy with him whom he calls his nephew. The boy sings like an angel.

Neville is very taken with him but he'll get no joy from that quarter because I would bet a month's wages that this nephew is a niece. Niece, that's a laugh! Most likely he's the dwarf's fancy piece. Now let me go to sleep, there's a good fellow. It's been a long day.'

Alarm bells began to ring in Nicholas's head. He sat up, his heart pounding.

'Wait, don't go to sleep. A dwarf did you say? Did he tell you his name?'

'Simon. The nephew's called Roderick. A likely story. Still it was good entertainment. I'll see if you can get an invitation tomorrow, if you like. It'll be fun to see what Lady Neville makes of you. But one thing I'm certain of is that Neville will be quite useless in commanding these troops. We'll have to fight this campaign for him. At least we should get a handsome reward when it's all over. King Francis will be very grateful and we'll not be in his way, like Neville, when he comes to claim the throne from the heretic.'

Then there was silence and Nicholas knew that Jacques was asleep and he was left alone with his thoughts. Simon! Could it be possible? Simon, the King's fool whom he'd seen many times at Court. And with a boy who could be a girl? Both musicians. Could he be here with Jane? No, the idea was madness. But he knew Jane had a mind of her own. Pray God he was mistaken, he thought. Jane here would put paid to all his plans. All thoughts of leaving the

285

castle now vanished until he'd found out who these two were. He tried to sleep, but as night wore on he became more and more convinced that Jane had come to find him and persuaded Simon to come as her protector. At all costs she had to leave before the fighting started. But how could he get in touch with her and not reveal himself to Neville? And there wasn't much time. At any moment the wind could start to blow and the present stalemate would be over.

CHAPTER TWENTY

It was already mid-morning and Simon was still asleep, sprawled out on his straw mattress, arms and legs spread wide to keep cool. The sun was high in the sky and the heat was oppressive, with not a breath of wind to disperse the stale air. Jane looked at him impatiently and tugged at one of his legs.

'Wake up, Simon. It's late. We've got to take a look round this castle. There's a lot going on here which we don't know about.'

Simon yawned and opened his eyes. 'Oh go away, lass, no one wants us right now. We've got all day to prepare for tonight's entertainment.'

'I'm not talking about entertainment; I'm talking about that contingent of French troops

286

billeted in the church.'

'Oh, give up, can't you? Don't start dabbling in politics. What do you want me to do? Go over to the church and ask the men who they are and where they come from? Don't be stupid. I'll be lucky to get out alive.'

'Those troops will provide more than enough evidence to send Neville and Montague to the block. My God, Simon, didn't your blood boil to see that arch-traitor sitting there last night eating his head off and enjoying our entertainment? The last time I saw Montague he was at Court enjoying the King's favours.'

'Well, times change, and the King must be more careful about choosing his friends. Now let me sleep. It's all right for you; you're not asked to turn somersaults and tie your body up into knots.'

He turned over, hunching himself into a ball, and shut his eyes. Jane looked at him in despair.

'Very well, I shall go over to the church myself.'

'If you go over to the church I can't be responsible for what the French pigs will do to you. Just face it, you shouldn't have come here, but now that we're here we may as well make the most of it. And I, for one, intend to enjoy myself while the going's good. Now, who's this fellow coming to disturb my peace?'

A man's face had appeared at the top of the stairs leading up to their sleeping quarters from the floor below. It was a young face, good humoured, clean shaven, with a mop of red hair on top of his pale, freckled face. He coughed discreetly.

'A message for you, master,' he said, looking at Simon who was struggling to sit up.

'Who wants me?'

'Lady Ursula, master. She wants to go out in the boat and she wants you to come. She says she needs fresh air. The tide's rising and there's no wind, so I've got to get the oars out.'

'When does she want to leave?'

'Now, master. If we're to get back on this tide, we haven't got a lot of time. I can't row against the ebb.'

Simon swore and ran his fingers through his hair. 'I've got to wash some of this sweat off. Give me a few minutes.'

'Better make haste. The lady doesn't like to be kept waiting.'

The head disappeared and Jane turned on Simon. 'No you don't, sir. You've got to stay with me and help me find out what's going on here.'

'Sorry, wench, my lady calls. Now, out of my way because I must clean myself up a bit.'

He pushed Jane out of the way, and was down the stairs before she could stop him. Buckets of water had been left for them on the ground floor, and draped over a chair was a splendid doublet that was obviously meant for Simon because when he picked it up he saw

288

that it was exactly his size. It was made of dark blue velvet with a beautiful, lace-trimmed collar. A row of mother-of-pearl buttons served as the front fastenings, and the sleeves were slashed with pale blue silk. Simon chortled and held the garment up for Jane to admire. Then he picked up a bucket and poured the water over his head and shoulders, rubbed himself dry and put on the doublet which fitted him perfectly.

'Don't get excited, lass. I'll not be long. The tide will see to that. Why don't you take Melissa out into the forest?'

'I'm not here on a joy ride, remember? I'll start investigating on my own.'

'Then, good luck to you. By the way, keep out of Neville's way. He's taken a fancy to you judging by the looks he gave you last night. Things might change when he finds out you're not what he thinks you are.'

Then he scuttled off, making for the watergate at the far end of the outer bailey, ignoring the ribald remarks of the soldiers enduring pike drill in the full glare of the sun.

The boat was moored at the bottom of the steps, its sail, impotent in the absence of wind, neatly furled, and the young man was waiting for him. Simon jumped down into the boat and took his seat in the bow, cheerful at the prospect of an hour or two's pleasure. He could see the soldiers up in the bastions and noted the number of cannon, their barrels protruding through the apertures. Lord Neville, it seemed, was expecting an attack. But they were safe for the moment, as no ships could get up Portsmouth Harbour and risk running aground on the mudflats in front of the castle.

Ursula appeared at the top of the steps and jumped into the boat, ignoring the young man's attempt to help her. She glanced at Simon appreciatively.

'You look handsome, dwarf. My dressmaker's done a good job with that jacket. You're going to be an expensive toy, I fear.'

Simon bowed. 'You are very kind, my Lady. May I return the compliment and say how well that dress suits you.'

'You approve? See how it shimmers in the sun.'

Her cream dress was made of silk, and when she held up her skirt for Simon to admire, the material seemed shot with shafts of light, like sunlight on water. The thin material left little to Simon's imagination and he gazed in wonder at her long legs and gently rounded belly. Her slim waist was encircled with a thin cord and above it her breasts seemed to flow out of her low-cut bodice. Her unbound hair fell around her shoulders like a dark cloak.

'You look like the goddess of the sea,' said Simon, quite overcome by her beauty.

She ordered the boatman to cast off and he rowed them across the main channel towards the opposite shore where a tiny reed-fringed creek ran into the harbour. She picked up Simon's lute which he'd brought with him, and handed it to him.

'Play something soothing; a song of love and desire suitable for such a perfect day.'

Simon obeyed. He sang one of the old songs of the troubadours about the longing for an unobtainable lady. His voice was sweet and seductive, perfectly suited to the gentle melancholy of the music. Ursula leaned back and rested her head in Simon's lap and closed her eyes.

They came to a halt at the top of the creek where the water disappeared into reed beds. Simon put aside his lute and picked up handfuls of Ursula's glossy hair which had spilled over on to the floor. She told the boatman to leave them, and he secured the boat to a tree stump and disappeared into the reeds.

It was hot and still, the only noise was the rustling of tiny birds in the reeds which surrounded them. The boat scarcely moved on the water which was as still as a mill pond. The air was heavy and languid with not a breath of wind to disperse the cloying sweetness of Ursula's perfume.

'Come, Simon, show me how you pleasure a lady. First, let me show you how to transform this little boat into a love nest. We only have to remove this seat and bring out the cushions in the bow. Come, help me.'

Simon, completely under her spell, did as he was told, and when the cushions were in place, he eased Ursula down beside him. Never before had he seen or felt such beauty. Her skin was satin smooth and cool to his touch despite the heat. He gently undid the single button which held the two parts of her bodice together and watched her breasts tumble out into his hands. He buried his head into their fragrance, marvelling at their perfection. He felt as if he was drowning in her scent and was scarcely aware of what he was doing. Ursula held his head down on her breasts and drew him on top of her. There he stroked her body, lingering over her belly and penetrating her secret places with his fingers. He felt her body grow tense beneath him and he began to kiss her more fervently, encircling each nipple with his tongue. She cried out with pleasure and tore off his jacket and unbuttoned his trousers. Still he caressed her with his hands and tongue until she became frenzied and almost uncontrollable. She tore at his shirt, ripping the thin material, clawing at his back with her long fingernails until the blood streamed down on to the cushions. He was oblivious to the pain, quite lost in the waves of pleasure which engulfed him. The sight of the blood seemed to arouse her even more and she bit and scratched him, tearing at his beard and clawing at his face. But still he caressed her, tormenting her with his strong fingers until she began to scream for mercy. Still he continued to stroke her, bending down to use his tongue as an instrument of pleasure. When she began to scream like an animal in pain, he took her with fierce, brutal movements, until she collapsed under him and sank back exhausted on the pillows. Simon sank down beside her, suddenly aware of the scratches on his body.

'My God, wench, you certainly know how to punish a man.'

'And you, dwarf, know how to pleasure a lady.'

'A lady? That's a laugh. Now I know why they call you a she-devil. Now, if you'll excuse me, I'll take a dip over the side to clean up these wounds.'

He slid over the side of the boat into the tepid water. When he looked up she was leaning over the side of the boat, her hair cascading over her breasts.

'Come back, dwarf, I've not finished with you yet,' she said.

He climbed back into the boat determined to punish her for the wounds she'd inflicted on his face and body. She was lying face down on the cushions, the smooth mounds of her buttocks gleaming invitingly in the sun light. This time he jumped on her back as if she were a horse. He faced her buttocks and began to caress each one with his hands, pressing his fingers into each crease, until she began to moan with pleasure. Then he flattened himself along her back and licked each buttock until she began to writhe under him. But he would not stop and she began to shout at him to get off because he was hurting her, but still he continued to penetrate each buttock using his strong fingers and muscular tongue. On and on he went, until she began to arch her body, trying to throw him off but he clung on like the old man of the sea and she screamed at him in pain and frustration.

An anxious call from the reeds finally stopped him. 'The tide's on the turn, my Lady. I can't row against the tide. We must leave now unless you want to walk ashore across the mud.'

The young man appeared, averting his eyes from the mess in the boat. Ursula covered herself and glared at Simon.

'You went too far, dwarf.'

'And you, my lady, have ruined my face. I think we should call a truce.'

The man put away the cushions, and re-fastened the seat. Then, using an oar as a pole, he punted the boat out of the creek and back into the main channel. Then he rowed them back to the watergate in silence. Ursula ordered the boatman to moor the boat by the steps and she went ashore not looking at Simon. He picked up his lute and followed her up the steps, feeling not displeased with himself, despite the clawmarks.

By midday the soldiers, lethargic and sullen in the heat, were only half-heartedly carrying out their military exercises, and Nicholas was soon aware that the general drift over to the keep for refreshments had become a stampede. Even Jacques had succumbed to the general malaise and had slumped down in a patch of shade by the outer wall. Nicholas went over to him and shook him impatiently by the shoulder.

'The men won't cooperate. It's too much to expect them to exercise in this heat.'

Jacques opened one eye and yawned. 'If you let them go over to the keep they'll start quarrelling with the English troops over there.'

'Then come and give me a hand to sort them out. They're spoiling for a fight and if they don't fight the English they'll start fighting one another. Pray God that this weather breaks soon. A storm's on its way and maybe that'll clear the air and the action can start. This inactivity is bad for everyone.'

'Well I can't do anything about the weather. And neither can you, so get over to the castle and bring the men back here. If trouble breaks out lock the English troops up in the keep and tell them to stay there.'

Nicholas, his mind agitated at the prospect of Jane being here with him, followed the men over to the main body of the castle, picking his way over the recumbent bodies of the French soldiers who had succumbed to heat and alcohol-induced torpor. He crossed the drawbridge to the gate leading to the inner bailey and saw, in front of him, Neville's house. He remembered the first time he'd seen it and how enchanting he'd thought it looked and how romantic Neville had looked with his handsome, dark appearance, waiting to receive him and play the gracious host. How things had changed in such a short time. Neville was now the arch-traitor, and the courtyard was no longer a haven of peace. A group of English soldiers was standing at the door of the keep preventing the French troops from going in. The English had been drinking and the level of abuse they were hurling at the French was increasing by the second. The message was clear enough. Nicholas had to take action. Leading the French was the giant Gilbert who had recovered from his beating and was desperate to get at the ale. Frustration made him reckless and he was goading one of the English, a great red-faced ox of a man who, as Nicholas went over, pushed Gilbert back on to one of his companions who promptly fell over. Gilbert, unsteady on his feet, landed on top of him. This was the signal. With roars of rage, the two sides fell on one another, at first using bare hands, but by the time Nicholas joined them, one man had drawn a sword. Nicholas drew his, and slashing at everyone around him with the flat of his blade, he separated Gilbert from his tormentors, and dragged him away by the scruff of his neck. He hauled him over to the gatehouse, and hurled him into the moat which was no more than a sewer for the discharge from the castle buildings. Gilbert sank under the filthy water then re-emerged coughing and spitting and shouting insults at Nicholas.

'Now keep away from here,' shouted Nicholas, leaving Gilbert to get out of the ditch as best he could. 'One more fight and you'll be locked up, do you hear?'

He walked back to separate the others who, now that the ringleader had been despatched, had lost their enthusiasm for fighting. And when one of the servants rolled out a cask of ale they pounced on it and carried it off as booty.

Nicholas turned to go back with them. Suddenly he noticed that a slim boy had come out of the tower in the corner by Neville's house. There was something familiar about him that made Nicholas pause. Then, at the sight of the cropped, copper-coloured hair, he realised who he was. Forgetting all caution, he rushed over to the tower. He hadn't made a mistake. It was Jane. And she was staring at him in horror, her eyes blazing with contempt.

'Jane,' he cried, reaching out to take her in his arms. She drew back.

'You,' she said, 'you, of all people, wearing the fleur-de-lys on your coat. You, in command of that rabble. So all the rumours are true. You are the worst of all traitors and you dare to speak to me!'

'Jane, let me explain.'

'No explanations are needed. Actions speak louder than words. Go back to your men. It seems they have some respect for you. And just keep away from me. Never did I think I should see a Peverell wearing the livery of a French soldier.'

She turned and rushed back inside the tower, slamming the door in his face. He turned round in despair and saw Gilbert, who had climbed out of the ditch, watching him, a grin of triumph on his face.

*   *   *

When Simon found her she was lying face down on her bed, her body racked with sobs.

'Jane, what's happened? As soon as my back's turned . . .'

'Oh go away, Simon. Just leave me alone. Can't you see I don't want to speak to anyone?'

Simon knelt by the side of the bed and put a hand on her shoulders. The action seemed to calm her because she stopped crying but still kept her face turned away from him.

'It seems to me that you need to talk to

someone, lass. Now sit up and dry your tears. Has Neville . . .?'

'Neville?' she said, sitting up and drying her eyes furiously. 'Don't be a fool. He wouldn't dare come near me.'

'Well, that's a relief anyway.'

She turned her head to glare at him and saw his face, usually so full of good humour, now drawn with anxiety and covered in blood.

'Simon, what's happened to you? Your face . . .'

'Just an encounter with a she-devil. It turned out to be quite a bloody business. But no harm's done and this blood'll soon wash off. But I think you've had a worse experience; not so bloody, but painful all the same.'

'Simon, I've seen Nicholas.'

'That's good news, surely?'

'No, terrible news. There was a fight just now out in the courtyard. Some French soldiers turned up wanting drink and our English soldiers who'd drunk too much wouldn't let them into the keep. A commanding officer came up and put a stop to it and when he saw me, he came over and called out my name. Then I recognised Nicholas. And Simon, you'll not believe this, he was wearing the livery of a French soldier. It was awful. Nicholas, who once saved the King's life, is now commanding the foreign troops who want to depose him. We've got to leave straight away. I can't stay here watching him betray his country any longer. I'll get Melissa ready.'

'Jane, stop,' said Simon jumping up and checking her with his hand. 'Don't jump to conclusions. You're sure this man was Peverell?'

'Of course. He called out my name. I saw his face under that repulsive French helmet.'

'Did anyone else see him?'

'No, the men had all left. Oh yes, there was one man. He'd been the ringleader when the men started to fight, and Nicholas separated him from the others and threw him into the ditch. He must have climbed out and stayed behind after the others had gone. He was watching Nicholas when he came over to me; I'm sure of that. He was one of the French soldiers.'

'Then this is more serious than you think, lass. And if you'd used that brain of yours locked away in that pretty head, and not gone jumping to conclusions, you'd know that Peverell is doing just what the King and Cromwell asked him to do—to spy on Neville and get proof of his treachery. He's done well. He's infiltrated the French camp and then you come along and upset the apple cart. Now his cover's blown, he's a dead man. And you, my dear, stupid Jane, are responsible.'

'How could I know?'

'You didn't stop to think, did you? But let me do a bit of thinking now. Someone's got to warn this fellow of yours that he's in danger.

And that someone has to be me. Don't worry, lass. I speak good French. The King likes French songs and the late Queen always spoke to me in French. Now don't start weeping and screaming at me that I'm deserting you and joining up with Peverell in his treacherous activities. I'll be back soon. But first I must wash off this she-devil's blood.'

Suddenly, there was a commotion outside. They heard men shouting and they rushed down the stairs, out of the tower, and into the outer courtyard. The English soldiers and the servants were pouring out of the keep to see what was going on. When they crossed the drawbridge to the outer keep they saw four covered wagons, drawn by oxen who stood there puffing and steaming after their exertions. As they watched, someone lifted up the flap of the tent-like covering and soldiers jumped down. Jane counted as twenty-five men jumped down from the first cart, and there were four carts. The soldiers, dressed in their dirty, tattered uniforms, stood there confused by the bright light. Soon the courtyard was filled with men, the French soldiers coming out of the church to jeer at the new arrivals and the English jeering at all of them. In the middle of the mob stood Neville and Jacques de Crèvecoeur trying to restore order. The German and Flemish mercenaries had arrived.

301

CHAPTER TWENTY-ONE

As the day wore on, and all attempts at keeping the soldiers occupied by military exercises were abandoned, the men began to light fires in the grassy area in front of the church and they sprawled on the grass drinking and playing dice. Nicholas was waiting for darkness. He had checked that Neville's boat was moored by the watergate and the oars were in it. High water, he knew, was at midnight, so he could, with any luck, slip away whilst the men slept. He could make use of the tide when the ebb set in and get down to Portsmouth by daylight. Then he would see Southampton. If Fitzroy of Arundel had raised the muster in Sussex there would be sufficient loyal men available to flush out this nest of vipers before the invasion fleet arrived. Meanwhile several hours of daylight had to be got through first, and by the look of the men, who were restless and bored and spoiling for a fight, there was a limit as to how long he could keep them under control, especially now they had heard the German mercenaries arriving and knew they were only a short distance away in the old palace inside the inner bailey.

As the sun went down and the soldiers showed no sign of retiring to their quarters inside the church, Nicholas became aware of a sudden change in the men's mood. Then he saw the reason for this lightening of the atmosphere. Simon had appeared to the accompaniment of loud cheers. News of his performance, along with his nephew Roderick, had spread round the camp and the men began to settle down for an evening's entertainment.

Nicholas tried to edge away but it was impossible. Some of them had cleared a space for an impromptu stage and had forced the men back making it impossible for Nicholas to beat a hasty retreat. The last thing he wanted was for Simon to recognise him and call out his name. Especially as Neville had come over to watch the show.

Seeing Simon brought back memories of Court life. How often had he seen Simon sitting at the King's feet being fed titbits by the Queen's ladies-in-waiting, and how often had he applauded his tumbling and clowning. Then another thought came to him, one that filled him with dread. Was Jane going to join his act? And would she turn away from him in hatred when she saw him standing in the crowd? The prospect was so alarming that he once more tried to force his way through the mob of soldiers but they shouted at him to sit down, and his neighbour made a space for him on the grass. Shielding his face with his hands, he gave himself up to despair whilst all around him the men were laughing and jostling one another to get a better of view of the stage and Simon.

Simon had brought a small drum with him which he began to strike as he strutted round the stage. This made the soldiers laugh simply because he looked so comic. He was wearing the doublet which Ursula had given him and his legs were covered in multi-coloured striped leggings. As he strutted round the stage, beating his drum, grinning at the men with his large, good-humoured face, all the men's resentment and boredom evaporated and they began clapping their hands in time to the rhythm of the drum and roaring out their approval.

The beat of the drum grew faster and faster until Simon was running round the stage. Then he put aside the drum and began to turn cartwheels at incredible speed until the whole stage seemed to come alive with flashes of colour. After a brief pause where he feigned tiredness, he began to turn somersaults in the air, and on the ground, until the men felt dizzy watching him. On and on he went, his muscular body flying through the air like an exotic tropical bird. Then, suddenly, he stopped and wiped his face with a scarlet handkerchief. He took off his doublet and took the lute which he'd given to Neville for safe keeping. The men shouted their approval, urging him on.

'*Chanson, chanson,*' they chanted until

Simon raised a hand and struck the first chord. Then silence settled over the camp.

He sang one of the lively student songs of Paris, popular all over France, a song which King Henry had introduced him to on his return from a visit to the French King. His French was good and the men laughed and bawled out the chorus. Nicholas watched in amazement as the unruly soldiers who had caused so much trouble that day suddenly had become peaceful and good humoured. After several more boisterous songs, Nicholas saw Jane, in her boy's clothes, step forward to more shouts of approval from the soldiers. He was appalled. Jane, coming to entertain this band of rough soldiers. They would tear her to pieces. He stood up, driven by some impulse to rush forward and save her, but at the sound of her sweet, boyish treble, the men fell silent, and Nicholas knew she was safe and he could only gaze at her in admiration mixed with love and longing for what he had lost. Jane, who'd come to find him, to be with him, bringing Simon with her for support. And now she thought him the worst of traitors and he couldn't speak to her. It was agony to see her and know that he had lost her. She most certainly hated him and would tell everyone that he was the worst of traitors who had gone over to the enemy. It was unbearable and once more he tried to edge his way out of the crowd. But suddenly Simon looked at him. Just one

305

look, but he knew that Simon understood what he was doing and why he was there. Simon was on his side, and wanted to speak to him. It was only a flicker of an eyelid but it was enough. Quietly, Nicholas began to edge his way nearer the stage. No one took any notice of him because they were all absorbed in Jane's performance. She had finished singing her sentimental love songs and picked up Simon's drum. She began to beat out the rhythm of one of the coarse drinking songs which Simon had taught her on their way to Portsmouth. Strutting round the stage she mimicked the walk of a woman of the streets, boxing Simon's ears when he tried to stop her. When he tried to take his drum away from her the men shouted their disapproval, and Simon retired in mock anger. Even Neville had lost his self-conscious aloofness and was absorbed in her performance.

Leaving Jane to hold centre stage, Simon began to resume his tumbling act amongst the audience, trying to regain their attention. He started to play the fool with the soldiers, knocking against them so that they fell over, then pulling their beards when they tried to get up. Then he darted away between their legs before the men could catch him.

One of these somersaults brought him close to Nicholas. He bobbed around him, playfully poking him in the chest.

'You are in danger, my Lord,' said Simon

cheerfully and bowing in mock respect. He spoke softly in French so that the men nearest Nicholas thought they were exchanging badinage. Even Jacques turned round and grinned at them.

'Get away from me, fool,' said Nicholas striking out at him, but missing him by inches. 'Go and pester someone else.'

'You were seen talking to Jane,' said Simon, mocking Nicholas's disapproving manner. 'The fat one over there saw you. He heard you speak English.'

'I'm leaving tonight. Don't worry.'

'Let me go instead,' said Simon, playfully aiming a punch at his body in imitation of the boxing matches which some of the men had been engaged in that afternoon.

'They'd not believe you. Go away, fool,' said Nicholas giving him a light tap on his chest, which made Simon squeal in mock pain.

'Then be careful. You'll be watched. No one would notice me.'

'I've had enough of this,' said Nicholas cheerfully picking Simon up and carrying him back to the stage amidst the delighted shouts of approval from the men.

Jane was singing a bawdy song in French about a soldier and a girl who loved him and followed him to the wars. She handed him the drum and he began to accompany her, shouting out to the men to join in the chorus. Nicholas watched them, smiling and clapping with the rest. But now things had changed. He suddenly felt a surge of optimism. Simon believed in him, and with any luck he might have persuaded Jane to change her opinion of him. But Gilbert would have to be watched. Gilbert would be waiting for his opportunity to denounce him. As darkness fell, and the camp fires began to die down, one by one the men crept back to their quarters. Soon Neville took Simon and Jane away and the performance was over. Jacques came up to where Nicholas was standing.

'Another day over. Pray God we shall soon see an end to this waiting. Another day of drinking and idleness will demoralise this rabble, and now we've got the German contingent to contend with. A pity the current brought them near the coast and they could be rowed ashore. They looked exhausted but they'll have recovered from the journey by tomorrow and will be looking for trouble. We can't keep this number of men locked up in this castle for much longer.'

'Tomorrow we'll hold a tournament, and gunnery practice. The cannons ought to be primed ready for action.'

'Alas, only the English are trained to use the cannons. And with all these reinforcements arriving, there must be over fifty English soldiers in the keep by now. More than enough to look after the cannons without having to train up the rest of the soldiers. Besides, it will take a long time to train a French or German pikeman how to aim and operate a gun.'

'It's worth a try, and would keep the men busy. But now, Jacques, my friend, I must get some sleep. The storm could break at any time, and when it does, the wind will come and the action will start.'

'Then, good night, my friend.'

* * *

Nicholas picked his way between the rows of men settling down for the night. They seemed relaxed and good humoured after the entertainment and called out to him to sleep well. He lay down on his bed and feigned sleep. In his mind he could see the tide sweeping up to the neck of Portsmouth Harbour. He knew that at midnight it would turn and, with luck, he would be in Neville's boat being carried down to Portsmouth. By daylight he would be with Southampton. By this time tomorrow night, Southampton would be in control of the castle, Neville would be under arrest and Montague's stronghold under attack. Simon would keep Jane out of harm's way until the fighting was over and they would ride back together to the King and his Court. His spying days would be over.

When all was quiet except for the heavy breathing of men who had drunk their fill of the potent English ale, Nicholas got up, picked up his sword, but left behind his helmet and breast plate. Never again, he thought, would he have to wear the hated livery of a foreign king. Then he picked his way over the bodies of the sleeping men and made for the west door which had been left open to let in the cooler night air. He had considered leaving the church by the tunnel, but that would mean going down into the crypt on the other side of the church, where he ran the risk of disturbing the soldiers. Also it brought him out in the wrong place and he would have to cross the outer courtyard to get to the watergate and therefore stood a greater chance of being seen. He didn't see Gilbert raise his shaggy head to watch where he was going. Neither did he see him get to his feet and follow him out of the church. Once outside Nicholas stopped and looked around him. The coast was clear. No one shouted a warning to him from the bastions. It seemed no watch had been set but then no invasion was expected that night. Keeping close to the church wall, he made a dash for the watergate. The gate was bolted on the inside but the bolt had been well greased and he was able to draw it back with ease. He opened the door and went out. Standing on top of the steps he saw the boat tied to the mooring post rocking gently on the water which had now reached its highest point. The oars were neatly stowed away under the seats.

He went down the steps. Then Gilbert

caught up with him. As Nicholas stepped into the boat, Gilbert grabbed him round the neck and dragged him back on the steps.

'Now I have you, English pig,' said Gilbert punching him in the face and kicking him as he fell on to the stone steps. Nicholas was conscious of a searing pain in his chest, and as the kicks continued, he doubled over trying to protect his body. There was no chance of defending himself as the attack had taken him completely by surprise. All he could do was try to protect himself as best he could. Gilbert gave a final kick which sent Nicholas rolling down the steps into the water where he finally lost consciousness.

*   *   *

When he came round he was lying on the flagstones in front of the keep. Neville was standing looking down at him with Jacques de Crèvecoeur next to him.

'So, Lord Nicholas, we meet again. Never did I think you would ever venture back to my castle. But it seems I misjudged you. But now you're here, I think it's time to get rid of you once and for all.'

He turned to Jacques. 'Kill him, Crèvecoeur. Any way you like. We'll send his body back to Henry Tudor after we've taken Portsmouth. That will show him what we think of his spies. And you, Crèvecoeur, can have his

Sussex estate. It's modest, but has a prime position.'

Nicholas heard this through waves of pain that washed over him and confused his mind. This was the end of all his plans. He was going to die an ignominious death and a foreigner was going to get his manor in the general shareout after the rebellion was over. He cursed his King who had brought him to this state and prepared himself to die.

Then he heard Jacques' voice, level and reasonable. 'No need to kill him, Lord Neville. He could be useful to us. For instance, he must know how many men Southampton has under his command and how many ships Henry Tudor has in his fleet. That way we shall, at least, know what we're up against. We could also use him as a hostage. The King would probably pay a lot for him. He is well thought of at Court, you say. Let's hold on to him for the time being and finish him off when we've no longer any use for him. Haven't you got some safe place to put prisoners? Mind you, he's in no fit state to attempt anything heroic.'

'I suppose he could be useful, if he survives this beating. Put him in the pit,' Neville said to the guard standing by.

Nicholas felt himself being dragged over the flagstones, then into a building. He heard the crash of a trapdoor being raised. Then he was lifted up and tipped over the edge of some deep hole. He fell on to the damp earth and the darkness closed around him. The air smelt foul and dank, and then he mercifully lost consciousness.

*   *   *

Jane lay awake for some time after that night's open-air performance. The sight of Nicholas had brought back all those emotions she had managed to suppress since Nicholas had escaped from the Tower and she had come looking for him with Simon. She knew that only by having a cool head would she be of any use to him. Now, seeing him in the middle of all those foreign soldiers, knowing that he was taking a great risk, she felt sick with longing to see him again. Simon had told her that Nicholas was leaving that night and she was saddened by the thought that he would leave without speaking to her. She understood, of course. Simon could play the fool and speak to him but it would not be appropriate for her to adopt the same ruse. Simon was Simon, and no one took him seriously. But if only, she thought, if only she had been able to speak to Nicholas, just three words would have been enough. But by now he would be on his way to break the news about Neville's treachery to the authorities.

Eventually she drifted into a deep sleep, only to be woken up by Simon returning to the room where they slept. She heard him slump down on the bed and, when she looked across at him, he looked the picture of despair. He sat on the side of the bed, hunched forward, his hands clasped round his head.

'Simon,' she whispered, suddenly terrified. 'Simon, what's happened?'

'Hush lass, go back to sleep. What's done is done. Better to wait till morning before I tell you.'

'No, tell me now. How can I possibly go back to sleep when you're in this state?'

She went across to his bed and sat down beside him, holding him in her arms. This was a Simon she hadn't seen before. Usually he was the one who comforted her but now he remained in her arms, making no attempt to disengage himself. Suddenly she realised he was crying and her terror increased. She'd never seen Simon weep real tears before. He was always the cocky, self-confident fool.

'They've got him, lass, just as he was leaving. That fat oaf, Gilbert, watched him all the time and followed him down to the boat. He's been kicked and punched, but thank God he's still alive.'

'You mean Nicholas?'

'Aye, lass, that impulsive fool of yours. I told him not to go. I could have gone instead of him, but he said no one would take me seriously. It's the story of my life. When I offer to do something really important, I'm told I'm only a fool. But I could have gone. No one would miss me in the day time. I could have slipped away from here and got to this Earl of Southampton and told him what's going on here. But he said they would only laugh at me. He was probably right. I'd only go and mess things up; but at least I wouldn't get caught. I know how to look after myself. As it happens I can't row a boat and I can't swim, but I have a wonderful way of making myself invisible. But he would go, and he's been injured. Lucky he wasn't killed outright, but that French chap they call Jacques suggested they dump him into some sort of pit and they dragged him off.'

'Where is he, Simon?'

'Some place where you're not to go. It's a dungeon of sorts over in a corner of the old palace. It's a great, dark hole. No light, and precious little air, I should imagine. And I can only think it's what he deserves for trying to play the hero and not listening to me when I warned him about that pig of a Frenchman. But, I'm so sorry, lass, because despite everything, I like that man and can see why you like him.'

Jane sat there numb with horror, her brain refusing to work. Suddenly, she felt Simon begin to recover his old cockiness and he moved away from her embrace.

'Well, lass, we'll have to start thinking of a way to get him out of there. Just let me think. I'm not altogether a fool, you know. Lord

315

Nicholas won't be much use for a few days, but at least he's alive and can't go blundering around the place getting in everyone's way. He'll need food and water—I heard them say that they didn't want him dead yet, so they will have to keep him alive. An old fool like me could offer to fetch him some water. Come on, lass, cheer up. It's not quite the end of the performance, although it seems like it at this hour of the night.'

CHAPTER TWENTY-TWO

The next morning, Simon got up quietly and went down into the courtyard. He could hear sounds of activity coming from the keep where the servants were busily preparing breakfast for the soldiers and the members of Neville's household. Preparing food for so many people kept them busy all day and throughout the night, but Simon was familiar with kitchens and was confident that he would not be unwelcome.

He opened the door of the keep and went in. He perched himself on one of the tables and sat there swinging his crossed legs and watching what went on. The head cook, a man named Black Jack because of his black mass of matted hair, luxuriant beard and dark complexion, was shouting at a reluctant workforce to work harder. Four bread ovens, tended by two young boys, were working at full pitch. Black Jack turned round and saw Simon.

'So, Simon the fool, if it's breakfast you're after then get down from your perch and give us a hand over here.'

'Couldn't I sing a song to pay for my breakfast?'

'Get away with you, this is no time for songs. We'll have songs enough when all these pigs have been fed. Now come over here, pick up that knife and slice these loaves. Then you can carry the baskets and the ale upstairs to our men. We feed them first. The others can wait their turn. No one mentioned I was going to have to feed a garrison when they hired me as chief cook. Now keep your eyes on that bread, you dolt,' he roared at one of the boys who was staring at Simon in amazement. 'Haven't you seen a little fellow like this before? Well let me warn you, he might be short on height but he's not short on brains. And I'm sure he's as cunning as a fox.'

Simon, looking long-suffering and playing up to the watching servants, slid down from the table, and went over to where a pile of loaves were waiting to be sliced and stacked in the bread baskets. He picked up the knife Jack had indicated and after a bit of fooling around during which he made playful lunges at Jack's back, much to the hilarity of the servants, he began to saw the bread up into slices. When the basket was full, Jack pointed to the floor above them.

'Up you go. Fifty of them up there, always hungry. Come back down again and I'll give you their ale to take up.'

Simon picked up the basket and climbed up the stairs to the floor above where the soldiers were waking up. When they saw him, they shouted greetings and told him to give them an early morning performance.

'Too much work to do, lads,' Simon said, dumping the basket on one of the tables. 'A couple of hundred foreigners to feed after you.'

'Let the pigs starve. What's it to us if they go hungry? Come lad, a song will wake us up.'

Simon was used to being treated as a child. They would be astonished, he thought, if he told them his real age, his birthday just a few months short of the King's.

'I've got to go back for the ale. You don't want the foreigners to drink the lot now, do you?'

'That's right, lad,' said one of the company, who, judging by the superior quality of his bed coverings, was their leader. 'Get on with your duties. I'm the one who gives the orders round here. Ned Smallbone's my name—Captain Smallbone to you. If you're going to be our new kitchen servant, then mind your manners, and we'll look after you. And tell that Jack fellow not to forget that Captain Smallbone's partial to a bit of cheese in the mornings.'

Simon did as he was told, and came back to eat his breakfast sitting in the midst of the soldiers.

'And what brings you here?' said Captain Smallbone, slicing off a hunk of cheese and handing it to Simon with the point of his knife. His hands were huge and covered with a fuzz of red hair, like fox's fur. Captain Smallbone was a massive redhead from the north of England with an aggressive red beard which made him look more ferocious than he really was.

'I needed a holiday from Court. Me and my nephew wanted to escape from London in this heat. There's plague and the sweating sickness up there and the sea air's a real treat. We sing for our supper and I suppose we've done well. So far, this is our best lodging, but we'll soon be on our way, because I can't be doing with all these foreign soldiers penned up here like a lot of cattle and eating their heads off.'

'We don't exactly like them, either,' said Smallbone. 'In fact, we hate the lot of them, and what's more, we can't fathom out why they're here. We're here to fire the guns. Now who are we supposed to be firing at? Why, Frenchies of course, and Germans and Burgundians. That's what we were told. But now, it appears that we're all pals together and they eat our food and drink our ale. It's right daft, Simon, and what we don't understand, we don't like, do we fellows?'

The men growled their approval and began to pour out their grievances to Simon.

'We're the only ones who can fire the guns. Now, take those German fellows across the way, we could mop them up in minutes with our ordnance. They've no right to be here. No right at all,' said the man sitting next to Simon.

'And what's going to happen,' said Simon, 'when the foreign pigs start firing on Portsmouth? Shouldn't you be down there stopping them from landing, not sitting up here keeping them company?'

'You've hit the nail on the head,' said Captain Smallbone heatedly. 'I tell you, little fellow, it's not right. In fact it smells as nasty as a dead dog at noon. I don't trust this Neville fellow. I don't trust him at all.'

'Best keep your voice down,' said Simon, alarmed by Smallbone's vehemence. 'He's got his orders. Perhaps he was told to hire foreign mercenaries to fight with you when the time comes.'

'And when's that going to be? Just think about it. We're supposed to be stopping an invasion. Now, just tell me, even if the foreign ships could get past the King's ships out at Spithead, how can they come up here on one tide and risk going aground? By God, lad, we'll blast them to bits with our guns whilst they wait for the water to come back. Sitting ducks, that's what they'd be. There's no commander in the whole world would be so daft as to risk an attack on this castle on the seaward side. No lad, that's not Neville's plan. I've got a feeling we're going to be used for a rearguard attack. On what? On Portsmouth? Now what does that add up to? It sounds like treason to me; and we'll not be traitors, eh lads?'

The men were now getting very excited and for a moment Simon feared that they were going to attack the German contingent straight away. 'We've taken one prisoner,' he said, trying to shift their attention away from the German soldiers. 'Captured last night. A pity he's an Englishman, one of us. He was sent here as a spy, it appears, and got caught leaving the place to make his report to Southampton. He's been dumped into a pit over there with our German allies, and no one's given him anything to eat or drink since he's been there. I don't know whether he's alive or dead.'

Captain Smallbone set down his tankard of ale and grasped hold of Simon.

'Now you look here, little fellow, Neville's no right to put an Englishman in prison whose only crime was to try to find out what's going on here. It sounds to me that our noble commander's got a lot to hide. Now, you get over to that prisoner, give him some bread and ale, Black Jack'll fix you up, and tell him that we'll look after him if he can get out of that pit. That's right, isn't it lads? And whilst we're looking after him, we'll find out what's going on here, and if necessary, take the law into our own hands.'

Simon scrambled to his feet, and made for the stairs. So far, so good, he thought.

'And tell our commander, that we'll only fight with Englishmen and we fight against foreign pigs. We don't fight with foreign pigs. Why? Because we don't trust them. Tell him that. And if he wants to sack us, that suits us. No need to remind him we're the only ones who know how to work them guns. Let him work that out for himself. Now, go and feed that prisoner and when he's ready, bring him up here to us. And it goes without saying that we'll keep all this to ourselves.'

Simon stopped at the top of the stairs and turned to look back at Smallbone. 'And how am I to get him out of the pit? I'm only a wee chap as you can see, and he's in a mighty deep pit.'

'You'll find a way. You're a bright chap. But don't be too long about it. We said we'd look after an Englishman, not a corpse.'

A roar from Black Jack below sent Simon dashing down into the kitchen where he was set to work again. By mid morning, everyone was fed and the servants were allowed a brief rest.

'Can I feed the prisoner?' Simon said to Jack.

'We don't feed prisoners. Besides, I hear

he's a traitor.'

'He's an Englishman. How can he be a traitor? Lord Neville's taken against him, that's all.'

'In that case, take him some food. We've no love for Lord Neville over here, but keep that to yourself. The man's a fool. He can no more command a garrison than control a pack of hounds.'

Simon took up a hunk of bread and pitcher of water. Then he picked up a piece of rope from a pile in the corner of the keep and went out. At least he could ensure that Nicholas didn't starve to death.

*   *   *

When Nicholas came round he thought he had been buried alive and was in his tomb. The darkness pressed down on him like an all-enveloping heavy blanket. He was lying on his side, curled up on a damp, mud floor and when he tentatively stretched out a hand, he felt the sides of the tomb very close to his body. And when he uncurled his legs, he immediately encountered another wall. Yes, he thought, it is a tomb, and he wasn't dead. He could still feel, and think and move his body.

He rolled over and forced himself to sit up, despite the agonising pain in his left side. Then he made the discovery that there was no lid to his tomb. Raising his right arm which

323

produced less pain than raising his left, he realised that the space above him went on indefinitely. He rested his back against the wall and tried to think back to how he'd come to be put in such a place. He remembered Jane, but somehow she looked different. And he remembered Simon, the King's fool, but he couldn't think what he'd been doing or why he should be remembered. Then he remembered the sea and a boat and some steps. Then nothing. Then he remembered hearing a man's voice suggesting that he shouldn't be killed. Yes, he remembered that. And the man had been Jacques, the amiable Frenchman who wasn't quite a soldier. So, he thought, that was it. He'd been caught, and kicked and beaten and dumped down here, and by the feel of it, it was a narrow pit not even wide enough for him to stretch out in. And it was deep. He was too weak to stand up and the pain in his side was excruciating when he put any weight on his left arm. However, he was sure no bones had been broken, except, possibly a rib had cracked. There was no food, no water, and the air smelt dank and fetid. Were they going to leave him to die a slow and agonising death? If so, it was his own stupidity which was to blame. He'd ignored Simon's warning, and Gilbert had been watching him and had followed him down to the boat. He should have watched out for Gilbert and despatched him before he tried to escape. Instead, he'd failed. He'd failed the

King, Jane, and himself. It was best he should die. Best that everyone should forget he had ever existed. But he wished he had spoken to Jane before he had been captured. He wished he could see her now before he died. He would tell her he loved her and he'd failed her and then she could go back to London and marry that passionate Welshman. The sooner she forgot all about Nicholas Peverell the better.

Giving himself up to despair, he fell into a deep sleep from which he hoped he'd never awaken.

A noise coming from above brought him back to consciousness. This time all the events of the past night came flooding into his mind. The noise continued and looking up, he saw a chink of daylight. Air, cool and sweet came flooding in and he breathed down great gulps which revived him. Slowly and painfully he dragged himself to his feet. Then a familiar face appeared in the opening above him, a large, good-natured face, Simon's face, looking at him anxiously.

'Lord Nicholas, are you still with us?'

'Simon! Thank God. Yes I'm alive. But how have you managed to get here?'

'Hush! With difficulty. But take heart, man. Here's bread and water and there are fifty English soldiers anxious to have you in their ranks. So don't go and die on us. Rest assured, we'll have you out of there. But I must go now,

I've been noticed.'

Bread and water were lowered down on a rope. Nicholas reached up and untied them. Then the rope was hauled up again. The lid clanged shut. But hope returned. Fresh air had entered his tomb, he had food and water and he had friends. But he realised that Simon was risking much by coming to see him.

*   *   *

'Simon,' a voice behind him said. 'What the devil are you doing? Are you meddling in affairs that don't concern you?'

Simon, turning, saw Neville standing in the doorway. His dark face was pale and tense with anxiety and Simon realised he was frightened. He looked like a man who had lost control of events and didn't know which way to turn. Simon tried to look unconcerned. He smiled and bowed to Neville.

'An errand of mercy, my Lord. Even dogs have to be fed.'

'That's none of your business. Don't come near the prisoner again or else I'll send you and that nephew of yours packing. You're taking liberties, Simon. Remember your place. I value your entertainments. You've kept the troops amused and brought relief to myself and my wife in difficult times. But looking after prisoners is the responsibility of the captain of the guard and no one else's. Tell

Captain Smallbone to bring the food in future. Now get back to your quarters.'

Simon bowed and walked back to his room in the tower, conscious of Neville's eyes upon him. From now on he'd have to be careful or else he'd end up in the same place as Lord Nicholas and that would leave Jane to fend for herself. As he went into the tower, he noticed that Melissa had gone. The straw she'd been standing on had been changed. All was in order. But Melissa had gone and when he went up to the first floor he saw that Jane had gone also. Damn the stupid girl, he thought. I can't abide these highspirited girls. They think they can do what they like. Why can't she be docile like other wenches?

*   *   *

Jane was furious with Simon. How could he desert her at a time like this? She could hear the soldiers laughing and shouting to one another in the keep and knew that Simon was in there with them, playing the fool like he always did as if he hadn't a care in the world. Had he forgotten that Nicholas was incarcerated in his dungeon without food and water? She would leave Simon to his selfish foolery, she thought, and start to sort out things for herself. It was time she stopped relying on him.

She fed and watered Melissa and groomed

her. She changed her bedding and decided to risk exercising her out in the castle grounds. She knew that the enforced inactivity was bad for Melissa and bad for herself and she thought that as long as she kept close to the castle walls, no harm would come her way.

She led Melissa out into the outer bailey and jumped on her back. The French soldiers had abandoned any pretence at exercise and were sprawled out on the grass near the church, too lethargic even to play dice. It was still very hot with an oppressive feel to the air which was a warning of the approaching storm. The sun had disappeared behind a think haze and even the birds were silent. There was no sign of life in the bastions. Even gunnery practice had been abandoned.

One of the soldiers sitting with a group in front of the church saw her and got up and walked across the grass to join her. She recognised him. He was the dark Frenchman who had been with them at dinner the other evening and was in charge of the French contingent. Everyone had called him Jacques and he seemed to be a cut above the rest of his men. He was a silent man, she remembered, an observer, but no fool. He gave the impression that he understood everything and was not taken in by anyone. He was attractive. Tall and slim, with dark Gallic looks, a lean face with an expression of world-weariness. He had listened to the performance and had watched her intently which had made her feel uncomfortable.

'Good morning, Master Roderick,' he said in English. 'A tiring day to be out exercising your horse.'

She reined in Melissa and looked at Jacques, forcing herself to remain calm.

'She has to be exercised, sir, or else she'll not be fit to carry us when we move on.'

'And when do you intend to do that?'

'When there is no more interest in our performance. I understand that an attack is expected and we should be away by then. A castle under siege is no place for songs and the tumbling arts.'

'Will you not dismount, Roderick, and walk a while with me? No action is expected yet; not until the weather changes.'

She was reluctant to talk to Jacques, but she didn't want to arouse suspicion. She slid off Melissa's back and led her to Jacques who stroked the horse's nose.

'A beautiful mare. How did you come to get hold of such a fine beast?'

'A wealthy patron gave her to me as payment for my singing.'

'The man has taste. You sing like a nightingale. You would be able to delight kings and queens, Roderick. This is not the place for you, amongst these rough soldiers.'

'They are fighting men, sir, and deserve some light relief. Besides, Lord Neville will pay us well.'

'And Lady Ursula has taken a fancy to your Uncle Simon, I hear.'

Much to her annoyance, she felt her face redden. 'What my uncle does is of no concern to me.'

'And you, Roderick? Have you no lovely lady to befriend you?'

'I keep to myself, sir.'

'A wise move. But come, tell me about yourself. Who, and where, are your parents? They must be of gentle stock. I'm surprised they let you roam around the countryside.'

'My father was a wealthy city haberdasher, sir. He died of the sweating sickness when I was ten and took my mother with him. Uncle Simon became my guardian and he has looked after me all these years.'

'And yet he takes you on tour with him and lets you roam round a castle full of rough soldiers?'

'He knows I can look after myself.'

'Where is he now? Asleep, I suppose, after an assignation with the Lady Ursula?'

'I don't know where he is, but I think he could be taking food and water to the prisoner.'

'On whose instructions?' said Jacques, suddenly stopping and looking at her keenly.

'No one's. He's a compassionate man, sir. He felt sorry for the man and acted out of Christian charity.'

'Then tell him to keep away from the prisoner. He's not worthy of anyone's compassion. He's a spy who got caught leaving the castle, probably to sell the information he's gathered here to the authorities.'

'He's not a spy,' said Jane, unable to control her indignation. 'He's a brave man who was only doing his duty.'

'So, you know the man, Master Roderick. Maybe he means a lot to you? Ah, now I understand. He is a friend of yours. You admire him, is that not so?'

Jane felt her face redden again and she became angry with herself for not being able to control her feelings. She turned away from Jacques and jumped up on to Melissa's back.

'Master Roderick, a warning. If this man is a friend of yours, then it would be best if you left this place immediately. I would hate to see that beautiful voice of yours lost to the world. Tread carefully, I beg you. These are dangerous times and people are not what they seem.'

Jane rode on to the corner of the wall. When she looked back, Jacques was walking back to the soldiers. She felt agitated and wondered what she'd done. How much had she said that would incriminate Nicholas further? And how much had she revealed about herself? She felt sure that Jacques suspected she was a girl. He would only have to voice his suspicions to Neville and she and

Simon would share the same fate as Nicholas. Yes, it was time to leave the castle, but she knew she could not leave Nicholas to his fate. If he were to die, then she would die with him. Then another thought flashed across her mind, a thought as blindingly clear as the flashes of lightning which were now penetrating the heavy clouds out at sea. She rode Melissa back to the keep and arrived there just as Simon was coming out of the tower to look for her. His face was unsmiling. In fact, his face was as dark as the thunderclouds outside.

'Well, lass, and where have you been?' he said, as she led Melissa back to her stall.

'Don't adopt that tone with me, Simon. I had to exercise Melissa.'

'She'll come to no harm. We'll be away from here soon. It's you I'm worried about. The men are restless and no one seems to be in control.'

'I spoke to the French captain. You know, the one who was at dinner with us the other night. He's a strange man and seems to know everything, yet keeps himself to himself. I'm sure he saw straight through my disguise and guessed that my feelings for Lord Nicholas were more than mere compassion for a prisoner.'

'You talked about Lord Nicholas?'

'Yes. He wanted to know what you were doing and I told him I thought you were on an errand of mercy to the prisoner. He warned me to tell you to keep away from him. He said Nicholas was a spy, and of course, I denied that, rather too emphatically, I think.'

'Then it's all up with us. We'll have to leave at once. If Jacques knows we're friends of Lord Nicholas he'll tell Neville and we shall all be in that pit together. Don't make that horse too comfortable. We'll be needing her very soon.'

'No, Simon, not yet. Something makes me think Jacques will keep his suspicions to himself for the time being.'

'He's hedging his bets, lass,' said Simon grimly. 'He's got no faith in Neville—no one in his right mind would have. If Neville's plans come to nothing, Jacques will have saved his skin by befriending Lord Nicholas.'

'That's what I think; but we can't be sure. But listen Simon. Nicholas was going to report to the Earl of Southampton. We're sure of that from what you told me after last night's performance for the troops. He got caught. Now someone must tell Southampton what's going on here. And that person is going to be you.'

'Me? My God, lass, you're out of your mind. Southampton'll take no more notice of me than if I were a fly on the wall. And you tell me how I'm to get out of his place. I can't just say goodbye to Neville and leave by the main gate. I can't row a boat and neither can I swim, and if you were thinking that I could ride that horse of yours, well forget it. Melissa and I like each other well enough, but she knows who's boss when it comes to riding her.'

'But you've got two legs, Simon, and it's only ten miles to Portsmouth. You can leave tonight. I'll help you over the old wall on the landward side. There's a storm coming, so everyone will be inside.'

'Great heavens, I'm to walk to Portsmouth in the rain, am I? You've got it all worked out. And what do I tell my Lord of Southampton when I find him, provided they let me see him that is?'

'I'll write a letter.'

'Bravo. I forgot about that brain of yours. And what will you do after I've gone? Run round and talk to the likes of Captain Jacques?'

'I shall look after Lord Nicholas.'

'Oh no, lass, not you. That'll be the end of both of you. Now leave this to me. There's a Captain Smallbone in the keep who looks after our men. He's a good sort. Give him some cheese and he'll look after you. Tell him you're a friend of the prisoner and he'll look after Lord Nicholas. You can trust him. He hates Neville and, by the looks of it, our soldiers do likewise. I'll go and talk to them again. Maybe something could come out of this. At least I've got more sense than Lord Nicholas. I'll not get caught. I like my comfort too much.'

CHAPTER TWENTY-THREE

Dinner was over. Ursula had withdrawn to her chamber. The three men continued to linger over their wine. Suddenly Neville got up, pushed back his chair and walked over to the window. He stared out at the camp fires still burning in the outer bailey. Flashes of sheet lightning lit up the sky out at sea and the rumbles of thunder which accompanied them were louder and nearer than they had been before. Henry, Lord Montague, a strongly-built man in his prime, watched Neville—his face dispassionate, his eyes calculating. His reddish-brown hair showed grey at the edges and was cut short like a soldier's.

'How much longer can you keep your men under control, Charles?' he said.

'As long as it's necessary. Probably only one more day. This storm will break tonight and the wind will get up and the ships can get under way again. Once we know they are coming, we can give the men their marching orders.'

'Almost to the day,' said the third man quietly. He was a neat, slim man dressed completely in black clothes. A silver crucifix hung round his neck giving him a priest-like appearance, an impression accentuated by his long, straight hair and lean, saturnine face.

335

'How have you reached that conclusion, Gallimard?' said Montague.

'Tyler gave the expected date as the twentieth of July, remember? In that letter which he wrote to Cromwell and Peverell didn't find. You still have the box, my Lord?' he said to Henry Montague who nodded his assent.

'Of course. The information contained in that box was vital to our plans. A disaster if it had reached its intended destination. I was interested to see your name mentioned in the list of secret agents Tyler had drawn up for Cromwell's benefit.'

'Then it's just as well we got Tyler out of the way when we did. A pity, though, we didn't get his box before Peverell appeared on the scene.'

'Peverell was too stupid to search the box thoroughly,' said Montague, finishing off his glass of wine and declining another.

'Peverell was still in the dark,' said Neville, coming back to the table. 'He didn't know what he was looking for. He thought Tyler had been murdered for his money.'

'And his curiosity has led him to his present state. Tomorrow we'll get him out of the pit and see what he can tell us about the strength of the English fleet.'

'However strong it is, it will be no match for the combined strength of the Imperial and French fleet. Tyler told of a great build-up of ships in the Channel ports,' said Gallimard.

'Besides, we have the advantage that God is with us. His holiness the Pope has given his blessing to our expedition, remember.'

'And the English ships will have the advantage of the wind behind them after the storm breaks,' said Montague impatiently.

'Provided they can assemble their ships in time,' said Neville. 'Gentlemen, we cannot fail. Let us have one more toast to the downfall of Henry Tudor and the restoration of the house of York, the rightful rulers of this kingdom. Come, fill up your glasses.'

Both Henry Montague and Gallimard declined. Montague rose to his feet.

'I think, Charles, there is no more need for me here. I ought to get back to my manor and see that the muster is as I ordered. When you have taken Portsmouth and the coastal towns, you will turn inland and then we shall join forces. You should have no trouble. Portsmouth will surrender without a fight because everyone there is looking out to sea and they won't be expecting an attack from the land. Now, I have a good way to travel and I want to get many miles behind me before the storm breaks.'

'Surely, it would be better to leave at daybreak?'

'Too late. There is much to do back home. The road is good and I know it well. There's enough lightning around to illuminate the way. Please order my horse, Charles.'

Gallimard carefully folded his linen napkin and rose to his feet. He didn't look at Neville.

'I, too, will leave with Lord Montague. I must report to King Francis about the progress of the expedition. It's been a long time since I have communicated with him. I must also see my contacts in Portsmouth again. My King will need to know the strength of the English defences. The castle at Southsea will soon be near completion and that will be an important consideration when it comes to future attacks.'

Neville looked from one to another. The expression 'rats leaving the sinking ship' crossed his mind. Why could neither man look him in the eyes? Panic began to flood over him at the prospect of his allies deserting him.

'Very well, gentlemen; but won't you stay for one more glass of this Bordeaux? There is no need for haste. We all know our instructions.'

'Every reason why we must now get on with the job,' said Montague, walking to the door. 'Gallimard will let us know when the invasion fleet is sighted. By that time, Portsmouth will be in your hands.'

'Gentlemen,' stammered Neville, trying desperately to control his panic. 'Don't fail me,' he ended lamely.

'Failure is a word I never use,' said Henry Montague. 'Nothing can go wrong. Have courage, man.'

Neville went down to the stables with the

two men. The French soldiers were still sprawled out on the grass. Most of them were very drunk. From the inside of the old palace came raucous singing and loud banging noises. No one seemed to be in control. Sadly, he watched Montague and Gallimard mount their horses and ride away. He felt very alone.

Upstairs in her chamber, Ursula who had been listening to the conversation from outside the door, and who had seen Montague and Gallimard ride away, began to assemble her jewellery.

*   *   *

Later that night when the camp fires had all died down and the soldiers were slumped in sleep, Jane and Simon crept out of the tower and made their way along the castle walls to the north side which was the oldest part of the walls and where, in some places, the masonry was crumbling. Successions of Constables had neglected repairs because they knew that any attack on the castle would most likely come from the southern, seaward side. Simon had a leather bag slung across his shoulder. In it was Jane's letter to the Earl of Southampton.

'Wish me luck, lass,' he said when they found a place where the stonework had crumbled sufficiently to allow Simon plenty of footholds.

'God go with you, Simon,' she said. 'I have

every faith in you.'

'That's more than I can say for myself. Look after yourself, lass. I've told Captain Smallbone what we're doing, and he will look after you. He's on our side, but he has to go carefully as long as Neville is still in command here. Now give us a push, and I'll be off.'

A jagged streak of lightning tore across the sky overhead as Simon climbed up on the wall and sat there for a second before sliding down the other side. The storm was now overhead. As he ran along the Portsmouth road, the clouds released their load of water, drenching him and Jane and putting out the last glowing embers of the camp fires. To the crash of thunder, Jane ran back to the tower. Her heart was with Simon, who hated discomfort and had no stomach for heroics. Knowing him as well as she did, she prayed that he wouldn't make for the nearest barn and shelter there until the storm was over. Time was running out.

*　　*　　*

As it happened, a farmer, with a cart laden with produce for the Portsmouth market, had made an early start, and saw Simon, head down, battling his way through the rain. He stopped the pair of oxen and leant down to take a closer look at Simon. Thinking that a chap of his size presented no threat, he told him to jump up and sit next to him under the tarpaulin which covered the contents of the cart. Simon didn't hesitate and as the dawn came shedding a bilious light over the scene, the two men sat together as snugly as mice in a hole and entertained each other with their stories.

*   *   *

The wait seemed interminable. Sometimes Nicholas slept, sometimes he stood up and moved his arms and legs around, feeling life returning. He tried to climb the walls of the pit, but the mixture of mud and gravel which the walls were made of was oozing with damp and he could find no foothold. He then tried to ease his way up by flattening his back against the wall and pushing himself upwards with his legs, but again the surface was too slippery and after several attempts, where each time he fell back on to the floor, bruising again the side where he had cracked a rib, he gave up. As time wore on and no more food and water came, he began to fear that Simon had been discovered coming to help him and had been imprisoned, if not killed. And with Simon no longer there, what had happened to Jane?

As his brain raced on, fuelled by his imagination, once again he cursed his own stupidity that had brought him to this state. Whatever he'd done so far seemed to have brought pain and suffering on the one person he held nearest to his heart. But this time, he didn't give way to despair. He kept his body moving so that when the time came, he would be ready for action. He couldn't believe they would just leave him to rot.

He lost all notion of time. No more food arrived, and he was just beginning to feel his optimism begin to evaporate with his increasing weakness, when suddenly he heard the door above him open and a man's head appeared. It was not Simon's, but another face, with Simon's red hair and beard. A voice with a strong north-country accent called down to him.

'Can you climb up if I send you down a rope, sir?' the man said.

'Of course. You might have to heave me up some of the way, though.'

The face disappeared. Then a thick rope fell on the floor by Nicholas's feet. He picked it up and tied it round his waist. Then he signalled to the man to start pulling. Holding on with his right arm and using his feet to climb up the wall, Nicholas was hauled out of the pit. He blinked in the pale light of the dawn and heard the rain beating on the roof overhead. In front of him was an English soldier.

'Captain Smallbone, sir. Come this way. We'll have to be quick about it. Things are going to pieces round here and someone could come at any moment.'

Smallbone made a dash for the keep, Nicholas following. He was taken upstairs to the first floor where the room was full of soldiers. Smallbone signalled to one of the men who had had some medical training and told him to check out Nicholas's broken rib. Food and drink was brought to Nicholas and, with his rib bandaged, he felt life returning. He went over to Smallbone.

'I'm much obliged to you, Captain. But now I must relieve you of my presence. You will all suffer if I'm discovered here.'

'It's no trouble, sir. It's my duty to look after you. No one comes here. But there is someone here who wants to see you. He's been nagging away at me to get you out of that prison and I think you ought to thank him for his concern.'

They went downstairs into the kitchen area. Over by the fire was a slim figure with cropped copper-coloured hair and a youthful face. They stared at one another for what seemed a long time, not daring to speak. Then, oblivious to the watching eyes of the servants, they moved towards one another.

'Jane,' said Nicholas, 'my own darling love.'

'Master Roderick to you, Nicholas. Quick, we've only got a second. If Neville comes . . .'

'I only need a second with you alone, Jane. I want to tell you how much I love you and always have. And you know why I'm here, don't you? You know what's happening, and why I have to leave immediately.'

343

'Nicholas, Simon's gone to Portsmouth with a letter I wrote to my Lord Southampton. He'll come as soon as he reads it. There's no need for you to go. Simon should be nearly there by now. At any minute fighting's going to start here and you'll be needed. Neville must not leave the castle. Now you must hide until it's safe for you to appear.'

'My dearest Jane, what would I do without you? You think of everything. But before you lead me away to some hiding place, let me hold you and tell you again that I love you, and whatever happens, we shall always be together.'

'And in these few seconds that we've got, Nicholas, let me tell you that I love you, too, and I expect I always shall. You and I, Nicholas, are made for each other.'

Seconds later, Smallbone, who had been watching the proceedings with a twinkle in his eye, coughed politely. As they drew apart, Nicholas grinned at Smallbone.

'Don't worry. Master Roderick is really Mistress Jane Warrener, my dearest friend.'

'No problem, sir. We all knew he was a lass. That little fellow of yours told us. Now we must get you safely out of the way. Trouble's coming and we shall need you alive. Master Roderick, because that's what I'm going to call you, ought to get back to his quarters because Lord Neville's going to create when he learns Simon's scarpered.'

Minutes later, Nicholas, wearing a doublet with the cross of St George blazoned on it, took Smallbone over to the bastion on the outer walls, next to the sally port. There, he found again the entrance to the tunnel which led to the kitchens and Neville's house.

'Here we are, Captain. Now bring me a flint and a candle, and some food and water and I am out of your way. Don't worry, I'll be around when I'm needed. Look after Jane, I beg you. She's very dear to me.'

'We'll do our best, sir. Now I must get back. The rain's stopping and the wind's getting up. It's a good wind, coming from the south-west. That'll make things a bit tricky for them foreign ships.'

In the tunnel, armed with a lighted candle, Nicholas made his way back under the keep where he could easily get into Neville's house. Meanwhile he had Jane's love to inspire him and the knowledge that Captain Smallbone would protect her.

*   *   *

But Jane had a mind of her own. When she left Nicholas, she went back to the tower and began to get Melissa ready in case Nicholas had to leave quickly. If he did, then she would leave with him.

She heard the door open and looked up from grooming Melissa to see Neville standing

345

there accompanied by one of the household guards.

'I sent for the fool and was told he's flown the nest. Where is he, boy?'

Jane, her heart suddenly beating rapidly, tried to appear unconcerned.

'I don't know, my Lord. I'm not his keeper.'

'Then you can come with me and I'll put you somewhere safe until you do remember where he's gone. Get him over to the house,' he told the guard.

The man seized hold of her and twisted her arm behind her. She screamed with pain, but he only responded by kicking her to go more quickly. Then she was dragged and kicked up several flights of stairs in Neville's house until they came to a small room at the top of the house. Here Neville took a key out of a small box and unlocked a door in the wood panelling which covered the walls. He opened the tiny door which just allowed a person to go through into the tiny chamber behind it. They pushed her in and she fell face down on the bare floor. Then the door closed and she heard Neville call out.

'You'll stay there until I send for you, and if I forget all about you, then you'll take a long time to die. Now, get Smallbone,' she heard him say to the guard, 'and tell him to bring the prisoner to me.'

Jane, in total darkness, thanked God that Nicholas was out of harm's way.

'Prisoner's escaped, sir. I took him some food and he's gone.'

'Gone? Who, in God's name, let him go?'

'It was nothing to do with me. My men will back me up when I say that I've been in our quarters all night, I only went out ten minutes ago to give the prisoner some food.'

'Why didn't you report this immediately?'

'Because I hoped we'd find out how he got out. None of my men left their quarters last night.'

Neville stared angrily at his captain of the guard who returned his stare impassively, his composure inflaming Neville even more.

'I don't believe you, Smallbone, and I'm sure you know where the prisoner's gone to. Is everyone against me? My friends desert me, the fool's gone, and my captain of the guard has suddenly become incompetent. Has the fool got anything to do with Peverell's escape, do you think?'

'It's possible, but he's a bit on the wee side to go hauling people up out of pits. However, it only takes a strong rope and the know-how to tie a knot. Peverell could have done the rest.'

'You seem to me, Captain, to take this matter too lightly. The escape of a prisoner is a very serious matter indeed.'

'I'm well aware of that, sir; but at least the prisoner was on our side.'

'What the devil do you mean by that?'

'He's an Englishman—that's what he is.'

'And who might you be, Captain?'

'I'm an Englishman, thank God, and I serve King Henry. Like we all do.'

They were standing in the courtyard in front of Neville's house. In front of the keep was a row of English soldiers, pikes at the ready. Smallbone nodded in their direction.

'King Henry's loyal subjects, sir. Just like you. And that's more than can be said for this rabble.'

Out of the old palace the German soldiers were emerging. They looked angrily at the English soldiers and started shouting insults at them.

'What the devil's got into them?' shouted Neville, beside himself with rage.

'It's the cooks, sir. They won't serve the foreigners any breakfast. Told them to come and get it themselves. They don't look too happy, do they? And, if I'm right, here's another lot who aren't too pleased. Best let me get back to the men, sir, and I advise you to get inside your house. I smell trouble.'

Neville whirled round and saw, on the other side of the drawbridge, a line of French mercenaries incensed at the prospect of no food. When the German soldiers saw them, a great shout went up. Smallbone strode over to his own men, pushed them back into the keep and shut the door. Without a word, Neville fled into his house. Then, suddenly, the first shot rang out.

CHAPTER TWENTY-FOUR

Sir Ralph Paget, Earl of Southampton and Admiral of the Fleet, stood back and surveyed, with a great deal of satisfaction, the castle he was building at Southsea. During the last month, the outer walls had been completed, and, through the turrets, the barrels of large cannon protruded. These guns, recently built in the King's arsenals at Woolwich, were capable of firing heavy iron shot over a longer range than ever before. Ships coming up the Channel from the east would have to run the gauntlet of these guns if they wanted to capture Portsmouth—an undertaking not many captains would choose to embark upon. Other guns were in place along the eastern defensive walls as far as Langstone Harbour, ready to pound any enemy ships to pieces as they approached Portsmouth. With the King's flagship, *Henri Grace à Dieu*, waiting at Spithead for any ship which managed to pass this formidable battery of guns, and the *Mary Rose*, updated and re-fitted only last year, accompanied by the *Peter*, the *Matthew* and the

Great Bargue bristling with guns of the latest design, any invasion fleet would stand little chance of landing troops along the south coast. Especially as he knew that King Francis and the Emperor had little interest in waging war at sea and paid little attention to guns and gunnery practice. Southampton, an artillery man through and through, had little patience with the French King's cumbersome ships over-laden with soldiers and short on trained gunners. What use were soldiers when you couldn't get near other ships to board them, nor get near the shore to land them? With any luck, this mighty fleet of foreign ships would get nicely caught between the *Henri,* and the *Mary Rose* coming up behind them. Smaller ships could then be let loose amongst the foreign ships which would be sitting ducks for the trained English gunners. He felt confident in his ships, his men and his gunners. He thanked God that the King took his fleet seriously and had not been penny-pinching when it came to modernising his ships, regardless of where the money had come from. Now, all that expense was to bear fruit. So, he waited, watched and saw that everything was ready.

A disturbance behind him made him pause in his reverie. He turned round and was confronted by a most extraordinary sight. Two of his captains were half-dragging, half-carrying a small man, who was looking bedraggled and bad tempered, between them. The little man's face bore an extraordinary resemblance to King Henry and suddenly Southampton remembered where he'd seen him before. It was at Hampton Court and he had been sitting at the feet of the King being fussed over by the Queen's ladies-in-waiting. He was the King's fool and chief entertainer; a tumbler, a juggler, a singer. What, in the name of God, was he doing here? Picking his way over the planks of wood and other debris from the carpenters' workshops, he went over to the trio.

'And who have we got here?' he said to one of the guards.

'Calls himself Simon, sir. Says he's got a letter for you. Shall we kick him out of here?'

'Let's see what it says, first. Who's it from, Master Simon?'

'Mistress Warrener wrote it, my Lord,' said Simon, shrugging off the restraining hands of the guards. 'She's a friend of Lord Nicholas who's got himself captured trying to leave the castle and report to you and is now down in a pit without food or water. Mistress Warrener told me to come in his stead; and here I am.'

'And you take orders from a woman, Simon?'

'Mistress Warrener's no ordinary woman, my Lord. She'll not take no for an answer. Pushes me over the castle wall in the pouring rain and if I hadn't been fortunate in getting a

351

lift in a farmer's cart I'd be dead of cold in a ditch. But you'd best read the letter. Mistress Warrener would be mighty put out if we let her down.'

Southampton took the letter and read it quickly. 'My Lord,' he read. 'This is to inform you that there are now two hundred and fifty soldiers in Porchester Castle under Sir Charles Neville's command. There are fifty English soldiers in the keep and they are almost certainly loyal. In the church in the outer bailey are one hundred French mercenaries, and in the old palace one hundred German mercenaries who have recently arrived. As soon as the invasion fleet is sighted, Neville intends to march on Portsmouth, and having taken the town, he will join forces with Lord Montague, and march on London. Both men are in the pay of the French King and the Emperor Charles. My Lord, I beg of you, come quickly. The soldiers are restless and Neville will, at any time now, order the attack on Portsmouth to commence. If you make your approach by sea, the English gunners will not fire on your ships. The watergate is made of wood; it would fall easily to cannon fire. Lord Nicholas Peverell is captured and I beg of you to make haste as his life is in danger.'

She signed herself, 'Jane Warrener, Lady-in-waiting to Queen Jane.'

Southampton read this, his face darkening with anger. He looked at Simon.

'Have you read this letter?'

'No sir. I am not familiar with the art of reading.'

'I take it this lady knows what she's talking about? She's not deluded, suffering from strange fancies? You know, the sort of things women suffer from?'

'Mistress Warrener deluded? She knows what she's doing all right. She might be a lass, but she ran away from Court dressed as a boy, cut off her hair, took me along for company, and went off to Porchester Castle to rescue Lord Peverell, who doesn't deserve such devotion.'

'This lass, as you call her, must think a lot of Peverell.'

'You could say that. She loves him all right, though what she sees in him I don't know. The man can't get anything right. He lands up in the Tower and then gets caught in Porchester Castle. And now, I expect, he's sitting there waiting for someone to rescue him. It'll take more than Mistress Warrener to get him out of his present fix.'

'And Neville? Is it true the place is swarming with foreign soldiers?'

'Aye, that it is. And a right carry-on they're causing. Captain Smallbone's loyal, though. He'll not let his men fire on English ships or English soldiers. But do as she says, sir, and, if you want my advice, beg pardon sir, no impertinence meant, get up there quick.'

Southampton turned to the guards. 'Get Percy here quickly. I want to know the latest time we can get up to Porchester today. Also, send Captain Drury to get down here straight away, and the Master of the Ordnance. This is a job for the row-barges and the culverins. Be quick about it, men!'

Then he turned to Simon, 'Get cleaned up and take some refreshment. Then take a rest whilst we go up to Porchester.'

'Oh, no, sir, I'm coming with you. I want to see Neville's face when his gunners refuse to fire. Besides, I don't know what's happened to Jane or that fool, Peverell. Who knows, I might still be needed up there.'

By noon that day, ten row-barges had assembled at Portsmouth Point, each one armed with culverins at the bow and along the sides. Each barge was packed with soldiers. When the time was right, sails were hoisted, and, under sail and rowed with oars, the ships glided up on the rising tide.

*　　　*　　　*

Inside Porchester Castle, the German soldiers had run out of patience. They wanted food and food could only be obtained from the keep. And the English soldiers had locked the heavy, oak door. Despite all their efforts with pikes and an improvised battering ram, the door remained closed. When Smallbone ordered his gunners to fire on the crowd, they hastily withdrew and vented their frustration on the French soldiers who were crowded on the other side of the moat. When one of the French hurled a stone at one of the leaders of the German troop and it hit him full in the face causing him to fall face down with blood pouring out of his nose, his colleagues, with howls of rage, charged at the French and fought like demons with pikes and swords. In the midst of the confusion, no one noticed Jacques de Crèvecoeur standing on the sidelines not attempting to stop the fighting. He had seen Neville retreat to his house, guessed the English had mutinied, and decided to escape whilst the going was good. He walked over to the watergate where Neville's boat was still moored. He pushed the boat out into the main stream, got in, picked up the oars and began to row to the shore. No use dying for a lost cause, he thought. Not when there were other, more rewarding things waiting for him across the Channel.

*   *   *

Upstairs, in Neville's house, Ursula heard the fighting. She looked across at her husband who was standing at the window nervously gnawing his fingernails.

'Aren't you going to stop them?' she said.

'It's useless, they'll take no notice of me.'

'No, dear husband, of course not; no one does. Your days as a commander seem to be over. What are you going to do? Stay here and sweat it out?'

'The fleet will soon be here. They'll soon put paid to this mob. Then we'll take Portsmouth and join up with Montague. He'll not let me down.'

'Montague will be back in his manor by now praying that no one knows about his involvement with you. He'll concentrate on saving his own skin. You'll see. I know the English aristocracy. They're not ones for lost causes, and you, my Lord, are the biggest lost cause of all. And I had the misfortune to marry you.'

'Then why did you, my love?'

'Because King Henry ordered me to. You are his son, remember. Even though he never acknowledged you, he must have had a guilty conscience because he wanted you provided for; but not at his expense. Instead, he chose me to do his dirty work for him. In return, he promised me a life at Court and a position for you. And what did he do? Why, nothing. He left us to rot here in this backwater. But it's over. I shall go back to my family, Charles dear. It's what you've always wanted me to do. You'll have to save your own skin. I value my own life too much to share what's coming to you.'

She wrapped herself in a cloak and picked

up the box she'd got ready, and walked over to the door. Neville turned to look at her, his face white with terror.

'No, don't go. Don't leave me, Ursula,' he pleaded, rushing over to her and grasping her by her cloak. 'It will be all right. The ships will come, Smallbone will put a stop to the fighting. For God's sake don't leave me here on my own.'

He fell on his knees in front of her, reaching out in a pathetic attempt to stop her. Contemptuously, she pushed him aside, and ran out into the courtyard. She ran across the drawbridge and out into the outer bailey where groups of soldiers were engaged in hand-to-hand combat, this time for real. She ran to the sally port which was the nearest exit point from the castle as the gatehouse was almost certainly locked, and disappeared down the steps and on to the mudflats. The rising tide had not yet covered the paths across the marshes, but the track had been made slippery with the recent, heavy rain.

Neville started to go after her, but, suddenly, he stopped. The cacophony of sounds coming from the kennels where the hounds had been cooped up and not fed for days, made him pause. Then he ran over to the cage where Gaston, the great mastiff had whipped himself up into a frenzy of rage and hunger. He drew back the bolt of the cage. The huge dog came leaping out. Neville seized him by the chain which was always round his neck, and dragged him over to the sally port. Out on the mudflats he could see the figure of his wife floundering over the soft ground.

'Go,' said Neville, 'get her.'

Then he released the chain. Gaston, rejoicing in his freedom, bounded down the steps. Then he was off over the mud, giving voice to his great baying call, the call of the hunter after its prey. Ursula, hearing him, turned and put her hands over her face. Neville heard a scream, a terrible sound, like one of Gaston's victims of the chase.

He saw Gaston leap on Ursula, saw her fall to the ground, saw Gaston push her down into the soft mud. He saw the hound seize hold of her throat, so white and slender, and watched with a smile of satisfaction on his face, whilst the hound shook her like a rat. He saw her dark hair tumble down over her face, he saw her hands lift in a futile attempt to push the dog off. Then her hands dropped down into the mud. Then he saw Gaston rip open the front of her dress and clamp his huge jaws in the centre of her chest. Not staying to watch Gaston enjoy his prey, Neville turned and ran back into his house, locking and barring the doors after him. They'd never get him now, he thought. He'd wait for just a little longer to see if the ships came, and if not, he knew just where to go.

By late afternoon, boats were seen making their way up the main channel. Each one flew the cross of St George from its mainmast. Suddenly terrified, the foreign soldiers bolted back to their quarters and locked the doors. Captain Smallbone decided it was time to get Nicholas. He marched over to the bastion by the sally port and pulled open the tunnel door.

'Come, sir, you're needed. Boats are on their way. Come and join in the fun.'

Nicholas, who had heard the fighting, knew what was going on. He knew that, when the time was right, the English soldiers would come out of the keep and help Southampton restore order. But there was one thing he had to do, and he had to do it on his own.

'Where's Neville, Captain?'

'Gone inside his house, sir. The hound killed his wife and he'd not stop him. A terrible thing to do.'

'And Jane? Where is she?'

'Haven't seen the lass since Neville took her into his house.'

'My God, Smallbone, couldn't you stop him?'

'I warned her to stay with us in the keep, but she took herself off. By the time we realised what was going on, it was too late. We had to guard the keep, sir, and not let those Germans in. I can't be responsible for the lass, whoever she is.'

'Then leave me to find Neville. You keep your men at the ready to help Southampton and tell him what I'm doing.'

'They've been ready for hours, sir. We've not been wasting our energies fighting that other lot. They've been fighting each other. There's not many left for Southampton's men to polish off. Where are you off to?' he said anxiously, as Nicholas disappeared down the tunnel.

'To get Neville, of course. And, pray God, to find Jane.'

*   *   *

Nicholas, down in the network of tunnels, heard the sound of gunfire. He felt confident that Southampton would take the castle with little resistance from the foreign mercenaries. Probably they would be taken prisoner and end up in the armies of King Henry because, to a mercenary, one king was very much like another. Some paid better, that was all. But Neville. He was another matter. At all costs he mustn't escape.

He crept along the tunnel until he was under the keep. When he emerged, he found the kitchen empty. All the servants had either fled or were in hiding. Glancing out of one of the tiny windows, he saw two of Smallbone's soldiers guarding the main door of Neville's house. Neville, he knew, wouldn't risk using the kitchen tunnel. The exits had been blocked; now to flush out the quarry. That is, thought Nicholas, if all the exits had been blocked. And there were other ways of escaping. He could lower himself down from a window and make for the north walls which were not so difficult to climb.

He was wearing his own sword, but he knew that, in close combat, he would need a dagger. Picking up one of the sharp kitchen knives, he dashed over to the far side of the kitchen and raised the trapdoor of the tunnel which led to Neville's house. He climbed down and emerged in the cellar area which was now familiar to him.

All was quiet. All the servants seemed to have left. No dog barked. Tapers were still burning in the wall brackets, casting dark shadows across the floor; shadows moved and jumped about in the strong draughts causing Nicholas to draw his sword and whirl round to face an imaginary attacker.

The rooms were full of cupboards and alcoves. Tapestries covered the walls, all excellent hiding places. Creeping up the stairs to the first floor, he opened doors and looked behind curtains. There was nothing. Just the creak of the floorboards and the flickering shadows. He looked out of one of the windows and saw Southampton and Smallbone rounding up the foreign soldiers. Out in the west, the sun was beginning its descent into the sea, staining the sky with blood-red light. Tomorrow, he thought, would be a fine day. The storm was over, the wind had freshened the air, the clouds had dispersed. But would he be alive to see it? He continued his search. Where, he thought desperately, was Neville?

He crept up the stairs leading to the second floor and began his search of the bedrooms. He found nothing. Had he arrived too late? Had Neville stolen a march on him, using his knowledge of the place to leave by a secret tunnel? After all, it was quite possible that there were other tunnels, some going under the defensive walls and out into the surrounding countryside.

Then, someone screamed. A high-pitched female voice. Then there were other sounds: the crash of furniture being overturned, the sound of heavy footsteps, more cries of distress. Then he heard Neville's voice, angry and panic stricken. The sounds were coming from the floor above. With sword at the ready and the knife in his left hand, he rushed out of the room he was in and up the stairs which he saw at the end of the corridor. As he kicked open the door, he saw a sight which could have been a scene from one of the masques which the King loved to watch at Hampton Court. Jane, standing there, a stool raised above her head, her face blazing with anger. Neville, with sword drawn, was steadily pushing her back to the wall. A small door in the wood panelling was open.

'This way,' shouted Nicholas, advancing into the room. 'No need to kill another woman. It's me you want.'

Neville turned round, his face distorted with fury. 'So, Peverell, you've had enough of your cowardly skulking. Well, make ready to die honourably by the sword instead of dishonourably in a prison.'

'Don't you dare speak of honour, traitor. You've raised arms against the King. Now, defend yourself.'

Nicholas closed with Neville who was an expert swordsman. Nicholas was certainly no novice but he was hampered by a virtually useless left arm due to the cracked rib on that side. But his right arm was strong. They held the centre of the room and neither gave way, but Neville was in no hurry. He knew Nicholas had been weakened by his time in the prison and the beating he had endured. It was only a matter of time before the right arm tired. Nevertheless, he pressed him hard.

Fending off Neville's attack, Nicholas sidestepped and crashed into a table, causing him to cry out with the shooting pain in his side. Neville, the panic in his face now giving way to a gleam of triumph, realised Nicholas's weakness, and came on more fiercely. Nicholas saw that it was going to be difficult to disarm him and the searing pain in his side was beginning to make him lose concentration. How long, he thought, could his right arm withstand Neville's attacks? And he knew that he must soon reverse the situation and turn his defensive position into an offensive. But already his right arm was tiring, and he was in danger of losing his balance.

Neville sensed Nicholas was weakening. He bounded forward and slashed viciously at Nicholas's head. Nicholas ducked and gasped at the agonising pains which shot across his chest. Slowly and surely, he felt himself retreating. Neville, with a shout of triumph closed with him and forced him against the wall. Nicholas dropped his sword.

'I have you, Peverell,' Neville shouted. 'Damn you to Hell.'

But he had not reckoned on Jane who was still standing by, clutching the stool. As Neville raised his dagger to plunge it into Nicholas's throat, she rushed forward and brought the stool down with all her force on to the back of Neville's head. Neville dropped his sword. Nicholas then transferred the knife to his right hand and, as Neville stood there swaying on his feet like an ox who had been stunned but not killed, Nicholas plunged the dagger into Neville's chest. Neville fell, a trickle of blood flowing out of the wound, down his chest and on to the floor.

Nicholas took a deep breath and looked down at Neville in his death throes. Then he gazed at Jane, who was standing there like an avenging angel still clutching one of the legs of the stool which had come off in her attack on Neville.

'So, Jane, you've rescued me again. It seems I cannot fend for myself.'

This time, she couldn't answer. She ran to him and he held her close, gradually feeling her trembling subside and the great sobs which racked her body began to die away. It was a moment which they would never forget; a moment where they felt completely united.

'Jane, my darling, tell me what happened,' whispered Nicholas after a few moments.

'I was in there,' said Jane, pointing to the door in the panelling. 'Then, after a long time when I felt sure I was never going to be released and I would be left to die there as I had no food and no water and very little air to breathe, the door opened and Neville dragged me out. He wanted my hiding place for himself and was going to kill me. I tried to escape but I was half blinded by the sudden light after being in darkness for so long, and I had no weapon. But I picked up the stool and he couldn't get at me. Then you came in. But how terrible to see a man killed. Is he dead yet?'

Nicholas glanced at Neville's body, the dagger still protruding from his chest. 'Yes, he's dead. It's better this way. Otherwise it would be the rack and the long road to Tyburn and an agonising traitor's death. Let's leave

365

this room and join the others. Simon will be pleased to see you.'

'So he did get to Portsmouth?'

'Oh yes, and he's brought Southampton with him on his return journey.'

*   *   *

On 30 July 1537, in St Paul's Cathedral, a solemn *Te Deum* was sung, giving thanks for the defeat of the French and Imperial ships in the Solent. Nicholas rode back to Hampton Court in the King's carriage. King Henry was in high spirits, waving to the crowds who had gathered along the route through the City of London. One arm was resting on Nicholas's shoulders.

'These are great times, Peverell. My ships reign supreme on the high seas, my enemies are defeated on land. What a wonderful thing it is to know that God is on my side. I feel invincible.'

'Long may it remain so, your Majesty. You are indeed fortunate to be served by so many loyal men.'

'Yes, Southampton's done well. He's a good commander and he cleared up that fracas in Porchester very well. He's right about our guns, you know. It's going to be artillery, Peverell, that will win our wars in the future. I hear that the French ships were like sitting ducks out there in the Channel. They were so heavily laden with soldiers which they couldn't use, and their ships were so cumbersome that they couldn't be manoeuvred. By God, Peverell, we chased them up and down the Channel like a pack of bloodhounds after foxes, and then when we caught up with them, we shot them to bits with our guns. We fired broadsides at them, Peverell. Did you know that? That's what Southampton calls it— broadsides. The French can't do that, you know. Ships can't be turned round quickly enough, and the French gunners are useless. Well, at least my appropriation of monastic property has been justified. All those cannonballs had to come from somewhere, eh? Cromwell tells me that the money we've acquired through the sale of monastic property has paid off our National Debt and will pay for our future wars. A good piece of work, don't you think?'

Nicholas, thinking of his own Priory, now neglected and abandoned with Prior Thomas gone and all the monks dispersed throughout Sussex, said nothing.

'But, come now, Peverell, don't look so gloomy. You didn't do too badly, you know. A pity you killed Neville. We could have done with his confessions. However, Southampton's caught Montague and he's to be interrogated tomorrow. They found that box, you know. Tyler's box. Montague had it. It won't be long before his head adorns Tower Bridge. Why do

367

they do it, Peverell? Why do they want to be rid of me?'

'Ambition, your Majesty. There have always been traitors and I'm sure there will be others in the future.'

'And you'll catch them for me, won't you Peverell? It's what you're good at.'

'I would appreciate it if, in the future, your Majesty, you would fully inform me of the facts of a situation before you send me off on an investigation. For instance, it would have helped if I had known Tyler was one of your agents. To start off with a murder investigation and end up uncovering an international conspiracy is a bit of a tall order.'

'Not for you, Peverell. You're quite quick on the uptake. Next time, you'll be quicker.'

'Next time?'

'There's always a next time, Peverell. But now let me tell you something to cheer you up. I think it's time you had a reward for all your efforts on my behalf. Southampton's been given the Priory which Neville wanted for himself. Montague's estates are mine now he's been arrested. They're yours, Peverell. My gift. Time you settled down and founded a dynasty, and thank God there's no Yorkist blood in you. But you ought to have some sort of honour and I've decided to make you one of my Knights of the Garter. We'll go to my palace at Windsor and we'll admit you to the Order. You'd like that, wouldn't you? Oh yes, and while we're there, you can marry your Jane at the same time. I shall be sorry to lose a singer but she can still sing to me when I come and visit you down in Sussex. Now, you can't accuse me of ingratitude, can you?'

'I am indeed overwhelmed, your Majesty. But how soon can I be released from my duties and return to my own manor?'

'Manors, Peverell. Don't forget Montague's place in Sussex. You'll be one of the biggest landowners in the country.'

Nicholas, thinking of his gardens at Dean Peverell, wanted nothing more. Jane would be there with him, and a picture of Jane with a cluster of children playing in the rose garden filled him with indescribable happiness.

'Well, we'll let you go for a short time. Just enough to start founding the Peverell dynasty. It's good for a man to have a family, Peverell. Think of the joy my children bring me, and will do so again when my Queen Jane gives birth to our son and heir. Don't look so surprised. God has been so good to me lately that I'm sure He'll grant me one more wish. I want a son, Peverell. God grant you many fine sons. Then you can die peacefully, knowing that your family line is safe.'

Nicholas, whose ambitions had not yet risen above the delights of taking Jane back to Dean Peverell as his wife, smiled at the King's optimism.

They drove back through the narrow streets

of the City and out into the fields leading to Westminster where crowds had gathered to watch the procession. The King ordered the coach to stop and told his guards to distribute money to the poor people who flocked around him. Then they drove on to Hampton Court.

'You know, Peverell, you and I are a good team. You stick to me and I'll see you are well rewarded,' said the King, leaning back against the cushioned wall of the coach.

And I, thought Peverell, will probably lose my life for you in the end. To enjoy the King's friendship was a mixed blessing. Wolsey? Sir Thomas More? Both had been the King's friends. And Cromwell? How much longer had he got?

'That Simon fellow,' said the King drowsily. 'That fool of mine who suddenly took it into his head to play the hero. What shall we do with him?'

'He'll be happy enough to continue to serve you at Court, your Grace.'

'Of course, that goes without saying. I know what we'll do. Tonight, after the feast we'll give him a knighthood. Sir Simon King. How about that?'

'It sounds good to me. He'll be delighted.'

'Then that's that, Peverell. Everything decided. Now it's time for a nap. You do prattle on, man. Just give me a bit of peace.'

The coach jolted on over the rough road to Hampton Court. Nicholas, looking at the sleeping King, thought what it must be like to have so much power. In the end, he decided, as he began to nod off, he much preferred his own country estate with its gardens and priory. And Jane.